Sun Storm

Marlow Kelly

Sun Storm
Published by Viceroy Press

COPYRIGHT 2017 by Marlow Kelly

This book contains an excerpt from the forthcoming book Fire Storm by Marlow Kelly. This excerpt has been set for this edition only and may not reflect the final content of the forthcoming edition.

ISBN 978-0-9952301-2-5

Cover art by Melody Simmons
EBook Indie Covers
https://ebookindiecovers.com

Edited by Corinne Demaagd
From CMD Writing and Editing
https://cmdediting.com

DEDICATION

For my editor Corinne DeMaagd, and my proofreader author Lori Power.
And as always, my husband, Steve, without whom this book would not be possible.

ABOUT THE AUTHOR

After being thrown out of England for refusing to drink tea, Marlow Kelly made her way to Canada where she found love, a home and a pug named Max. She also discovered her love of storytelling.
Encouraged by her husband, children and let's not forget Max, she started putting her ideas to paper. She Loves to write about strong women in crisis.
She is an award-winning author, and a member of the Romance Writers of America. For news of Marlow's next release sign up for Marlow's Newsletter at: www.marlowkelly.com

Chapter One

The storm was building, growing in strength. A mist of warm air streamed from Marie's lips as she blew on her frozen fingers. She was a cerebral, solitary, and creative person. And now she could add overwhelmingly stupid. She hadn't considered how hard it would be to kindle a flame at five in the morning. A shudder racked her body, causing her to drop the matches. She gave up trying to light a fire and paced the room, flapping her arms in an attempt to generate some heat. She'd flown to Montana and rented the remote log cabin with no running water and no heat because there *was* a blizzard coming. She needed the worst possible conditions in order to test her solar panel. The place did have a generator, but she had chosen not to hook it up, not yet anyway.

She'd attempted to sleep in her one-piece thermal long johns, but the frigid temperature had forced her to wear her coat and boots. She fingered her socks that hung on the back of a wooden chair. They were still wet. It was her own fault. She'd shed her boots and then walked through a puddle of melted snow, by the front door, no less, where one would expect the floor to be damp. Of course, most people would've remembered to pack extra socks, but she wasn't most people. She was a scientist on the verge of a breakthrough.

The musty cottage was really just one room. At the back was a counter for food preparation, a hand-pump sink, and a hot plate. A wooden table stood near the door, and in front of the stove sat an oak-framed futon couch. The owner had described the small house as rustic, which she assumed was another word for neglected. Maybe it was pretty in the summer, but when the snow sat five feet high outside her front door and the wind whistled through a cracked window frame, causing the candlelight to flicker eerily, it was just miserable.

She sunk onto the decaying couch. There was one blanket, which stank of mold, rendering it unusable.

To reach the cabin, she had flown to Granite City, Montana, rented a car, and survived a white-knuckle drive on icy county roads.

The little house might be miserable, but it was the perfect location to test her solar panel. Tomorrow she would connect her prototype, power the cottage, measure the energy output and prove her hypotheses correct. Professor Hargreaves from Montana Tech would join her around lunchtime. His recommendation would go a long way toward securing funding and gaining recognition for her work.

She pulled her hair into a ponytail and then plucked her backpack from the floor. She unfolded the flexible, gold sheet. Checking for any signs of damage, she ran her fingers along the concentric squares that had been pressed into the soft plastic. Some plastics became brittle at low temperatures. That was something she would have to consider for future models. Then she inspected the small black box that protected the inverter, but there was no way to tell if the cold had caused condensation to build up on the inside and damage the components.

There was a rustling noise outside, and Marie stilled to listen.

There it was again, a sound almost like footsteps crunching on the snow.

A crack of splintering wood and the door crashed open. Marie jumped to her feet, her heart pounding. A scream lodged in her throat as four men burst in, filling the tiny space. She raced to the fireplace and grabbed the poker.

A handsome blond-haired man led the way. He was so good looking he could be an actor. He had a square jaw and wore a well-tailored leather jacket. Even his fair hair was perfectly trimmed. Two burly men followed, both with dark, short-cropped hair. They could be twins. Their thick bodies and the way they swung their arms reminded her of a pair of gorillas. They also had the same flattened nose and malicious, small, dark eyes. They moved to the back of the room near the sink. The last man had unkempt, long, sandy-colored hair. He wore a crumpled, hooded camouflage jacket and baggy gray pants. A long scar ran across one side of his face, starting at his ear and running through his beard, parting it with a jagged white line. He didn't say a word. He simply nodded at the poker in her hand and shook his head, silently telling her to drop her weapon.

Sensing that any attempt to fight him would be futile, she let it fall to the ground. "You can take the money. I don't have—"

"Shut up," the handsome blond barked. A vein on his forehead bulged as he scowled.

Her heart hammered against her ribs. She prayed they would take what they wanted and leave.

Handsome stepped in front of her and placed the barrel of his handgun between her eyes. "Tell us where it is."

"What are you doing?" The man with the scar strolled over and stood next to her. In her peripheral vision, she could make out his intense, pale, lifeless eyes.

He leaned close to her face so his warm breath touched her cheek. "This is all wrong."

A small squeal emanated from her throat. He was too close. Too scary. *Killer.* The word rang through her mind. The scar, those dead eyes, and his demeanor gave the impression of a lethal, terrifying man.

"What do you mean? Our intel is good." The vein on Handsome's forehead throbbed to life.

With one finger, Killer nudged the pistol away from her head. "First, how can she tell us where it is when she's too frightened to talk?"

Handsome shrugged, revealing a smile with perfect white teeth.

Marie released a huge breath. She needed to do something, but couldn't focus, couldn't form a coherent thought.

"Second," Killer continued, "what do we really know about this situation?".

Handsome sneered. "You were in the army. You know how it is. We don't make the decisions. We follow orders."

"And what exactly are our orders?" Killer asked, his voice low and calm.

"We're to retrieve what was stolen and eliminate the girl."

There had to be a misunderstanding. She was a *scientist*, not someone who needed to be *eliminated*.

"Does she seem like a threat to you? Someone we should murder? She smells like"—Killer sniffed her hair—"coconut."

Not wanting to attract more attention, she resisted the temptation to pull away. She had to concentrate, control her fear, and escape in one piece.

The two other men, the musclemen, stepped closer.

"What are your plans?" Killer turned his nose into her hair and sniffed again, but the question was directed to the others. "Are you planning to use her before you kill her?"

She stepped to the side, trying to put some distance between her and the scarred man with the dead eyes, but he gripped her arm and tugged her toward him. She wanted to pull away, but her muscles were the consistency of string cheese and refused to respond.

Handsome smiled. "Retrieving the prototype is number one on my to-do list, and then if these two want to have some fun, I won't stop them."

She swallowed bile, suppressing the urge to vomit.

They were going to rape and kill her. *Oh God.* Her vision blurred, and her ears rang. Was she going to faint? Killer's hand tightened around her arm, causing her to wince. No, she could not allow that to happen. If she lost consciousness, she wouldn't be able to defend herself. She inhaled, held her breath, and then exhaled. She repeated the process, forcing herself to focus on the men.

Killer's gaze flickered to the two bruisers and then back to Handsome. "Either way she's going to die? Those are our orders?"

Handsome nodded. "Do you have a problem?"

Killer ignored the question. He released her arm and hooked her chin, forcing her to stare into his pale eyes. "These men think you have a stolen prototype. Do you know what they're talking about?"

Cold beads of fear dribbled down her spine. She pointed a shaky hand to her backpack, which sat on the floor next to the futon.

Handsome slipped his gun into his belt holster and then flipped the bag upside-down, emptying its contents onto the couch. Out dropped her wallet, a hairbrush, her smart phone, a pen, a tampon, a memory stick, the solar array, the inverter, and a lint-covered collection of dimes and nickels.

"It's not here." Handsome threw her bag across the room and then kicked the futon. The couch moved back a couple of inches.

Killer stepped forward, placing himself between her and Handsome. "What sort of prototype are you looking for?"

Handsome's upper lip curled into a sneer. "A solar panel and a gizmo."

"A gizmo? Seriously? You don't fucking know what we're looking for?"

Handsome rolled his eyes. "I'm looking for a prototype of a solar panel."

"A solar panel? That's not going to fit in her bag now,

is it?"

Marie took a step toward the door.

Killer glanced over his shoulder and shook his head, stopping her in her tracks.

****

How the hell had he gotten himself embroiled with this fucked-up assignment? This was David Quinn's first day on the job, and it looked like it would be his last. He wasn't going to execute a woman, especially not a pretty little thing who wore pink long johns and smelt of coconut. Not that he had planned to kill anyone. Marshall Portman, the president of Public Domain Energy, had asked David to help retrieve some stolen property, but there had been no mention of murder, at least not to him.

The woman looked ready to bolt, but she needed to wait. If she took off now, the other three members of his detail would chase her down. Inside the cabin he could immobilize them and control the situation. Once outside, they would be harder to overpower, and the chances diminished of her getting away unscathed.

Her long, brown hair stuck out at odd angles, some of it falling in clumps around her face as it escaped her ponytail. Her coat had fallen open, revealing a curvaceous body clad in tight-fitting thermal underwear. Never mind lacy lingerie, the soft cotton clinging to her breasts did a number on him. Her shape and soft brown eyes converged into a mind-blowing, sexy-as-hell combination, which made her position here even more dangerous.

The biggest problem was his team leader, Brad Harper, whom David secretly called Pretty Boy. He was an idiot. The guy looked like he would be more at home modeling clothes in a magazine than operating a team of ex-military personnel who'd been sent to recover a stolen prototype before it could be sold on the black market.

David eyed the two chimps that made up the other members of the four-man team. Alex and Shane, the twins. Both were big and muscular. Alex had a scar across his chin.

Both rested a hand on the weapon in their shoulder holsters as if they were getting ready for a quick draw. Did they see him as a threat? They should. Everything had gone to hell the moment they'd stormed through the door. Brad didn't have a clue...about anything, and the chimps seemed more intent on rape than retrieving a stolen solar panel.

Shane, the one without a scar, favored his left leg, possibly a bum knee. Alex took his hand off his revolver and absentmindedly massaged his shoulder. David stored that information away, too.

He strolled to Brad, who stood at the couch rummaging through the contents of her backpack. Glancing over Pretty Boy's shoulder, he said, "Why are you still looking through her things?"

"Look at this frou-frou shit." Brad unfolded a gold plastic sheet that was about a yard in diameter. "What do women use this shit for?"

It reminded David of the foil emergency blankets paramedics used on hypothermia victims. "Does it matter? A solar panel is not going to fit in a backpack. Are you sure she has it?"

"Yeah."

David studied the girl. "What's your name?"

She'd backed up until her butt was against the table. "M-M-Marie." She was scared, but holding it together—just.

"Marie what?"

"W-Wilson, Dr. Marie Wilson."

He turned to Brad. "Is that the name you're looking for?

"I think so?"

"You think so." What kind of a dumb-shit answer was that?

Brad held up his smartphone. "These are the GPS coordinates, see?"

David didn't bother to look. He didn't care if they had a signed order from the Pope. He wasn't murdering anyone.

"Alex, Shane, make her talk," Brad ordered as he jerked his semi-automatic, a Glock 19, from his belt and slid the safety off.

The chimps smiled.

Alex strolled toward Marie, unzipping his pants.

Shit.

Marie's lips trembled. She blinked, unable to tear her gaze away from the two meatheads closing in on her. She fumbled behind her, reaching for the car keys that lay just out of range.

Brad aimed his gun at David's chest. *What the fuck?* Without thinking, David pushed the Glock to the side and pivoted out of the line of sight. He then grasped the weapon and twisted it back toward Brad until he relinquished the gun. Using his fist, he punched Brad hard on the nose. Pretty Boy's cartilage snapped.

David fired the Glock at the ceiling above the table. Chunks of wood rained down on the chimps, stopping them.

He stepped away from Brad, gripping the semi-automatic. "I'm all for you guys getting your property back, but I can't let you harm her."

Marie darted to her jumble of possessions on the couch and stuffed them in her backpack.

"What are you? A knight in fucking armor?" Brad shrieked, clutching both hands to his bloody nose.

"I'm a soldier, not a rapist, and definitely not a murderer. I don't want to be a part of this." He sounded tired even to his own ears. He wanted everything to stop, the operations, the missions, the fighting, and most of all the death. Taking a position with Public Domain Energy had been a mistake. He saw that now. All he had to do was disentangle himself from this mess, quit his job, and go on his way. "Okay, here's what's going to happen—"

Before he could finish, Marie ran out of the cabin.

David stared after her. "Shit, she'll freeze to death. You know what you're looking for isn't in her pack, right?"

Brad nodded, still clasping his nose.

"Then search the rest of the house. She obviously doesn't have your stolen prototype on her. If you find it, great. I'm outta here." He grabbed Marie's car keys off the table and marched out into the early morning darkness.

Chapter Two

The long, plowed driveway from the main road to the cabin had looked quaint when she'd arrived. Now the isolation only emphasized her vulnerability. She should've grabbed the car keys. Luckily, the men hadn't recognized the solar panel. What if they realized their mistake and came after her? She needed to get to safety. She scanned the darkness, searching for house lights, but there weren't any. She had deliberately chosen this cabin because of its remote location, and that meant she didn't have neighbors.

Her muscles were weak, and her knees threatened to buckle. She concentrated on running as every step became a chore.

Thank goodness, she'd been wearing her coat when they attacked, but her ears, nose, hands and toes stung. She was in danger of freezing. How long could she survive out here before her body succumbed to hypothermia?

A bright orange, compact VW Bug drove up beside her. Her rental car. She didn't look, just kept running.

The driver opened the passenger window. "Get in."

Oh, God. Killer had come after her. She veered off to the side, climbing onto a snowbank. Cold sliced her hands with pain. She curled her fingers into a ball to protect them. Her panicked gasps rang loud and clear in the frozen night.

Just as she breeched the top of the bank, strong arms clamped around her middle, pinning her hands to her side. She hadn't heard him get out of the car or run after her, so either he was as silent as the night or she was making so much noise she eclipsed all other sounds. She fought, kicking him in the shins, but he held tight. He carried her in front of him to the vehicle.

"No!" she screamed when he stuffed her into the passenger seat.

"Dammit, I'm trying to save you. You'll die if you stay out in this cold."

She sat sideways on the seat and, coiling her knees to her chest, kicked out, not looking or caring where she hit, as long as she forced him out of the way.

He twisted to the side, absorbing the impact with his hip. "Son of a—" He placed a hand on her chest and shoved hard.

She flailed, one arm hitting the steering wheel. She tucked her legs up under her chin ready to defend herself, but he'd stepped back out of range.

He tossed her backpack on the floor by her feet and then shrugged out of his jacket, cursing as he did. Then he threw it on top of her and slammed the door.

The driver's side opened. "Get out of the way." Using his shoulder, he nudged her to the passenger seat. "I want to get away before the others come after us."

Her heart raced. She needed to stop…everything, before her fear robbed her of her ability to think and rationalize. *One, two, three…*

Once she'd counted to ten, she focused on her situation. She was trapped in a car with a bad man. It was freezing outside, and she was in a remote location. She needed to remain warm and calm. She should stay in the car and save her energy until they were closer to civilization. Then she would make her move.

When he settled himself behind the steering wheel, she flinched. He was too near. Heat radiated from him, and the faint aroma of soap surrounded her. Men who forced women into their cars should not smell good, and yet paradoxically, he did. She leant against the passenger window, wanting to increase the space between them, but that was impossible given they were in her tiny rental.

He hauled his coat over her like a blanket, put the car in gear, and drove.

"W-w-who are you?" Unbidden tremors wracked her body.

"I'm David." They bumped and bounced down the rough, snow-covered driveway to the main road. He stopped at the entrance and rolled down his window. "Cover your ears." He pulled a gun from his pants pocket.

Oh God, he has a gun. Before she could move or scream, he leaned out the window and shot the front tire of a truck that was parked on the road then tossed the pistol into a nearby snow bank. "That should slow them down."

He'd thrown the weapon away. That seemed significant, but she couldn't figure out why. Everything was a chaotic blur, a jumble of questions, and reactions with no logical reason. "Who-whose—"

"That's the truck we came in." He rolled up the window and turned onto the icy highway.

Shudders once again racked her body, and she tensed in an attempt to control her shivering, not wanting him to think she was scared. *Show no fear.* Wasn't that what you were supposed to do with people who frightened you? But was easier said than done, especially for her.

He turned some knobs on the dash, and warm air blasted from the vents. "Let the shakes come. They'll help you warm up. You're not just cold. There's the adrenaline crash, too."

It obviously hadn't occurred to him she might be terrified. Not that it mattered what he thought because she had no control over him or his actions, but she could control herself.

"Is this a rental?" he asked after they'd been driving for fifteen minutes. "It's front wheel drive, which is good, but the car company should've put snow tires on this little vehicle."

She didn't answer, but instead asked a question of her own. "The other's... Did you...?" She couldn't finish. If he admitted he'd killed them, then he had overwhelmed three men. On the other hand, if they were still alive, they might come after her. Either way she was still at risk so her question didn't matter.

She placed her hands flat under her knees, being sure to leave her fingerprints on the vinyl seat. If she disappeared, then the police would know she'd been here in the passenger seat, being driven rather than driving herself.

If she survived, she would need to give a description of David. It was still dark out and the light from the dashboard wasn't great, but she could ascertain his scar started high on his cheekbone. On closer examination, she could see it wasn't thin and jagged, but was a large gouge carved out of his skin and was slightly thicker than the width of a pencil. The edges were white, but the deeper parts of the wound were darker.

His intense gaze slanted toward her. She jerked and stared straight ahead, trying to regain control. Now she knew why she was so scared of him. It wasn't the scar, his long hair or beard. It was his cold, penetrating gaze.

She heaved her backpack onto her lap to form a barrier between herself and her captor. He was tall, muscular, and radiated power so the idea she could overpower him was ludicrous. She needed a plan, a way to escape a moving car. Sooner or later he would slow down for a stop sign or a traffic light. He couldn't keep driving indefinitely. Once he stopped, she would be ready to jump out and run, but she had to choose her moment. There was no point in escaping if there was no one around to rescue her. And she would need to reach safety before he recaptured her.

She jogged for half an hour every day. But a run to keep in shape was very different than a sprint for her life. His knees poked out of either side of the steering column, his legs so long they barely fit behind the wheel. She had to assume he could outrun her. To think differently would be foolish.

He touched her shoulder. "Are you okay?"
She flinched, but didn't answer.

"Look, I want to put some distance between us and them before I pull over. Do you understand?"

She remained silent, turning her face to the window just as they passed a gas station. A gas station meant people. They needed to stop—now. She made gagging sounds with her throat.

"Are you sick?"

If he thought she was ill he might pull over. She put a hand to her mouth, pretending to vomit. *Be strong. Escape.*

He steered the car onto the shoulder of the highway. Marie released her seatbelt, grabbed her pack, and opened the door in one fluid motion.

The cold hit her like a sledgehammer. She slipped on the ice, slamming down hard on her right knee. She stifled a yelp as she pushed up with her toes like a sprinter at the beginning of a race. She had taken only a few strides when she crashed into something solid. She bounced off David's hard body. He clasped her shoulders, forcing her to stand still.

She slapped at him. "Get your hands off me. Let go—"

"Get in." He forced her back to the car and stuffed her into the vehicle. He cursed as he snapped her seatbelt in place. "What's wrong with you?" His moist breath warmed her frozen ear.

She could see the sky through the open door. It was dark. There were no stars, no illuminating moon. The only light came from the headlights, the interior of the car, and the glow from the gas station canopy only a hundred yards away. When she turned to face him, she noticed another tiny, white scar on his eyebrow. "I do not need to talk to the man who is kidnapping me."

"I'm not kidnapping you. I'm saving you. I'm not interested in hurting you. Somehow we've both been caught up in something that's...that's..." He scrubbed a hand over his face. "To be honest, I don't know what's going on."

"Leave me at the gas station."

"Normally, I would, but it's closed, and you'll probably freeze waiting for it to open."

"I'll take that chance."

"Really? And what if the others come by while you're waiting?"

She pictured the handsome man with the gun and the other two closing in on her. She didn't want to meet them again *ever*.

"Look, I'm taking you somewhere safe."

"And where would that be?"

He captured her hands in his, blew on them, and then held them between his palms, warming them. "The FBI."

"But your friends—"

"They're not my friends."

"But you arrived with—"

"First day in a new job, last day, too. Look, I'm a soldier and I've seen combat. But there's a huge difference between fighting an enemy and barging into a woman's house and raping and murdering her."

He placed her hands in her lap and stood. "Stay in the car for fu—God's sake, and do up your coat. The cold will kill you, especially the way you're dressed."

Although her body was mostly covered, the exposed skin of her hands did hurt, as did her cheeks and ears. And she didn't want to think about her painfully cold toes.

He slammed the door, walked to his side of the car, and climbed in.

"You forced me into this car. How is that saving me?" Marie kicked off her boots and pulled her knees up to her chest, curling her fingers around her feet.

"You're not wearing socks," he accused as if she were the one who'd committed a crime instead of him.

"I wasn't expecting company," she snapped.

"Show me your feet."

"What? No." She shifted away from him.

He rolled his eyes. "You need medical care if you have frostbite."

"And you can tell if I have frostbite?"

"Yes, as a matter of fact, I can."

"You have medical training?"

"Yes, all Special Forces personnel have some medical training."

"You were a medic with the Special Forces?" It was easy to imagine him as a heavily armed soldier who worked in dangerous situations, but she couldn't picture him with a caring bedside manner. He was too distant and dispassionate for that.

"No, I was a communications specialist. Now show me your feet." He growled the last sentence, which in any other situation might have made her smile. He definitely lacked the rapport of a medical professional.

With her knees still tucked against her chest, she shifted so he could see.

He ran a surprisingly gentle finger along her big toe. "Are they numb?"

"They hurt."

"That's good. It means there's no permanent damage to your skin. You have frostnip. It's an early stage of frostbite. They'll hurt as they warm up, but it's nothing to worry about as long as you keep them warm."

He slid the driver's seat back, removed his boots and socks, stuffed his bare feet back into his boots, and passed her his socks. "Here, put these on."

Marie did as she was told and moaned with pleasure as they encased her icy toes. She couldn't believe how happy she was to wear someone else's pre-worn socks. His gaze flashed to hers, and his pale green eyes softened and then focused on the road.

She had considered him to be cold and emotionless, but his actions had proved the opposite, and maybe he had a point about the cold. She'd misread him. It wouldn't be the first time she'd misjudged a man. Seven years ago, she had been naïve enough to believe that when a man said "I love you," he meant it. But those were just words, lies, to keep her from seeing the truth.

David plucked a cell phone from his pocket, flicked it open, and punched in a number. "Finn, it's David."

He waited a few seconds and then said, "I'm bringing in a woman. She's involved in the theft of a solar panel."

"I didn't steal anything," she said and then clamped a hand over her mouth. She had to stop being confrontational. This wasn't the time to grow a backbone.

"Hush." He scowled at her and then put the phone back to his ear. "Look, I need to hand her over to someone I trust. I trust you." He disconnected without saying goodbye.

"I'm not a thief." Dear God, she needed to stop talking now. She didn't need to antagonize him. He was the one who'd broken the law, not her.

"Good, you can tell that to Finn Callaghan."

"And who is Finn Callaghan?"

"He's an FBI agent stationed in Granite City." He steered onto the highway.

"Why the FBI? Granite City is a good size. They must have a police department."

"I trust him."

"And then what?"

"Then you'll never see me again."

Marie clutched her backpack to her chest and stared out over the dark, frozen landscape. If David was telling the truth, soon she would be safe, and this whole terrible night would finally be over. She should be pleased, ecstatic even, but she wasn't. David had shielded and looked after her on what was the most traumatic, terrifying event of her life. This type of selfless protection wasn't something she'd ever experienced. No one had ever endangered themselves for her, until now. Not that she'd ever been in this kind of trouble before. Despite the fact he was connected to the men who had threatened her, part of her wanted to stay with him. She shook away the notion. It was an irrational reaction to the aftereffects of the night.

Once he left her with the FBI, she would be alone again, and her short time with her terrifying protector would be over.

Chapter Three

David resisted the urge to wrap his arm around Marie's shoulders as they walked into the red brick building that housed the Granite City-Elkhead County Police Department and the small FBI office. She didn't want his protection or comfort.

The desk sergeant scrutinized them over his mug of steaming coffee.

"She's here to see Finn Callaghan," David said, trying to seem relaxed, and not someone who had burst into a young woman's cabin and scared her half to death.

Marie unzipped her coat to her waist, revealing the soft cotton fabric that was virtually transparent. He inhaled, looking away from her erect nipples, not because he didn't enjoy the view, but rather because she had been through enough without him ogling her breasts.

"It's six a.m. Special Agent Callaghan probably isn't in yet," the desk sergeant said.

"I just spoke to him. He's here."

The young officer, who showed signs of teenage acne, shook his head. "I haven't seen him."

David sighed, "Look, it's been a long night. Finn will be here because he's an asshole, and no woman will have him. And if he has his teeth into a case, he's like an obsessive pit-bull—he can't let go."

The officer gawked at him and then picked up the phone.

Marie placed a hand on David's arm to get his attention. "Is the agent a friend of yours? You said you trust him."

He was gratified by her touch. It meant she wasn't scared of him anymore. She met his gaze, not flinching from his grotesque face the way most people did. In the harsh, bright lights of the police station, her eyes were brown with gold striations, reminding him of dark gemstones. They held a hint of vulnerability, but no fear. He wished he were still handsome and whole the way he used to be. Then he would've whispered comforting words and held her until the feelings of powerlessness disappeared.

Her head came to his chest. He estimated she was about five-six. She had the perfect figure, all curves. Only the longest tips of her shiny, dark hair remained in the ponytail, the rest hung about her face.

"I don't suppose you have a change of clothes on you?" he asked, although he knew she didn't.

She glanced down. A deep crimson flushed her cheeks. She was so different from the women he usually found attractive. They tended to be a little more obvious. He enjoyed ladies who taunted him and teased him until he sated his desire in a prolonged session of mutual pleasure. But he hadn't engaged in a bout of lovemaking since before the scar and his self-imposed exile.

She clutched her zip and tugged it higher. "Oh, God."

"Don't worry. I didn't look," he lied.

She nodded. "Thanks." Her bright eyes faded into a blank stare.

He'd seen that look before. Psychologists probably had a technical term for it, but he called it shock, trauma, or just plain done-in. Marie needed rest. She needed this day to be over.

With any luck, Public Domain Energy would rectify their mistake in sending Brad Harper and the Chimps after her, and everything would be sorted out.

She stood in the small entrance, clutching her backpack, as if it held the crown jewels of England. He hooked her chin, forcing her to look at him. She didn't recoil and turn away but, once again, met his gaze.

"Those men last night were under the impression you

stole something. Tell Finn everything. Come clean."

"I didn't—"

"Here." He stuffed the car keys into her hand. He hadn't decided to leave until that very moment, but it was necessary. She was safe here, but she needed an end to this nightmare, and for that to happen Marshall Portman had to call off his men. The President of Public Domain Energy was David's mentor, a man who had saved him from poverty and a life of crime. David owed Marshall the opportunity to make this right. He deserved the chance to deal with the situation and talk to the police on his own terms.

Marie put the keys in her pocket without looking at them. "Where are you going?"

"I have to talk to an old friend. Then I have to quit my job and collect my truck. Tell Finn I'll call him later to arrange a meet." He forced himself to step away from her. His work was done. It was time to let Finn do his job. It didn't matter if she'd stolen the prototype or if this was all a big mistake. Either way, he wasn't in a position to help. He'd protected her as best he could and brought her to the FBI. The rest was up to her. The police and FBI could sort out the mess. If she really was a thief, then David didn't want any part of it.

He took another step back. She stood in the middle of the lobby. One hand grasped the neck of her coat, the other a tight grip on her bag. Her embarrassment from a moment ago was gone. Her face was now pale and ashen. Once again, he was assailed by the overwhelming need to put his arms around her and comfort her, but he resisted the temptation. Instead, he turned and headed for the door.

He couldn't picture her as a lowlife thief. She seemed too innocent. This must be a terrible mix-up. Maybe they had gone to the wrong location. And he doubted that Marshall knew the kind of tactics Brad Harper employed.

An icy gust hit him as he stepped out into the dark

winter's morning. He didn't turn around to get one final glimpse of Marie. The last thing he needed in his life was a lady who stood neck deep in trouble. If the past year had taught him anything, it was that he wasn't anyone's savior. He couldn't save himself, let alone a woman with pretty brown eyes, crazy, messed-up hair, and a curvaceous body clad in long johns.

****

Marie watched David thrust open the door and march out into the cold January morning. He hesitated for a moment, his unkempt hair lifting in the frigid breeze, and then marched across the street toward Granite City Square.

She was safe in a police station, and yet a shiver of unease tingled down her spine. She had been in danger since the moment she'd met him. He had terrified her, forced her into her car, and threatened her. No, that was wrong. He hadn't threatened her. Yes, he had shoved her into the car, twice, but both times she'd had been in a dangerous situation. Men were menacing her, threatening to rape and kill her. And then once she'd escaped, there'd been the relentless cold. David had also cared for her, giving her his coat to use as a blanket and his socks when he realized her feet were bare.

She wiggled her toes. The memory of him running his finger along her feet while he checked them for frostbite sent a rush of heat through her body. It had been so long since she'd had any physical contact with the opposite sex that even the touch of a man who looked like he'd just crawled out of a cave was enough to excite her.

She had formed an opinion about him based on his appearance. It wasn't so much the scruffy hair, beard and scar, although they didn't give a good impression. It was his penetrating, emotionless stare. Or perhaps that was his reaction to the intense situation. After all, he had arrived with her attackers. Yet, he had rescued her. When she thought back to that awful moment in the cabin, when Handsome held a gun to her head, she realized David had been trying to protect her even then.

The young desk sergeant held the phone against his shoulder. "Will your friend be back?"

"No." She shook her head.

David was one of the good guys, and she hadn't even thanked him for his help. This again proved she wasn't a good judge of character, especially where men were concerned. That was one of the reasons she worked alone, so she wouldn't make further costly mistakes.

She needed to see if the frigid temperatures and last night's activities had damaged the prototype. She was about to take it out and examine it when a tall, broad man with cropped, dark hair and startling blue eyes appeared in front of her.

"I'm Special Agent Finn Callaghan, and you are?"

"Marie Wilson, Dr. Marie Wilson."

"Medical?"

"No, mechanical engineering and organic chemistry."

"Impressive. How can I help you?"

"I was attacked, and the man who saved me said I should talk to you."

His sharp eyes narrowed, assessing her. "Are you the woman David called about?"

"Yes."

"Please follow me."

After going through security, Agent Callaghan led her to a shabby room with a chunky mud-colored couch, a scratched coffee table, and two chairs. There was a counter in one corner that held a half empty coffee pot and a stack of disposable cups. He motioned for her to sit.

"I'm surprised the FBI would have an office in a town like Granite City." As soon as the words slipped out, Marie inwardly groaned. Whenever she was nervous she engaged in small talk.

"We have several offices in Montana." He sat opposite her and placed a pad of paper and a pen on the table.

"I never realized—"

"We don't specialize the way they do in big cities. We have to deal with everything from domestic terrorism to fraud, sometimes in the same day. Now, down to business. The desk sergeant said that an unsavory character walked in off the street, asked for me by name, and described me perfectly." Callaghan's brow wrinkled. "I assume he's talking about David Quinn."

"Yes, he said you were a pain—difficult, and no woman would—you aren't married."

The agent scowled. "Describe him to me?"

"He's tall with shaggy, sandy-colored hair. He has a scar that runs down the side of his face, he wears a beard, and he has these intense pale eyes. Oh, and he said he's a soldier, or he was a soldier, Special Forces. At first I thought he was going to kill me, and then I thought he was a kidnapper, but he brought me here. I guess I was wrong about him." There was a dull ache in her chest, a reminder that she'd misjudged him.

"That's Quinn."

"He said he would call you to arrange a meeting."

"Good, did he say where he was going?"

"He said he had to quit his job. Is he a criminal?"

"I've known David Quinn for over sixteen years, and he's always been honorable, forthright, and direct. I don't see him being part of a plan that involves harming a woman. Can you tell me what happened? Start at the beginning."

"Around five this morning, four men burst into my cabin."

"What did they want?"

"They were looking for a prototype."

"Ah yes, David mentioned the theft of a solar panel."

"I didn't steal it. It's mine. I invented it."

Agent Callaghan picked up his pen and clicked the end. "Where are you staying?"

"I rented a cabin about an hour out of town, off route eighty-nine. The men emptied my backpack. One of them put a gun to my head, and two of them were going to rape me, but—"

"David stopped them."

Her mind flashed to the man with the scarred face as he nudged the gun away from her head. "How did you know? I thought he was there to kill me. It wasn't until he brought me here I knew I was safe. I thought he was dangerous."

"Oh, you're right, he is dangerous. But the man I know would never hurt a woman. To be honest, I find it hard to believe he was part of a home invasion."

"He said it was his first and last day on the job. How do you know he wouldn't hurt...?" She clasped her arms across her chest to ward off a sudden chill as cold radiated down her body.

"Tell me, were you staying in a one-room cabin with a red roof on Deerborn Road?"

"Yes, that sounds like it."

"I know the place. It's out in the county. This case comes under the jurisdiction of the police, but lucky for you, Granite City and Elkhead County consolidated thirty years ago."

"What does that mean?"

"It means the bean counters thought it was a good idea, and I have to admit, when it comes to law enforcement, it does simplify things."

"How?"

"Although it has a small population, Elkhead County covers a large area. It seems that before consolidation, someone could commit a crime in the city and then hideout in the county where they didn't have the funding for a large police force. Now the police don't have to worry about jurisdiction in the county. They can chase the bad guys over the county line. I'll just grab an officer. Okay?"

"David said he trusted you."

"I don't have the authority to investigate a home

invasion, but I'll ask if I can sit in on your interview if that'll make you feel better."

She nodded. "Please."

"Can I get you a coffee or maybe a glass of water?

"No, thank you."

Agent Callaghan left the room and returned a few minutes later with a man who wore a police badge and a gun, and a set of cuffs were attached to his belt. He had short, gelled air and sharp, dark eyes. An intricate tattoo peeked out from the open neck of his grey dress shirt.

"Marie this is Detective Ramirez. He's with the Granite City-Elkhead county police department. He'll be conducting your interview." Agent Callaghan stood by the door.

Ramirez sat in the armchair opposite her, pen in hand. "Why don't you bring me up to speed?"

"Four men burst into the cabin I'd rented." Her hands shook as she recalled the moment when she'd been so helpless, so defenseless.

"And you said this happened an hour out of Granite City on route eighty-nine?"

"That's right." She told the detective everything she could remember, which wasn't much. She tried her best to describe the handsome leader and the two thugs, but her memory blurred. Most of the time she had been focused on David, believing he was the biggest threat.

"What was the purpose of your visit to Montana?"

"I've developed a solar panel that uses plant technology. I was to run tests on the prototype today and then meet with Professor Hargreaves from Montana Tech tomorrow—I mean today. He's interested in my research. I couldn't miss the opportunity to talk to him."

"Why's that?"

"He's well respected because of his work in developing electrical conductive polymers. The Department of Energy will consider funding my work if I can prove it has merit. I'm out of money, and without funding from the DOE, there's no way I can develop my prototype into a viable product." And the last seven years of work would be for nothing.

"And have you?"

"Have I what?

"Made progress."

"I've made leaps in developing a new photovoltaic cell—"

"And Professor Hargreaves thinks your work has merit." The detective tapped his notepad with his pen.

"I hope so. I planned to bypass the cabin's generator using my solar panel and measure the amount of electricity produced."

"Is there any reason you chose this location?"

"Yes, I needed to know how the prototype handled the cold, and I also wanted a location away from the urban heat created by large cities."

"And if your tests were successful, the professor will endorse your work?"

"Yes, we were supposed to look at the data together."

"Is he the only person in Montana who knows about your prototype?" The detective glanced up from his notes, observing her with kind eyes.

"Yes…I mean no. Public Domain Energy contacted me. They're interested in sponsoring my research, too. I agreed to stop by their offices here in Granite City with an analysis of the trial."

"Public Domain Energy, the power company? The same outfit who provides most of Montana with electricity and natural gas?"

"Yes. But I've been holding off. My father—he's a lawyer—says they will want control over my discovery."

"What does that mean?"

"It means that although I conceived it and developed it, they will own the patent and be able to market it as they wish. I will get a percentage, but I won't have any say in how it's developed."

"What's the name of the person you were supposed to see at PDE?"

"Hold on, I have his card somewhere." Marie searched through her backpack until she found the small, white business card with shiny blue letters. "Marshall Portman."

She handed the card to the detective who scribbled the name and phone number on his report.

"Do you have a phone number for Professor Hargreaves, too?" Ramirez asked, not looking up from his paperwork.

She retrieved her smartphone and tapped the screen, then placed the phone on the coffee table in front of him.

The detective stood. "I'm going to make some calls. Are you sure I can't get you something?"

She shook her head.

Then he addressed Agent Callaghan. "Can I talk with you outside?"

They left the room, shutting the door behind them.

She collapsed back in her seat. Her feet were heavy, as if her boots were weighing them down. She unzipped her coat a fraction in an effort to relieve the chest-crushing sensation of suffocation. She wanted to leave. Every nerve, every fiber screamed at her to run, to go home to Seattle.

She covered her face with her hands. Maybe she could scrounge up the money to return to Montana and arrange another meeting with the professor. If not, then all her hopes for her future were gone. Over. The past seven years of work would be for nothing unless she could think of a way to find additional funding. But at this moment, she was done, exhausted. All she wanted to do was curl into a ball and sleep.

Chapter Four

"Ms....I mean Dr. Wilson, I'm sorry to tell you, but Professor Hargreaves is dead," Detective Ramirez said as he entered the interview room.

Marie shot to her feet. "What? No. That can't be." This must be a bad dream. It couldn't be real.

"I don't have all the details yet."

"How? What happened? When did—"

"It seems he was killed last night in a single car collision on an icy road. I won't know more until I look into it. How well did you know him?"

She sat. Then stood again. "Not well. I contacted him a couple months ago, asking him to read my research. He emailed me saying he needed concrete data to prove my theories. That's why I'm here. I was supposed to..." She stared at the detective. He'd returned to the room alone without Agent Callaghan. "Is it connected to...? No, that's not possible. Is it?"

"If you're asking if his death has anything to do with the attack on you, I don't know. As I said, I need to look into it. What were you supposed to do?" Ramirez poured himself a coffee.

"I'm sorry?"

"You said, 'You were supposed to...' and then you trailed off." He took a sip of his drink, grimaced, and then added some sugar.

"Oh, just as I told you before. I was going to set up my prototype at the cabin. He's well respected in the field of electrochemistry. I was hoping he would—"

"Recommend your work to the Department of Energy. Yes, you've said that. What else?" He pointed to the couch, indicating without words that he wanted her to sit.

She crumpled onto the lumpy cushion. "Nothing."

"And you weren't involved with him in any other way?" He took the seat opposite her and opened his scribbler.

"No, we've never met in person. I only talked to him on the phone once to confirm our appointment tomorrow. He sounded nice. He said he was looking forward to meeting me. Are you sure this had nothing to do with—?"

"Do you know where Quinn planned to go after he left?" Ramirez recorded something on his notepad. His writing was indecipherable. The long, scrawled characters resembled an intricate spider's web more than letters.

"He said he had to go and quit his job."

"Do you know who he worked for?" He pinned her with his incisive gaze. She doubted Detective Ramirez had any trouble when it came to character assessment. He probably would have recognized David as one of the good guys.

Her brow crinkled. "I don't remember him mentioning his employer. I only know that it was his first day on the job."

"He told you that?"

"Yes, I tried to run away, but he caught me. He said we were both caught up in… something."

"Something?" He raised an eyebrow.

"I don't think he knew what was going on. Look, I've told you everything I know. I'm tired, and I want to go home. Can I leave?" She needed to put some space between herself and this place. Yesterday when she'd arrived, she'd been so full of hope, and now she was beaten. Her life's work was destroyed. She would try to go on. She'd get a job and work on her panel in her spare time, but she was crushed. The only academic who'd shown an interest was now dead. His endorsement would have repaired her damaged reputation within the scientific community.

The detective examined the report in front of him.

"You're not a suspect. You're a victim. I have no reason to keep you here. The fact they were looking for a solar panel suggests you were targeted. Where do you intend to go?"

"Home to Seattle." She couldn't afford a hotel, and even if she could, she wasn't sure she should remain here. Her time in Montana had been terrifying, and even if she wanted to stay, there was no point. She should go home and assess her options.

"Okay, how are you getting there?" He gave her a thin smile.

"Plane, I have a return ticket."

"Is there someone who can meet you at the airport?" He rubbed the back of his neck, his concern for her almost palpable.

"I'll call my father." That was a lie. Her relationship with her father was distant at best, but if a small fib gave Detective Ramirez some peace of mind, then it was worth it.

"Please be careful. If you spot anyone suspicious, I want you to call me, or better yet, dial nine-one-one. And I suggest you stay with a friend or family member until we clear this up."

She nodded, zipped her coat, and then slung her backpack over her shoulder.

"Are you sure you want to leave? I really don't think this is a good idea." He passed her his card.

"What else am I going to do? I can't hang out at a police station all day. Besides, I'm probably safer in Seattle than I am here." She pulled her hair back from her face. "I came here to test my solar panel and meet with Professor Hargreaves. Neither of those things is going to happen. As it stands right now, my career in the field of photovoltaics is over. I've wasted seven years of my life and spent all the money my grandfather left me chasing a dream, and now that dream is dead."

Ramirez opened the door for her. "I know it seems pretty bad, but you're actually very lucky."

She frowned.

"It would've been so much worse if Agent Callaghan's friend hadn't been there."

She inhaled and straightened her shoulders. "You're right. I'm sure you've seen some terrible things in the course of your career. You don't need to waste your time watching me wallow in self-pity. I apologize. I'll get out of your hair."

Ramirez smiled. "If you think of anything else, call me. I'll have an officer give you a ride to the airport."

"That'll be great. Thank you."

Chapter Five

David wiped crumbs from his mouth as he left the coffee shop, heading for the PDE building. He figured he might as well have breakfast while he waited for Marshall to arrive at his office. The café had changed hands since he'd slept in its doorway as a teen. It was newly renovated, boasted modern décor, and served a nice selection of pastries and breakfast sandwiches.

He rubbed his knuckle, recalling the moment in the cabin when Pretty Boy had pointed his weapon at David's chest. That was careless and unprofessional. You never aimed a gun at someone unless you were prepared to use it. Thankfully, David's instincts were still honed, and he'd managed to disarm the idiot. He needed to remember to tell Finn about the gun he'd tossed back at the cabin. Let the FBI deal with the mess.

It had been four hundred and two days since he'd handled a weapon, which meant three hundred and fifty sleepless nights, and fifty-two nights where he'd used the age-old remedy of straight Scotch whiskey to cure his insomnia. The metallic feel and weight of the Glock, the vibration when he'd fired at the ceiling, had been so familiar, like an old friend, and he hated it. He didn't want to be knowledgeable about weapons, didn't like the fact his instincts were still sharp and lethal.

He inhaled and then exhaled, releasing the bad memories. He didn't do guns and death anymore. That was all in the past. Although, at this moment, he wouldn't mind a shot of Scotch. That path was tempting, but he knew it led down a dark road.

The last time his sister, Sinclair, had visited, she'd warned him to get his act together or she'd kick his butt.

He smiled at the idea of her trying to beat him. She was tall, lean, and well trained in hand-to-hand combat. He knew how good she was because he'd taught her himself, but her role as a linguist with Child Seekers International did not involve any direct conflict, whereas he was a master sergeant with the Special Forces. There were some things you couldn't unlearn, just as there were some memories you couldn't forget.

Granite City Square was cleaner and less run-down than when he and Sinclair had lived here. They'd spent three long years living on the street, avoiding cops, begging for spare change, and sleeping in doorways. They'd met another homeless kid, Tim, about a year after they'd arrived, and Michael about eighteen months after that. They'd called themselves the Granite City Crew. The four of them had guarded and protected each other. They had shared their recourses. Although life on the street for Michael was more of an experiment than a necessity. It had always been a puzzle to David why a genius from a good home would spend one night sleeping rough, let alone six months. It wasn't a surprise when they woke up one day to find him gone. They hadn't seen him again until basic training at Fort Leonard Wood.

Pretty LED lights twinkled in the leafless trees. They really had done a good job on the downtown cleanup. David suspected that Marshall Portman was the driving force behind the rejuvenation. There was a fountain in the center of the square, which was surrounded by a small garden. It was probably pretty in the summer when the flowers and shrubs bloomed.

David knew firsthand that Marshall was a man of solid principles. Despite being born rich, with the proverbial silver spoon, the millionaire businessman had started a charity that took street kids in and helped them reenter society.

One of the best days of David's life was when he, Sinclair, and Tim had been offered a place in Marshall

House. The staff had been smart enough not to try and separate them. They had given them a room, squeezed in three beds, and allowed them time to acclimatize. For the first time in years, they were fed, clothed, and had a bed to sleep in. They even had books to read. He smiled remembering how much he'd enjoyed that first book, a spy thriller by Ken Follett.

Marshall had been a regular visitor. He had taken a special interest in the three of them and had encouraged them to join the army and serve their country, but in retrospect, joining the military might have been a mistake.

David entered the ornate, white stone building that housed the PDE headquarters. He nodded to the kid on security, flashing the company ID he had received only the afternoon before, and carried on walking, as if he were a PDE executive. Ninety-nine percent of the time if you acted like you belonged, no one stopped you.

He stepped into the elevator, hit the button for the fifth floor, and allowed his mind to wander back to Marie in her pink thermal underwear. His body warmed as desire flooded his veins. Those long johns along with the unkempt hair were a turn-on. They made her both innocent and sexy at the same time.

He shook away visions of her when his cell phone vibrated. He looked at the display. It was Finn again. This was the fourth time he'd called. He ignored the call and slipped the phone back in his pocket. He wasn't avoiding his friend, but he wanted to talk to Portman first and tell him how everything had gone to shit in the last twelve hours. David owed him that much. Once Portman knew the kind of tactics Harper and the Paxton brothers employed, he would put a stop to it.

It was by pure chance he had bumped into Marshall a month ago at the VA hospital in Granite City. His former mentor had been attending a program for homeless veterans. They'd chatted, and David had enjoyed reminiscing about his time at Marshall House. Inevitably, the talk turned to the present. Once Marshall learned David needed money to build a cabin and start a beekeeping business, he had gone out of his way to find David a job.

Unfortunately, the bad luck that had followed him for over a year continued to haunt him. He hadn't completed his first day before it had gone to hell. Their brief had been to retrieve a stolen prototype. It was supposed to have been stolen by some lowlife thug who was going to auction it to the highest bidder. The minute he set eyes on Marie, he knew he was in trouble. It was weird how Pretty Boy and the Chimps took it all in their stride. It never occurred to them their information was wrong.

He stepped out of the elevator into an overwhelming onslaught of orange and brown, making him feel as if he'd walked into a seventies sitcom. The decor was probably the work of one of those interior designers who thought butt-ugly meant chic.

There was no receptionist on duty yet, which wasn't a surprise considering it was not yet eight in the morning.

"I want him dead. Do you hear me?" There was no mistaking Marshall's distinctive upper-class New England accent or the urgency in his voice. A rush of adrenaline surged through David as he dashed to the door of Portman's office.

"You were supposed to shoot him as soon as you got to the cabin. Before he suspected—"

David stopped. The old fashioned oak door wasn't open, but it wasn't completely closed either. The latch hadn't caught, leaving the door ajar.

There was something about Marshall's tone. David could picture him clenching his teeth while he talked. The president of Public Domain Energy wasn't in danger—he was angry.

David held his breath as he listened.

"You said he was burned out—he had no fight left in him." The effect of Pretty Boy Brad's combative tone was lessened by his nasal wheeze.

"He's a hot-shot Special Forces screw-up. Do you really think he would stand there and let you——?"

"You said he was broken after that incident where he shot his own man. According to your intel, putting a bullet in him should have been easy."

They were talking about him. David dug his fingers into his palms to establish he was awake and this wasn't some awful nightmare. A cold vice tightened around his chest, making it difficult to breathe.

"There were three of you and one of him. How did he get the better of you? You were supposed to kill him, the woman, and make it look like a murder-suicide," Portman spat.

"I couldn't very well shoot him in the back, could I?"

"Yes, damn it, you should've shot him as he walked across the threshold. I own the Granite City-Elkhead County police, for God's sake."

"You should have told me that. I thought we needed to make it look as if he was part of the attack. You know, get his fingerprints on her belongings and stuff like that. I put up with that bastard talking his face off when I could've just shot him."

"You idiot. How could you not know? Half the cops in the department went through Marshall House."

There was silence.

David wanted to turn and run, but his feet wouldn't move. His friend and mentor, the man who had saved him from the streets, had also set him up and planned his death.

Leather creaked as Marshall sat in his chair. "Okay, enough with the blame. Let's move onto damage control. Where's Dr. Wilson now?"

"Not sure."

Fuck, they were going after Marie.

"Have you talked to the tech department about tracking her phone, or are you trying to do it yourself?"

Marshall's chair creaked again. David pictured him sitting behind his expensive antique desk with his large beaked nose and steel-gray hair.

"Tech department."

"Then I'll look into getting better people. There are hackers on the dark web who can track her through street cams and that sort of thing."

"Tracking Quinn won't be difficult. I have men stationed at his house. As soon as he returns home I'll have him." Brad sniffed. His nasal passage was probably blocked with blood from where David had punched him.

A ringing cell phone sounded in the office.

"Hello," Marshall answered the phone. He listened for a minute and then said, "Thank you. Keep me up-to-date."

There was a dull *thunk*, which David assumed was the phone slamming on the desk.

"That was one of my contacts in the Granite City PD. He's just informed me that she went to the FBI."

"Do you own the FBI, too?"

"No, I do not," Portman bit out the words.

"Damn it."

David breathed a sigh of relief. At least he knew he could still trust Finn.

"This isn't an FBI matter. As soon as the case is passed to the police, I'll have my people bury it," Marshall announced.

"We burned the cabin so there's no evidence left."

"Did you destroy the panel?"

"We couldn't find it. Do you think she has it hidden?"

"Maybe. I think she needs to become an eccentric scientist who, when her research fails, commits suicide."

"What about Quinn?"

"You and the Paxtons concentrate on the woman—"

"I want Quinn. I owe him for breaking my nose." Pretty Boy sniffed again.

"Go to medical on the ground floor and get them to look at it. Send the Paxtons after Dr. Wilson. Before they kill her, make sure they destroy her solar panel. Then we'll deal with Quinn."

"Yes, sir." Heavy footsteps stomped toward the door.

David backed away. *Son of a bitch*. It was a lot to take in. Marshall Portman, David's mentor and friend, wanted him dead. The job offer was a setup. They had planned to murder Marie and blame him.

He needed to get out of town and hide. He had to find Marie and warn her. Marshall owned the police, so Finn and the FBI were his only hope. He had to tell Callaghan what he'd just heard.

He glanced back at the office door. Harper was backing out as he talked to Marshall. A bright red exit sign caught his eye. *The stairs*. He crashed through the door to the stairwell and hurled himself down the steps.

Chapter Six

Marie tugged the collar of her coat over her mouth as she tried not to slip on the ice-covered sidewalk. The wind blowing through the city square made it too cold to talk to her police escort.

The downtown was pretty. Small lights covered buildings and trees, twinkling in the dim early morning light. They gave the impression of a fairy grotto rather than the heart of a city. A fountain sat dormant in the center of the square, the surrounding pond frozen. A sign in front read, *Skate responsibly*. A space surrounding the makeshift ice rink was complete with tables and chairs. Snow had been plowed into huge piles at the edge of the park. Another billboard said, *Play at your own risk*. Marie couldn't imagine anyone skating, sitting outside, or playing in a pile of snow; it was simply too cold.

Surrounding the large square was a coffee shop, the police station, the city hall and law courts, and the classical architecture of the PDE building. The only gaudy business in the city center was Big Sky News. A two-story cement and glass building boasted a large neon sign that read, *Montana's only independent news station*.

They reached the street that traversed the south end of the square and waited for the light to change. Images rose unbidden of the moment in the cabin when a gun had been pointed at her head. A fine sheen of sweat dampened her body. She shut her eyes, squeezing them tight, to drive back the nightmare.

"Are you okay?" Officer Calder, the young, serious policemen who'd accompanied her from the station, touched her arm.

She opened her eyes and inhaled a deep, calming

breath. She could break down once she was home in Seattle, but not here, not now. "I'm fine. Thanks again for walking with me. I'm sure you have more important things to do."

"No, as long as I drop you off at the airport by nine, we're good." He was wearing a uniform-issued navy blue parka and high quality rubber-soled winter boots. The cold didn't seem to bother him.

"I don't think that'll be a problem. Mr. Portman isn't expecting me so I'll probably just leave a message at reception, but I can't afford to come back to Montana so I have to do this now."

The light changed. They crossed the street, and then started up the massive ornate stone steps of the PDE building.

Trying to secure funding now was definitely in poor taste. The professor hadn't even been dead a day, and here she was looking for a sponsor, another way to keep her work alive. But as it stood, the Department of Energy would not fund her work without Hargreaves recommendation.

Perhaps if she stretched her budget, she might be able to continue for another two months. After that she would be forced to shelve her project and give up on her aspirations of creating a cheap source of electricity and receiving scholarly recognition for her work. She didn't want to let go of her dream, especially when she was so close to proving her theories and publishing her findings. Her solar panel was viable, unique, and might even revolutionize the way people harvested electrical energy. If only she could get it in front of the right people.

She reached for the ornate wood-framed glass door. Suddenly, a man charged through the entrance, heading toward her. He was tall with shaggy, sandy hair and wore a crumpled green and beige jacket. As he neared, she saw the scar that ran through his beard.

"David? Is that you? What are you doing here?"

His face was deathly pale. "Marie," he gasped and then glanced behind him. "You're coming with me." He grabbed her hand.

"What are you doing?" She tried to yank her arm from his clasp.

The policeman grabbed her other arm as he reached for the gun at his waist. David released her. With one hand, he gripped the weapon in place and with the other he shoved the officer—hard. The cop let go of her as he flailed, teetering on the edge of the top step, and then he lost his balance and fell backward, rolling down the steps.

David clutched her elbow and dragged her in his wake. She tugged back, forcing him to slow, but she couldn't make him stop. He was too strong. Her feet slipped on the icy sidewalk as she slid along.

He turned. His intense gaze flickered over her body and then to the building behind her. He gave a hard jerk that propelled her forward and quickened his pace. "They want to kill you."

"What? No—"

"Yes." He sped up.

"You must have that wr—"

"I heard Portman give the order. I'll explain later." They stopped at a rusted, black truck. "Get in." He opened the door.

"But he offered to sponsor—"

"Who? Marshall?" He grabbed her around the waist and tried to hoist her into the vehicle. "Get in."

Marie pushed against him. This was madness. He must've gone insane. She'd read about soldiers who came back damaged, who imagined they were still in the thick of the fighting. She twisted, trying to jab him with her elbows. "Stop shoving me."

The sound of a balloon popping caught her attention. She stopped fighting. Gun raised, Handsome stood at the entrance to the office-building.

"Shit." David rammed her into the vehicle. Another

pop sounded, followed by a small, flat ding.

She tumbled in, head first, diving for cover.

A firm hand shoved her butt, propelling her upside-down into the passenger seat.

More loud pops sounded.

Marie righted herself in time to see Handsome, his face bloody, raising his gun for another shot. Beside him, the young police officer also had his gun raised.

David didn't bother to back out of the parking space. Instead he drove over the short cement divider that separated the parking lot from the sidewalk. With a hand on her shoulder, he forced her down in the seat as he stepped on the gas. They plowed through a snowdrift and swerved onto the road.

Chapter Seven

"Was that the same man from the cabin?" Marie inhaled a shuddering breath as she eased herself up and onto the seat. Thank God she was sitting down because her legs were as floppy as a pair of nylons.

"Yes." David kept his eyes on the road.

"What happened to his face?" She was numb. Her mind was a complete blank, unable to focus on anything except Handsome with his battered nose.

"I broke it." His voice was impassive, as if he'd taken no pleasure in the act. "Actually, you were there when it happened."

"Oh." She didn't remember that. She craned her neck to see through the rear window. "Are they following us?"

"Not that I can see."

All she could picture was that awful face and the gun. The interior of the truck felt cramped and tight, as if it were closing in on her. She cranked on the handle to roll down the window. Frozen air blasted in.

"Are you hurt?" He concentrated on the road, steering the beat-up truck in and out of traffic, zipping from lane to lane.

"I'm fine." She slotted the seatbelt into its receptacle while gulping in large, calming lungfuls of frigid air. "Why are they shooting at us?"

"Portman wants your solar panel destroyed and us dead." He slanted his gaze in her direction and then turned his attention back to the traffic.

"But he said he wanted to sponsor my work—"

"Look, I don't know what to tell you. I know what I heard. If you don't believe me, then think about it. Those men, last night, were looking for a solar panel, and they were definitely going to kill you, which is a little heavy-handed considering the fucking solar panel has already been invented." He turned his intense pale green eyes toward her.

She felt as if she'd been slapped. She wanted to question David's logic and find some flaw in his reasoning. She tried to put the pieces from the last six hours together. "Professor Hargreaves—"

"Who's Professor Hargreaves?"

She hadn't realized she'd spoken aloud until he asked the question. "I was supposed to meet him today, but he was killed in a car accident last night."

"Are you sure?"

"That's what Detective Ramirez said."

"Who the hell is Detective Ramirez?"

"He's with the Granite City-Elkhead County Police. He—"

"You were supposed to talk to Callaghan."

"He was there, but a home invasion doesn't fall under FBI jurisdiction."

"Callaghan, you by-the-book son of a bitch." He punched the stirring wheel.

She flinched, but kept silent.

"Is there anyone else who knows about your work?"

"Sure. Lots of people know about it, but…"

"But what?"

"Most of my colleagues don't believe my research is valid. I'm considered a dilettante." Coming to Montana was her chance at redemption, an opportunity to prove the lies and scandal from her past were unfounded, and her ideas and research were groundbreaking.

"A dilettante?"

"It means—"

"I know what it means. It means that everyone thinks your ideas are half-baked. Where does this professor fit in?"

"I contacted him and asked him to read my paper on

semiconducting materials with photovoltaic properties. He must've liked what he read because he asked to see my research."

"Don't you have any lab assistants or anything like that?"

"No, I built a lab in my garage. I've been working alone, funding my own research."

"The only person who took an interest in your solar panel is dead?"

"It would appear so, yes."

"Shit." He stepped on the gas, once again zigzagging through the morning traffic.

"Would you stop swearing? She didn't like his brusqueness. He was terse and gruff. He put her on edge in more ways than one.

"Stop swearing?" He pinned her with his icy green gaze. "People are shooting at us, and you're worried about a few curse words. Well fuck me. In fact, fucking, fucking, fuck, fuck. How's that for swearing?" He hammered his fist on the steering wheel again.

"Stop the car. I want to get out here." She shifted toward the passenger door in an attempt to distance herself from him.

"No."

"No?"

"Do you think the men with the guns don't know how to drive? They will come after us."

"There is no 'us.' For all I know, they are after you, and this violence has nothing to do with me."

"Nothing to do with you," he shouted. "This is all about you. They want to destroy you and your fucking solar panel."

"You're the one who broke into my cabin. I didn't make you associate with criminals. And for the record, my life hasn't been all sunshine and flowers since you crashed through my door," she shouted back, shocked by her own reaction. What was wrong with her? She never argued, raised her voice, or confronted anyone. David was making her crazy. It was the only explanation. For some reason, she had no problem arguing with him. Maybe it was because he was so aggravating.

"No kidding, lady."

She pointed a finger at him. "And I'm really sick of you forcing me into cars." It was as if all her fear and stress were curled in her chest waiting for an outlet, and he was it.

"What?"

"I've known you for less than twelve hours, and you've pushed me into a vehicle three times." She knew she was being unreasonable, but couldn't stop.

He rolled his eyes. "Where are my manners? The next time someone's trying to kill you, I'll just politely ask if you'd like to get in my truck. Do you want me to curtsey while I'm at it?" He shouted the last part.

"There's no need for sarcasm." She sat straight, folding her hands in her lap, hoping if she gained control over her body, then she would gain some much needed restraint over her emotions.

"I think there is, and do up that window. It's freezing in here."

She did as she was asked, but only because her fingers were numb with the cold.

They reached the city limits where the town gave way to the treed foothills of the Rockies. She could tell they were heading west because the white tips of the mountains edged the horizon.

David took the on-ramp for the highway and turned south. This whole situation was insane, staggering and totally out of control. Surprisingly, she felt better, as if the argument had been a safety valve releasing some of her pent-up fear and confusion.

With the window closed, she was enveloped by the intoxicating scent of soap, honey, and man. Her body clenched in a nerve-jarring sensual reaction. He shouldn't be allowed to smell so good that she responded to him in this deep, spine-tingling way. Behind the unkempt, long hair, beard, and scarred face, he struck her as being utterly male. He threw her off balance. The logical part of her brain registered that her attraction was just a physical response to his pheromones and an emotional backlash in the face of danger, nothing more. She needed to get away from David and the conflicting responses that came from being in his company. He made it hard for her to think and consider what to do in the aftermath of this latest catastrophe. She closed her eyes and pictured her lab and small, cozy house in Seattle. It was modest, but she had spent some of her inheritance ensuring that it was well maintained and filled with comfortable furniture. Above all, it was home. She wished she were there now, safe in her sanctuary, away from men with guns, policemen, and a virile ex-soldier.

"I want you to let me go," she demanded.

"I'm not holding you against your will. Marshall Portman is trying to kill you, and I'm trying to save you. You do remember the man with the gun back there, don't you?"

"Why aren't we going to the police?"

"I heard Portman say he owns the Granite City-Elkhead County police. We can't trust them. I can't drop you off at the police station like I did before. We need to get out of town—"

"Take me to the airport."

"What?"

"You heard." This nightmare was fast becoming ludicrous. It was illogical to think that someone would go to such great lengths to hurt her. Although, Handsome had shot at them, or maybe he was shooting at David, and she just happened to be in the wrong place at the wrong time. Either way, this whole situation was completely irrational.

"That's a terrible idea."

"No, it's not. I can contact the police in Seattle and fill out a report there." She hadn't thought it through, but as soon as she said the words, she realized how reasonable they seemed, especially when compared to the absurd situation she was in now. She'd studied a map of Elkhead County when she'd arrived. Canada lay to the north and the Idaho border was in the Rocky Mountains to the west. From what she could remember, the county spanned a large area with terrain that included lakes, mountains, and federal and state parks. Maybe they could drive to the nearest large city and file a report there, but that would take hours. Getting on a flight was her quickest way out of here.

"I still don't think—"

"Are you forcing me to go with you?"

"No," he sighed, "but for the record, I don't think going to the airport is a good idea." He sounded calm, less combative.

"Why not?"

"Because it's a corral where you get herded through specific doors. There's no leeway, no other avenues to take. Plus you need to give a valid ID when you travel. There will be a record. There's a good chance Portman and Harper will know where you're going and what time you'll get there. They could be waiting for you as you get off the plane. Is there anyone who can meet you? Someone who can handle themselves?"

"My father. He's a lawyer. He'll know what to do." She pictured her only living relative at his desk in the penthouse of his downtown Seattle office building that overlooked Puget Sound. On a clear day, he could see Mount Rainier.

"A lawyer, huh."

"He's also a man who knows people. If anyone can fix this mess, it's him." She didn't add that her father hadn't returned her recent phone calls. More importantly, he was a detached man who liked working more than spending time with his only child.

David blew a long breath between pursed lips "Must be nice."

"What must?"

"To have a rich daddy to look after you."

Marie ignored his remark. Her relationship with her father was one-sided. She believed he loved her deep-down, but he wasn't a man given to displays of emotion. She dialed his number, praying he would answer her call.

"Wilson." Her father's curt voice answered on the first ring.

"Daddy, it's me. I'm in trouble."

"What kind of trouble?" The telltale flick of papers told her she did not have his undivided attention.

"Someone's trying to kill me. They burst—"

"Don't be ridiculous. You haven't left your lab for years. Why would anyone want to hurt you? Is this an attempt to get me to finance that damn thing of yours? I told you it's time to move on."

Her heart sank. He didn't believe her. "They broke—"

David snatched the phone out of her hand. "Sir, my name is David Quinn. I want you to listen. Your daughter's in deep-shit over this solar panel."

Marie tried to snatch her phone back, but David blocked her by lifting his elbow.

She reached for the phone. "Will you give me that?"

"Be quiet." He gave her a cold, hard stare.

"Don't give me that look. It doesn't frighten me," she spat and then realized the truth of her words. She wasn't scared of him. Moreover, she argued with him when she didn't argue with anyone. That somehow seemed significant, but at this moment she couldn't figure out why.

"Look, we don't have much time before they put a trace on our phones. I need him to listen."

"Oh." *Trace our phones.* This sounded like something out of a movie.

He lifted the phone to his ear. "Sir, do you have

contact with anyone who can protect your daughter."

David was silent for a minute.

"Granite City, Montana. I estimate we have about thirty minutes tops before they track us down—"

He listened again.

"I don't think that's a good idea—"

She couldn't hear her father's part of the conversation, but David held the phone at arm's length and stared at it as if it were an alien, then held the phone to his ear once again. "Listen, I will put her on the next available departure heading west. She will call with her flight number. Have at least two security personnel meet her at the airport. Men you trust, or better yet, meet her yourself." He didn't wait for an answer. Using his thumb, he pressed the disconnect button, ending the conversation.

"I hadn't finished talking to him."

"We're out of time."

She stared out the window, hoping he wouldn't see the hurt look she knew was in her eyes. Her father didn't believe she was in danger. He thought she was pretending to be in trouble in order to obtain money. Her heart ached as she was reminded her father didn't know anything about her.

Keeping a hand on the steering wheel, David slid the back off the phone, pried out the battery and SIM card, and placed all three in his pocket. Then he grabbed his flip phone out of his pocket and followed the same procedure, removing the battery and the SIM card, his movements smooth and practiced.

"What are you doing? That's distracted driving. You should be concentrating on the road."

"I can multitask. Besides, there are no distracted driving laws in Montana. It's important they don't use our phones to trace us. I'll put them back together later and give them a false trail to follow."

"I need my phone. It holds my contacts, emails, and all sorts of other pertinent information. More importantly, I can't afford to replace it."

"You can buy a prepaid cell from Walmart for ten bucks. There's nothing that can't be replaced."

His idea of a phone was vastly different from hers. But she would gladly sacrifice it to ensure she never came face to face with the men from the cabin again, especially if he was right about their ability to track her. "Do what you have to."

He grimaced. "Listen, I want you to be wary on this flight. Don't talk to anyone. That includes little old ladies and children."

"Children?"

"Yes, you'd be surprised what a child can be persuaded to do."

"That's sad." Marie continued to stare out the window as David took the exit off the highway that led to the airport. She had to wonder if her father cared enough to obey David's instructions. If he didn't, then once she landed, she was on her own, but that was nothing new.

Chapter Eight

David glanced at Marie as he parked his truck in the short-term parking. Every muscle, every sinew of her small body seemed coiled tight.

"You should've just dropped me off." She opened the door of the truck with one hand, while the other hand clutched the strap of her black backpack. Her gaze drifted to the terminal building.

"I'll walk you to security." She royally pissed him off. He'd put himself on the line to protect her, and she couldn't wait to get away from him, as if he were a lower form of life. Never mind that he'd saved her pretty little butt. One look at him, and she wanted to get as far away as possible. It wasn't that he expected or wanted her gratitude. He'd done what he'd done because it was the right thing to do. He'd learned that a man had to be able to live with himself and the consequences of his actions. He had a hard enough time living with his memories. He didn't want to add her death to his overburdened conscience.

Portman's betrayal screwed with his ability to think. How could he have been so blind? He should have seen it. Portman's incessant phone calls. The pleas for help. It was all a ruse.

Marshall figured David was expendable in his present condition. Well hell, he'd always been expendable. That was why he'd been sent from one hellhole to another, to kill and be killed for his country. He didn't want thanks for that either. He'd been proud to serve. Even if it hadn't ended well.

He sighed. He shouldn't have lost his temper and sworn at her. It had been petty and small, but her prissiness in the face of mounting danger had touched a nerve. Maybe parting ways was for the best. He was just getting his life back together, and the last thing he needed was trouble, especially when it came in the form of a beautiful, curvaceous, naive scientist. He would get her on a flight out of here and then call Finn and arrange a meeting.

Clutching her backpack, she walked around the front of his truck and then stopped. "Thank you for everything. It's all so—so…"

"It's a lot to take in," he said, letting her off the hook as they made their way through the ice-covered parking lot.

"Yes, it is." Bluish-purple shadows darkened the skin under her eyes. She was traumatized by the night's events. It would take a while for her to recover.

If he considered things from her perspective, then he probably did seem menacing, especially with his scar. Maybe she thought he was as ruthless as the men he'd arrived with. She would be right—he was a bastard. He just didn't kill people anymore.

He clasped Marie's cold hand as they headed across the one-way street that separated the Granite City airport from the parking lot. Her touch comforted him, and he was gratified when she didn't pull away. Instead, she squeezed his fingers, tightening her grip.

Like most civilian airports, it was a newer glass and steel structure with baggage claim on the ground and flight departures on the first floor.

"I just don't understand why anyone would want to hurt me." Marie kept pace, still clutching her bag in her free hand.

"Did you steal the solar panel from Portman?" Somehow he couldn't picture her a thief. She seemed too innocent, but he wanted there to be a reason, some rationale behind his friend's betrayal.

"I didn't steal anything. My panel is in existence

because I thought it up and did the research and experiments to make it happen."

"There's more to owning an invention than actually conceiving it. You have to patent it and go through a lot of legal loopholes."

"Not that this is any of your business, but I had a problem in the past, which is why my father took over my legal affairs. I funded all the experiments, materials, and research myself. The solar panel is mine." She tipped her small, delicate nose in the air as if she had a whiff of something distasteful.

He ignored her snippy answer. "What kind of problem?"

"I'm sorry?"

"You said you had a problem in the past," he asked as they entered the building and rode the escalator up to departures.

"I developed a small solar charger that could be attached to any window and generate enough electricity to power a computer. It could fit into the palm of your hand." Her eyes sparked with renewed energy as she talked.

"Sounds useful." He let go of her hand as they approached the automated check-in computer.

"I thought so." She rummaged through her bag, searching for ID.

"What happened?"

"I was in university at the time, and my professor took credit for it." She pressed her lips into a thin line and averted her gaze, giving him the impression there was more to the story.

She produced her driver's license from her bag. "Legally, there was nothing I could do. I was in his department under his supervision. Once I graduated, I decided to work for myself so there would be no doubt who owned my creation. This solar panel is mine. There's a flight to Seattle leaving in twenty-five minutes."

"Sounds good." The hairs on the back of his neck rose, reminding him the airport, a place where Portman's men were bound to check, was risky. But what else could he do? She'd made her decision. He wasn't capable of doing what it took to keep her alive. He was a shell of a man who couldn't trust his own decisions, and he didn't want to be responsible for her survival. Besides, this was what she wanted—to be free of him. He would put her on a plane and send her to her father. All he needed to do was ignore his unease and forget about her pretty brown eyes.

He had sixty dollars in his wallet. Once he left her at security, he'd call Finn and then get away from the airport as fast as possible. He'd dump his truck, change his appearance, hitch a ride west, and hide out in the mountains for a while. They were in a flight or fight situation, and his only option was to run. "Take my advice and lay low until you can figure out what's going on."

She nodded.

He winced when the check-in machine scanned her ID as she changed her return ticket. Then it spat out a boarding pass. If PDE employed a competent hacker, they would know she'd been here. Come to think of it, they didn't need a hacker. They had the police.

He tried to drink in every detail. Hiding her curves was her black, down-filled coat zipped up to her neck. Her legs, clad in pink long johns, were stuffed into thermal boots. She was probably still wearing his socks. He liked that idea. He wanted her to have a reminder of him, even if it was just an old pair of socks.

The lineup for security stretched for two hundred yards. She took a step toward the end of the line. He put a hand on her shoulder, stopping her.

"What's wrong?"

"Nothing, I just want to check…" He scanned the area. Nothing seemed out of the ordinary. People from all walks of life filed into the line. There was a mix of business types, tourists, and families. A little girl wearing a tiara informed the security personnel she was going to see a princess. There was nothing threatening or out of the ordinary as far as he could tell. His stomach lurched at the idea of her going on without his protection. He inhaled. They had just come from PDE headquarters. There was no way Portman could have tracked them down in such a short time. If she left now, she should be safe.

He turned her toward him as he tucked a wisp of hair behind her ear, enjoying the soft texture on his fingertips. He stared at her mouth and then brushed his lips against hers. He straightened, shocked by his actions. "Stay safe."

He walked away before he could do something stupid like give her a real kiss.

Chapter Nine

Marie stared at David's retreating back and then touched her lips. It had been a chaste kiss, the kind a relative might impart. And yet, she felt it deep in her core, and her body wanted more. And that was the problem. His nearness caused an erotic reaction that made it hard for her to think. An unerring sense of loss told her she'd allowed something important to get away, which was madness.

As she moved with the queue, her mind flashed to him checking her toes for frostbite. His touch had been so gentle. Under all that hair, she suspected there was a handsome man with a strong, rugged physique.

He was argumentative and confrontational. She had to let him go and put this whole ordeal behind her. She inched forward, slinging her backpack over her shoulder. There was only one scanner in operation, and six passengers waiting to be patted down and searched by hand. She shouldn't be surprised by the delay. Small airports like Granite City probably didn't have the budget for the efficient full-body scanners she'd seen in SeaTac.

She scrutinized the procession of people going through the scanner and collecting their belongings from the conveyor on the other side of the x-ray machine. An elderly couple helped each other. The wife grabbed her husband's belt and shoes, while he hefted their carry-on luggage. Having set off the metal detector, a young woman took off her cowboy boots and walked through it a second time.

A man caught her eye. He stood in the lineup three people ahead of her. He seemed familiar, which strange because she didn't know anyone in Granite City.

She scrutinized his broad back and short-cropped dark hair. He turned, stared straight at her, and smiled. Her heart stopped, and a scream lodged in her throat. It was one of the twins from the cabin.

She took a step back, trying to put some distance between them, but the person behind pushed against her backpack, moving her forward. She recoiled at the acrid smell of body odor that stung her nose.

At that moment, the security personnel opened another scanner. People dashed from her lineup, desperate to be the first to go through the newly opened lane. She whirled around, ready to make her exit, and found herself staring into the face of the other twin—the one with the white, jagged scar across his chin.

"Hello pretty lady. Imagine meeting you here." He gripped her arm. "We're going to walk out of here, nice and slow. You don't want me to use my knife, do you?"

He hauled her out of the line-up. She glanced behind. The first twin was working his way back through the crowd. Once he joined them, she would have no chance to escape.

Strong fingers dug into her elbow, catching the nerve that ran to her shoulder, making her wince. He leant close to her ear. "Don't make a fuss."

A cold trickle of fear crept down her spine as her vision blurred. She had to think. *Don't make a fuss.* The words echoed through her mind. That was it. There were people here. If they didn't want her to make noise, then that was exactly what she should do.

"Help." But what she hoped would be a loud roar sounded more like a dull croak. No one looked at her or offered her help. The other passengers continued going about their business. The security personnel didn't spare her a glance. She was being taken under their very noses, and no one noticed. The second twin was ten feet away. Soon it would be too late.

She couldn't let them drag her out of the airport. Once

they had her alone, they would do terrible things to her. She swung her backpack as hard as she could, aiming for the twin's stomach. He bent forward, absorbing the blow. Then she stomped on his instep. He yelped and released her arm.

"David," she screamed, and then ran.

****

David stood on the sidewalk, staring at the terminal building. He needed to leave. There were cameras everywhere. If Marshall owned the police, then he had access to the cameras. *Get in the truck and go.*

He would feel better if he could talk to Finn. He wanted to hand himself over to the FBI and let them deal with it, but Finn's line had been busy so he'd left a message.

He pictured Marie with her pretty dark eyes and messy hair. He should've obtained a gate pass and made sure she made it to the plane in one piece. *Hell,* he ought to have purchased a ticket and accompanied her on the flight. Then he would know she was safe instead of standing here, wondering.

He groaned. He was a burnout who was no good to anybody. Shaking his head, he headed back into the building. Maybe he could still catch the flight.

He turned to his left at the sound of a high-pitched scream. His heart slammed against his ribcage—Marie.

Alex Paxton was tearing after her. "Come back, you bitch."

Her unseeing eyes were wild with fear as she ran down the escalator toward him and sprinted past. Alex didn't even make eye contact with him. His whole focus seemed to be on his target. *Unbelievable.* He could understand Marie not seeing him. She was a civilian with no training, but he'd been told the twins were ex-military.

David didn't stop Marie, but when Alex reached the bottom of the escalator, David whirled around, aiming a kick at Alex's head. The twin's upper body stopped, while his legs kept going. He slammed to the ground, landing on his back, gasping for air.

Shane dashed down the escalator steps, coming to his brother's aide. His small beady eyes took in the situation in a glance. As he reached the bottom, his hand went for his sidearm.

David kicked him in the stomach so he couldn't draw his weapon. Then before the twin could recover, David grabbed his arm, straightened the elbow, and twisted until he heard a snap. As Shane collapsed, screaming in pain, David relieved the twins of their weapons and tossed them in a nearby garbage can.

He glanced at Alex, who was still lying on the ground. The twin clutched his head. David knew a kick to the face could do a lot of damage to the soft tissue of the neck, and he doubted the twin would be able to threaten anyone for a while.

Marie ran through the exit a hundred yards ahead. He chased after her and caught up to her in the middle of the one-way street that ran in front of the terminal building. He grabbed her shoulders and spun her around. She swung her bag, aiming for his head. He managed to deflect the blow with his elbow. She stopped, stared at him for a moment before recognition registered in her gaze. A small cry escaped her throat, and she threw her arms around him, pressing her soft body to his. He reciprocated, holding her close. God, it was good to see her again. From now on, he was keeping her by his side. He'd keep her safe even if it killed him.

"Time to go, sweetheart." He tugged her to the side of the road and flagged down a passing taxi.

"Where to?" The driver asked.

"Granite City."

The driver nodded and stepped on the gas.

As the car pulled away, David saw Alex through the glass windows. He was helping his injured brother. Shane's face was pale and distorted with pain as he cradled his broken arm. They didn't look happy.

Chapter Ten

A blast of warm air welcomed Marie as she trudged through the sliding glass door of the truck stop. It was a large gas station. The entrance led them into a central hallway with a convenience store on the left and a diner to the right. She headed for the coffee counter near the back wall of the store.

They'd trekked along the ice-covered side road for what seemed like hours, but was probably only ten minutes. The extreme cold made everything hurt, not just her hands and feet. She'd pulled up her collar so that it had covered her mouth, which prevented cold air from entering her lungs. David had held one of her hands, keeping it warm. She'd stuffed the other into her pocket to prevent frostbite. But her ears hurt, not just the lobes, the pain seemed to have seeped through her ear canal into her brain.

His beard encrusted with ice, David stepped next to her at the counter. He grabbed a Styrofoam cup and poured himself a hot drink. She did the same. She didn't need the hit of caffeine. She was still tense after her near escape at the airport, but a warm coffee would help her thaw out.

"Are you okay?" He took a sip of the hot, black liquid.

She nodded, adding three packets of sugar and two servings of cream to her cup. "Tell me again why you ordered the taxi to stop on the highway before we reached Granite City?"

"They have tracking software in cabs. I didn't want them to trace us to this spot."

"How do you think they knew we were at the airport?" She tried not to think about her close call. Instead, she inhaled the scent of the sweet brew, hoping it would replace the memory of the twin's foul body odor.

"Maybe they put a tracker on my truck."

"They can do that?" Her chest constricted. Her life was out of control. It was as if she were inside a tornado, being tossed about, with no idea where, or even if, she would land.

"Sure, we live in a digital age, and we're being chased by a man with unlimited funds. He can afford the latest technology and experts."

"They'll know we were here even though we walked?" She had never felt so powerless. "We're not going to get out of this, are we?" With a shaky hand, she lifted the cup to her mouth and took another sip. Panicking was not going to make the situation better. She needed to think clearly, but that was beyond her at the moment.

She wished she could call the police, but David's concerns gave her pause. Those horrible men at the airport had attempted to take her in broad daylight, in a public place where there were an abundance of cameras and security personnel. They seemed to have no fear of being arrested. What if David was right and Marshall Portman had bribed the police? Had he only perverted the Granite City-Elkhead County Police or did his corruption reach farther afield?

"What now?" She glanced at David who stared blankly out the window, lost in his own thoughts.

He leaned in close so that his breath warmed her ear, sending an unexpected shiver tingling down her spine. "First we need to get away from Granite City and Elkhead County.

"Why did we come back here? Shouldn't we have gone in another direction?"

"First, the nearest city is over an hour from here, and I can't afford the cab fare. And second, the dispatcher at the taxi company would be able to track the car. It's all done by GPS."

"That's why we got out on the highway."

"Yeah. My original plan was to hitch a ride out of the state and hide out until Finn can sort out this mess. I think it's still viable."

That made sense. All they needed to do was stay alive long enough for the FBI to catch the bad guys. "Good plan."

"There's a cabin northwest of here on the Idaho border. It belongs to a friend. I haven't been there since I was in basic, so it's doubtful anyone will look for us there."

"I like the sound of that." She stepped back, needing to put some distance between them, not wanting to be distracted by his intoxicating scent and her attraction to him.

"Good, cause I wasn't asking. As soon as I can, I'm handing you over to Finn, and then he can protect you."

The thought that he couldn't wait to be rid of her stung, which was strange because she wanted the same thing—to be away from him. That was why she'd insisted on going to the airport. David wanted to pass her off to the FBI as soon as possible. He wasn't interested in her in a romantic sense. They had been thrown together, and he was just doing his best to keep them alive. She'd been behaving like a self-important little brat when she should be helping.

This whole situation was so insane, so over the top, she struggled to comprehend Marshall Portman's reasoning. It left her shocked and bewildered, and her only option was to go along with this hard, confrontational man who'd warned her that going to the airport was a bad idea. "How are we going to get there?"

"Like I said, we're going to catch a ride, but no one will help us if we seem too desperate. The drivers will know something's up. I think we need to sit and eat just to appear ordinary."

"That makes sense, but I really don't want to stay here too long." She scanned the store again. Everything looked normal, but would she be able to spot a deviation—an anomalous or strange customer? Probably not.

"I hear you. From now on, we're a couple. Our car broke down. We're heading to Libby. I have a job waiting for me there."

"What kind of job?"

"Does it matter?"

"I'd ask if I were giving us a ride. People like to know that kind of thing. We define ourselves by our professions."

He tilted his head. "We do?"

"Yes, we do."

"Okay, I work in the family store."

"Selling what?"

He rolled his eyes. "Styrofoam cups. Does it matter?"

"Oh yes, I'd—"

"Ask if you were giving us a ride." He threw his cup in the garbage and grabbed a wire shopping basket. He loaded it with Band-Aids, aspirin, a small emergency foil blanket, waterproof matches, toothbrushes, toothpaste, a pack of razors, a pair of scissors, two knit wool hats, two pairs of thermal mittens, a cheap purple backpack, and some feminine hygiene products.

Marie picked up the sanitary napkins. "Do you know something I don't?"

"I have a twin sister. I've learned that it's essential to stock up on these kinds of things."

"You have a twin? Is she like you? No, don't answer that. I can't even begin to imagine what the female version of you would look like. Right now, I'm picturing your sister as a hairy woman in a skirt."

His mouth twitched in what could have been characterized as the beginnings of a smile. "Do you have any allergies I should know about?"

She shook her head.

"Good." He pushed the basket into her hands. "Get some food and water. Energy bars, jerky, trail mix, stuff like that. Don't buy anything that won't fit in the purple bag. We need to travel light. And from now on we'll have to pay cash for everything, no credit cards. How much money do you have?"

She rifled through her wallet. "Forty dollars."

"Okay, you can pay for breakfast. Here's some money for our supplies." He stuffed three twenty-dollar bills in her hand. She deposited the cash in her wallet as he retrieved their phones from his pocket and reassembled them before heading for the door.

Marie hunted the aisles for food that would boost their energy. She collected some protein bars, a box of crackers, a small jar of peanut butter, three large bags of nuts, and some jerky. Then she added a few chocolate bars to satisfy her sweet tooth. She eyed the popcorn and chips. Both were filling, and the chips were high in calories, which might be handy in the cold, but she doubted they would fit in the backpack. She grabbed two half-gallon water bottles. It wasn't enough. The average human needed eight glasses of water a day, but they were limited in how much they could carry, so these would have to do. She joined the line-up to pay, watching David through the window.

He stood at the gas island, seemingly intent on throwing away garbage. With his other hand, he dropped something, probably one of the phones, into the back of a pickup. If she hadn't been watching, she wouldn't have noticed.

He then strolled toward the entrance. She was struck by how much he knew, how prepared he was for their current situation, whereas she was an ill-equipped mess.

She paid for their items, not forgetting to add their coffees, shrugged into her black backpack, and then stuffed everything into the new purple bag.

David waited by the entrance to the diner. There was no way he could be described as handsome, but there was something about him, an intensity, that drew her. He was powerful, strong, hard, and serious. He made her feel on edge and yet safe at the same time. It would be a lot simpler if she weren't attracted to him. When he stood too close, her body came alive as every molecule and nerve ending vibrated, and tremors tingled down her spine, making it impossible to focus.

He scrutinized her as she walked toward him. Using her free hand, she tucked her hair behind her ear, hoping she looked presentable. She could probably make herself more attractive if she tried. She could do her hair, learn how to apply makeup, and she could stand to lose a few extra pounds.

Get a grip. She was a scientist who analyzed data and drew conclusions. Obsessing about her looks and her physical reaction to him must be her mind's way of distracting her from the reality of their situation. It was a protective response so she didn't become overwhelmed with the stress. She'd allowed herself to be sidetracked instead of dealing with the reality. Dangerous men were chasing them. She needed to concentrate and work through the variables, and then she could find a resolution.

"Let's hope that worked." David grabbed the purple backpack from her and headed into the diner. Red, plastic tabletops with chrome trim gave the restaurant a retro sixties feel. Windows ran along the front and side so customers could sit in the booths and look out at the parking lot and gas pumps. A counter in the center acted as a waitress station and extra seating for customers.

He didn't wait to be seated. He grabbed some menus from the cash register near the lobby and headed to a booth by the window.

A waitress, sporting a nametag that read *Hildy*, threw silverware, napkins, and two cups in front of them. Without asking, she filled the mugs from a steaming carafe of coffee.

"You two look cold. Are you ready to order?" She placed her glass coffee jug on the table and reached into her apron pocket for a notepad and pen.

"Yes, our car burned down on the highway. We lost everything." David shook his head.

Marie's jaw dropped. He'd just changed their story.

"Oh my." Hildy put a hand to her chest and shook her gray head. "You poor dears."

"We'll be fine." He gave the waitress a dazzling smile that softened his features. It gave the impression of a charming, attractive man and was a side to him she hadn't seen before. "I'm just glad no one was hurt. The insurance should pay for the damage. We just need to get where we're going, then we can get started on the paperwork. Do you know anyone heading northwest toward Libby?"

"Is Libby home?" She stuffed her pen and notepad into the pocket of her apron.

"No. Not yet anyway. I've got a job waiting there."

"What will you be doing?"

Marie cut in. "He's been hired with the sheriff's department."

David blinked and then said, "My first shift starts tomorrow."

Hildy narrowed her eyes. "You're going to need a shave and a haircut."

"Yes ma'am. I was planning to shave my beard tonight. He glanced at the menu. We'll both have eggs, bacon, and toast."

Marie bit her lip. She wanted to tell the waitress to change her order to a waffle with syrup and butter, but he was supposed to be her husband, and a husband would know what kind of food his wife ate. Not that she had much experience when it came to relationships. She only had one former boyfriend, Daniel. He had been middle-aged, flabby, and distant. She had adored him until the moment he stole her research. Then he had smeared her name in the mud, destroying her reputation as a scientist. But more importantly, he had broken her heart, and with it, her ability to trust. It had taken her years to recover.

Her scientific colleagues tended to be pale, anemic

types, and her father's friends were odious businessmen who thought nothing of backing their friend's underage daughter into a corner and slobbering all over her. David Quinn was unlike any man she'd ever met.

"I'll talk to some of the regulars, see if anyone's going your way," Hildy said, bringing Marie back to the present.

Once their waitress was out of earshot, David leaned across the table and whispered, "Sheriff's department?"

"You have this whole dangerous thing going on. No one's going to believe you work in a store, or behind a desk for that matter. Besides, you changed the story first, and I went along with that."

He shrugged and stood.

"Where are you going?"

He pointed to a beat-up payphone that hung on the wall by the entrance. "I need to call Finn and tell him what's happened. This won't take long."

She noted his long legs, the powerful way he moved— tense and contained—as if he'd harnessed raw energy and controlled it with sheer willpower.

Don't just stare at him. She made herself watch the vehicles, looking for anyone suspicious, as travelers filled their cars with gas. Most were pickup trucks and SUVs, but there was one small red car. It had spots of rust along the bottom and was stuffed full of household belongings: pillows, blankets, a percolator, and boxes.

David slammed the receiver onto the phone and marched back to their table.

"I left a message," he said as he slid back into the booth. His light green eyes flickered to the window. His shaggy hair curled around his collar. Strands of blond blended with brown, giving him what appeared to be natural highlights.

Needing a diversion, she unfolded her napkin. She'd been staring at him, drinking him in, when she should be watching for the men who'd tried to snatch her.

****

"Now explain why a solar panel is worth killing for." David pinned her with what, he hoped, was a cold, piercing gaze.

"I don't know. My prototype is different, revolutionary even, but it isn't threatening in any way. It's a very efficient solar panel, but at the end of the day, it's just that—a solar panel." She shrugged.

"Tell me about it."

She straightened her cutlery. "It's small, portable, and is made of recycled plastic."

"How small?"

"About a yard square. You've seen it—"

"Son of a bitch. It's that gold plastic sheet, isn't it? Brad had it in his hands, and he didn't know. What an idiot." He sipped his coffee. "I guess he should've done his homework. Do you still have it?"

She unsnapped her backpack and peeked inside. "Yes." Then she angled the bag and held it open to reveal a flash of gold.

"I still don't understand why anyone would want to kill over it." She closed her pack and then picked up her napkin, unfolded it, and flattened it out with her palm.

"All I know is what I heard. Portman told Harper that he wanted you, the prototype, and the plans destroyed. You'd think you were working on a bioweapon the way he talked." His gut twisted as he remembered his friend's treachery. "Are there any military applications?"

"Oh yes, it's a source of mobile power. I thought it could be used to power hospitals, command centers, and that sort of thing. You said you were a soldier. What would you use a small, portable solar panel for?"

"Everything. In fact, we already have small, mobile units we use in the field. I think Portman has lost touch with reality."

"Is there any way to convince him that he's gone insane?" She refolded her napkin in crisp, precise creases.

There was probably some psychological reason behind

the folding, but he'd be damned if he knew what it was.

"I don't know. We stayed in touch, but haven't been close for almost twenty years." Once again, he remembered the phone calls. Portman had begged for his help. David should've seen his duplicity. There was no way the president of a power company needed the help of a washed-up ex-soldier.

"How do you know Portman?" she asked. "How are you involved in all this, and don't tell me first day on the job again—"

"It was my first day on the job. At least I thought it was a job. Turns out it was something else." He took another sip of his coffee, not ready to share his past with her.

"I need to know why you were there last night." She pressed her lips together as she thumbed another crease into her napkin. She probably needed to know what kind of a man she was dealing with. He couldn't blame her. If it were the other way around, he'd have asked the same question.

"Fair enough. Like I said, it was a job. About a month ago, I came into the city—"

"Why?"

"I had a doctor's appointment at the VA hospital to check on this." He pointed to the scar.

Her eyes narrowed as she leaned in, assessing what he knew to be a deep, misshapen gouge carved into his cheek. He waited for her to recoil, to shudder and turn away, but she just studied his face and then nodded. "Go on."

"We chatted for a bit. I told him I had some land near Missoula. I think I mentioned I needed to get some money together. To be honest, I can't remember all the details of the conversation. Anyway, last week Marshall called me and told me someone had stolen the plans to a project he'd sponsored. He asked for my help getting them back. He gave me the impression that some criminal element was involved."

"And that's what you do for a living, retrieve stolen

items?"

"No. I had a good chunk of money saved when I got out of the army. I purchased a ten-acre parcel of land west of Missoula and five beehives. I cleared a spot near a stream and put an old camper on it. I don't need much. I can hunt for my meat and cook over an open fire. I'm used to roughing it, and I have some money put by for incidentals. I'm in good shape."

"How did you end up at my cabin?"

"As I said, Portman contacted me. He said he needed my help. I told him I wasn't up for the job and I don't carry weapons anymore, but he kept insisting. He offered to pay me enough so I could build a cabin and invest in more hives." The coffee burned his gut. He'd been lured into a trap by a sense of obligation to an old friend and the promise of a few thousand dollars.

"And that's how he convinced you?"

He shrugged. "That, and I owed him."

She frowned. "Why?"

"He saved my life."

He could see by the way she tilted her head she wanted to ask more, but they'd been sitting here long enough. The question and answer portion of their conversation was over. They needed to concentrate on their survival. "We have to keep a low profile, no smiling at strangers, no small talk, don't make eye contact, just keep your head down and try to be invisible."

"You make it sound as if everyone is after us."

"When you make a connection with people, even a small one, they are more likely to remember you."

"And you think just because they remember us, they'll run to PDE and tell them where we are?"

"Don't forget about the police. It's a risk we can't take."

"Well, I think you're wrong. People are basically good, and someone will help us."

"You're talking about a fantasy. I deal in reality."

Portman had helped him, saved him, and in the end, he'd come to collect.

"That's not reality. It's distrust and skepticism. Look at you. You could have turned your back, but you stayed and helped me."

"Yes, and it was a mistake. We are not in this together. I do not fight other people's battles anymore. I do not carry weapons, and I'm not going to prison for you. As soon as I can arrange for Finn to clear up this mess, we will part ways, and I will go back to my land and my bees." He pictured his camper parked by the small creek that ran through his property. He imagined the silence and the peace.

She swallowed hard as she stared out of the window. He'd hurt her feelings. He really was a bastard, but he wouldn't sugarcoat the truth. He simply wasn't in a position to help her. Plus, she was in deep-shit, the kind of crap that required help from law enforcement. It didn't matter how he felt. Sooner or later, he needed to take a step back and allow the authorities to do their job. Until that time, he would keep her close and protect her. "Is there anyone in your life you can trust? And don't say your father because he's an idiot."

"Why do you say that?"

"He thought this was some kind of trick to get money. Maybe I'm wrong, but you don't seem the type to commit extortion."

"I'm not. That's just how he thinks."

"Back to my question—who can you count on?"

She stared out the window. "My friend Ella and her husband, Nick. We all met at university. She's blunt to a fault and tells me the truth, even if it's not what I want to hear, but I trust her." Her hand went to the neck of her shirt. "Nick's cool, too. They have a baby, Matt. He's a cute, little drool machine.".

There was something about her body language and the way she averted her gaze that told him there was more to this friend than she wanted him to know. He could press her, insist she tell him everything, but in all fairness, he didn't want to explain every facet of his life to her either, so he let it go. Given her mannerisms, he had to conclude she was on her own, and there was no one who cared about her.

"Jake, this is the young couple I was telling you about." Hildy hustled to their table with a baby-faced man in tow. "Jake, here, is going to Spokane and will give you a ride in his semi."

"Hi, I'm David, pleased to meet you. This is Marie. We're grateful for any help you can give us." David had no doubt about his ability to overpower Jake if necessary. The trucker was young, tall, slim, and not overly muscular. He wore a fleece-lined check shirt, jeans, and work boots. Strands of short dark hair poked out from his red baseball cap. His shirt fit tight and left no room to conceal a weapon.

Jake nodded hello to Marie. "If you want that ride, we have to get going. I want to get across the state line before the blizzard hits."

David stepped out of the booth. "There's a blizzard warning?"

"Yep, the storm's supposed to roll in from the west. The radio said it would reach Granite City by three this afternoon." Jake's gaze didn't meet David's, but instead he stared at David's chest. David buried his suspicions, not because he thought Jake was harmless, but because he experienced this reaction on a regular basis. Most people avoided looking directly at his ravaged face. He was learning to acclimatize, but there were times, like now, when he faltered before recognizing the response for what it was, an attempt to avoid looking at his scar.

Hildy dumped two brown bags on the table in front of them. "I figured I'd package your food to go. Jake's in a hurry." She placed the bill on the table.

"I'll get that." Marie reached into her pocket and found

some bills.

He'd used the last of his money to pay for their supplies. The lack of cash could be a problem in the short term. Once everything was sorted out, he would have access to his account. Then he could go back to his life. He grabbed the brown bags and the purple backpack and gave Hildy a bright smile.

The waitress's cheeks reddened as she smiled back. It was good to know he still had the ability to make a woman blush.

Marie frowned at him, her eyes hard. She was angry with him. He had no idea why. One minute they were getting along fine, the next he was a lower form of life. There was no way a smile would work on her. He followed Jake, wondering what it would take to melt Marie's defenses and make her blush.

Chapter Eleven

Marie held David's hand as they followed Jake to a big red semi attached to a long, gray trailer. As much as she hated to admit it, being close to him comforted her on a very basic level, reminding her she wasn't in this alone, which was a strange notion now that she thought about it. She'd been alone since her mother's suicide when she was five years old. It was all she'd ever known. She'd had various nannies who had tended her, but they were distant, going through the motions of caring without any feeling behind their actions. That was probably why she had fallen so hard for a jerk like Daniel. Her loneliness was a protection and a liability.

She'd always been different from the other children in her class. While they were learning their letters, she was reading books on Albert Einstein. It wasn't unusual for her to bear the brunt of hurtful taunts. No matter how old she'd gotten, she'd never learned to deal with nasty remarks. They always hurt. Isolating herself and becoming self-reliant provided her with a buffer from the outside world, but it also caused problems. She wasn't worldly and didn't understand the nuances that were plain to others. She suspected her isolation also made her more likely to become overly involved. That was why she had lost herself with Daniel. When she fell, she fell hard. It wasn't that she didn't want to love again, but surviving the humiliation and hurt that came with it was another matter. And unfortunately, she was especially susceptible to attractive, scarred ex-soldiers.

"I'm empty so it'll be a bumpy ride." The trucker smiled, unlocking the doors.

"We're just grateful you can take us," David said.

Jake stepped out of the way. "You guys get comfortable. You'll have to share a seat, but I figure that won't be a problem. I'll just be a minute. I have to check the airbrakes before we leave."

David grabbed her around the waist and hoisted her up into the cab.

She swatted at his hands. "Stop that, and what's with all the smiling?"

"What? He followed her into the small, cramped interior. There were two captain's chairs in the cab. The dashboard curved around the driver's seat with a gearshift in the middle. Most of the space was taken by the bunk, which was concealed behind heavy red curtains. A photo of two young boys peeked out from the visor.

Marie perched sideways on the edge of the chair with her legs around the gearshift. She looked over her shoulder at David. "If I'm not allowed to smile at people, then you aren't either."

"That's why you're in a snit. Stand up." He gave her a hard stare.

"Don't give me that look. You smiled. Hildy blushed. She'll remember you." She stood, bending so her head didn't hit the roof.

"You jealous?" He seemed to be enjoying himself.

"Jealous, no." She couldn't begrudge a middle-aged waitress a pleasant goodbye, but a twinge of envy festered in the back of her mind. She wanted more than the emotionless glare he tended to throw her way. "The rules have to be the same for both of us. And by the way, not smiling is a stupid rule. You're too memorable with your light eyes and the scar—"

"I'm memorable? You're the one everyone will remember with your curvy little body, wearing nothing but long johns—"

"Well, pardon me, the next time men burst into my cabin in the middle of the night, I'll be sure to dress first. Would you like me to do my hair and put on lipstick, too?

Besides, my coat is done up so they can't see anything."

He sat behind her, held her waist, and drew her down so she rested on his thighs. "It doesn't matter. You've got those sexy bedroom eyes—"

"I've never heard anything so ridiculous in my life."

He grinned as he placed an arm under her knees, swiveled, and elevated her legs so she lay across his lap, bridal style.

For a moment she was distracted by his smile. It was genuine, bright and devastating. "What are you doing?" She tensed, holding her body rigid. He really was the most annoying man. She'd stated her case, and he'd tried to distract her with a lot of nonsense about bedroom eyes and a sexy grin.

"Getting comfortable. You'll need to put your arm around my neck if we're going to convince Jake we're a couple." He reminded her of a cheeky little boy. The muscles on the uninjured side stretched in to the correct position, while the scar seemed to prevent the corresponding movement, giving him a lopsided smile.

She was not ready to let go of her anger, even if he was. Although why she was so upset, she couldn't say. Maybe because it was something she could hold between them and use as a barrier to prevent her from becoming too attached. She jabbed him in the ribs with her elbow, so he knew he wasn't off the hook. "He's more likely to believe we're a couple if I'm mad at you, so I'm going with that."

"Why are you so angry?"

"I'm not," she lied. "I'm—I'm frustrated."

"Why?"

She needed to come up with something. She needed to exercise some restraint, but not because she wanted to be rid of him, but because she liked him a little too much. Each time he smiled, cared for her, or seemed genuinely interested in her, she became even more drawn to him. The way iron filings were drawn to a magnet. She couldn't trust herself in this situation. There was a chance she would get too emotionally involved, and she couldn't let that happen. "B-because I'm not equipped to deal with this. I don't know about tracking phones and being chased. You're prepared. Fearless. I'm not. I'm just a scientist. I study, research, and experiment. I also examine the facts and draw conclusions. I don't dodge bullets and fight bad guys. I've never been bold and daring in my life." It was the truth as far as it went.

He tilted his head. "You haven't?"

She gazed out of the window as her cheeks burned. She was ashamed of her cowardice, but it was easier to explain than her attraction.

The truth was he couldn't count on her in a fight. She wished she were different, but she had to face whom and what she was—a coward. He needed to know that so he could protect himself. "No, I live a very safe, orderly life. In fact, my father's nickname for me is Mouse. He calls me that because I'm scared of everything." She cringed at the admission. One of her father's taunts echoed through her mind. *"You're a mouse who never leaves your house."*

"Really?"

"Yes, I was frightened when you burst in to the cabin, and I was terrified at the airport."

"Being afraid is normal. When we invaded your cabin, you didn't freak out. When those bastards were going to rape you, you reached for the car keys. And then at the airport, you got away from Alex. Every time you're in trouble, you don't freeze, you do something to help yourself. You handle yourself well."

"I do?" Could that be true, or was he just being kind? She went back over the events in her mind. "I managed to get away at the airport, but you're the one who fought them."

"I'm trained. You're not. It would be suicidal for you to take them on. And while we're being frank, I want to know how come you're not scared of my death stare?" He gave her the cold, hard stare he'd used earlier.

"You had that look on your face when you burst into my cabin, and you've used it a few times since."

"I know. I've practiced and perfected that look over the years. The ability to make people back off with a glance is invaluable and has saved me from a fight on more than one occasion."

"I need to learn that."

"My friend, Tim, has nicknamed that particular expression my death stare. All those years of practice wasted because it doesn't work on you."

"To be fair, it did. That was why I was so terrified of you, even though you put yourself in the line of fire. It wasn't until you left me at the police station that I realized you weren't dangerous, at least, not to me.

"There are grown men I've known for years who are still scared of that look. You've known me for less than a day, and it has no effect on you. I think you're wrong."

"About what?"

"You are brave. You just don't know it."

"That's so-so…" It was probably the nicest thing anyone had ever said to her. She put both arms around his neck and gave him a small, quick hug. He returned the embrace, rubbing his warm hand down her back. She pulled away, aware that she enjoyed being held by him a little too much. Oh boy, she was in big trouble.

****

"I think Jake's coming. Now remember, we're a couple," he whispered into her ear as he allowed her to lean back and put some space between them. Not that she could do it effectively when she was lying across his lap. As displays of affection went, her hug was small, but it was genuine, which was a surprise because he hadn't said anything flowery or romantic. He'd simply stated the truth, but for her it had been significant. He would have thought a scientist would be more aware of herself and her capabilities, but Marie's reaction suggested she had no idea how competent she really was.

Jake slid into the driver's seat, put two fingers to his lips, kissed them, and then put them on the photo of the boys, which was attached to the visor.

Jake had a pocketknife attached to his belt. That wasn't a big concern. Pocketknives were mainly used as a tool. Plus, you had to pry the blade out of the handle, making it slow and awkward as a weapon. David would bet his property there was a handgun close by. It wouldn't be in the glove compartment. That was too far away. Maybe under the driver's seat.

Jake turned to David. "My boys are my lucky charm. Do you two have any kids?"

"No, but we're thinking of it. Aren't we, sugar?" He kissed her hair again, enjoying the feigned intimacy.

Marie smiled and shrugged, but didn't reply.

"You should," Jake said. "Being a daddy is the best thing in the world. It's hard being away, but knowing I'm providing for my family is worth it."

They bounced on the ice-rutted road and took the exit onto the main highway. Soon they would be away from Granite City. Once Jake dropped them off, David would look for a phone and call Finn. Maybe he could help them figure out their next move.

When Marie wiggled, trying to get comfortable, her soft body curving against him, an erection throbbed to life. He stifled a groan as he imagined her breasts pressing against the soft cotton of her thermal underwear. With a shake of his head, he forced away the vision of sucking her pert nipples into his mouth. This wasn't the time.

He leaned back in the captain's chair, pulling Marie with him. He wished he could relax, but that was impossible. He'd known Portman for nearly twenty years and had believed he was a friend. The man had rescued him, fed him, educated him, and given him a future. David couldn't even fathom why he would go to such lengths to rescue the children of Marshall House if he considered them disposable. David's gut twisted again. He had to compartmentalize and deal with the emotional crap later. Right now they needed to survive, and getting out of Granite City was a good start.

Marie squirmed in his lap and flicked her hair over her shoulder. It was a uniquely feminine gesture, which made him wish he'd met her under different circumstances. If he'd bumped into her at a grocery store, or maybe a coffee shop, he might have made an excuse to talk to her. They could've discussed their plans and dreams with no mention of killers or being chased. Regular life—it'd been so long since he'd experienced it, he didn't know what it was anymore or if it even existed. He longed to be normal and whole, instead of a washed-up ex-soldier.

He nuzzled Marie's hair. "We should eat and then get some rest. You must be tired. You didn't get any sleep last night."

"I'm fine."

"Eat," he insisted.

She eyed him as if she'd like to gut him like a fish, but said nothing. Instead she plucked a brown bag off the floor and passed it to him. Then she levered herself into a sitting position and searched the purple backpack until she found a chocolate bar.

He liked it when she got prickly and sharp. He'd wanted her to eat, but instead of eating breakfast, she'd chosen a sweet. It was an act of pure rebellion, and he loved it, although he couldn't say why. Maybe it was because every person he'd met since he'd been shot either pitied him or treated him as if he was a monster. There was no middle ground. But now that Marie had gotten over her initial reaction to his appearance, she had no problem showing her displeasure. That didn't mean she was completely comfortable with him. There was something she wasn't telling him, something to do with her father and friends. She'd flinched when they'd talked about him in the diner. It was a small movement, almost imperceptible. She probably didn't even know she'd done it.

On a purely emotional level, it annoyed him she didn't trust him enough to explain her feelings, although he wasn't about to explain his deepest emotions to her either. They'd known each other for less than a day. He'd have to be patient and get to know her.

Now there was an idea, he could become intimately acquainted with her. It was selfish to drag her down into his bleak world, but there was something about her. She was an intriguing combination of feistiness and inexperience. She made him want to be whole again. He wanted to save her, protect her, and love her because she gave him purpose. He didn't know if those feelings were temporary or if they could develop into something permanent. One thing was certain; if he didn't take the chance, then nothing could happen.

She didn't seem to be repulsed by his appearance, but that didn't mean she was attracted to him. Nothing could happen without mutual attraction. As it stood, time was on his side. While they were hiding out, he would charm, cajole, and nag her if necessary until she was comfortable enough to share everything with him, even her bed.

The nickname, Mouse, bothered him. It wasn't that bad. He'd heard parents call their kids far worse. He couldn't put his finger on what it was about it that troubled him, but he knew it was something important.

She finished eating, and he was about to tell her to eat more when she relaxed against him. Within minutes, her rhythmic breathing told him she'd fallen asleep. Her body molded to his, as if they were a married couple and not just acquaintances. He stared at the icy highway as the truck sped west. They were in one piece, and they were leaving Granite City. Things were definitely looking up.

Chapter Twelve

Supervisory Special Agent Finn Callaghan had just finished unpacking the last of his boxes. As the newly promoted senior agent at the Granite City resident agency, he was still remembering names and faces. He needed to learn the players, the influential businessmen, community leaders, and most of all, figure out who were the good guys and who were the bad. Something that was hard to tell by position alone.

His second-floor office in the Granite City-Elkhead County police station was nice as ex-storage rooms went. His superiors in Salt Lake City had assured him the space was temporary until something more suitable could be found.

A large filing cabinet with a small television on top stood in the corner behind the door. The size of the cabinet was a testament to the amount of paperwork inflicted on all law enforcement officers. His desk sat on the opposite side of the office, and behind it a luxurious, ergonomic swivel chair he'd given himself two Christmases ago. If he was going to put in sixty hours a week, he wanted to be comfortable.

But the thing he enjoyed most about his workspace was the large south-facing window with a view of the square. The town fathers had done a decent job planning the downtown. The police station was situated on the north side, with the town hall and law courts to his left, and a coffee shop and news station to his right. The grandiose building that housed the headquarters for Public Domain Energy was located on the south side of the square.

Twenty years ago, when executive Marshall Portman had moved his power company headquarters to Granite

City, he'd taken over a derelict hotel, saving beautiful architectural work and handcrafted moldings from the wrecking ball. He had revamped and modernized the building into a unique five-story structure that was both elegant and functional.

Finn stood at the window, squinting at the sky. It was a beautiful, sunny day. Mounds of snow glistened in the square as if they'd been scattered with tiny diamonds.

He pictured David sleeping in the city center as a teen. A twinge told him something about David's situation didn't add up. The fact he had been part of a home invasion went against everything Finn knew about his friend. And Marie Wilson had been terrorized and threatened because of a solar panel. If this was a puzzle, then the pieces didn't fit. The solar panel was not new technology. People all over the country used them.

A knock at his open door interrupted his thoughts.

"Good morning, Agent Callaghan." Agent Kennedy Norris, the junior FBI agent assigned to Granite City, stepped into his office.

She was tall with strong shoulders and a trim torso, a swimmer's body. As usual, she wore her shoulder-length, light brown hair neatly tied at the nape of her neck. Her practical cargo pants were coupled with a long-sleeved turtleneck sweater, and an expensive down-filled coat hung over her arm. She seemed relaxed, her disposable coffee cup in hand. But after working with her for two weeks, he knew she was a whirlwind of impulse and insight disguised as a sensible woman.

As striking as she was, he found he wasn't attracted to her, which was a surprise, and a relief. He was a normal, healthy male with all the usual urges, but there was no chemistry between them. Sexual chemistry had to be the most noxious, toxic, and inconvenient bioweapon ever unleashed on mankind. He smiled at his underling, thanking his lucky stars it hadn't reared its ugly head. Dealing with Kennedy's sharp instinct was enough. He didn't need to be involved with her, too.

"Morning." Finn crossed the room and sank into his chair.

"I heard you had a visitor."

"A scientist named Marie Wilson. She was the victim of a home invasion."

"We don't do home invasions. That's a PD matter."

"She was saved by a guy I knew in basic training."

"How did he save—"

"He was part of the gang that invaded her home—"

"And then he rescued her? How likely is that?" Kennedy took a step closer.

"That got your attention, didn't it?" Finn smiled.

"Who starts a home invasion and then changes his mind halfway through?"

"David Quinn, apparently." He leaned forward, propping his elbows on his desk. Once again, he questioned the likelihood of David being part of a criminal act. It just didn't reconcile with the man he'd known for fifteen years. David had always been honest, direct, and straightforward. He wasn't a criminal, and he was very protective of women.

Finn could believe he had saved Dr. Wilson. He just had a hard time understanding why he was involved in the first place. "Anyway, the Granite City-Elkhead police are dealing with it. I just sat in because she asked me to."

Detective Ramirez knocked at his door. "Do you have a minute?"

"Sure."

"Your friend, Quinn, hasn't come to see me. Has he contacted you?" Ramirez closed the door behind him.

"No, but I've been in a meeting with the federal attorney for most of the morning." Finn picked up his phone, five messages, and two from unknown numbers. "Hang on. I'll see if he's called." He swiveled his chair so his back was to the detective as he entered the code for his voicemail.

The first three messages were from Kennedy concerning items she needed for the office, toilet paper being at the top of her list. Two were from David and included some choice curse words. It was the tone of the message that really got his attention. Quinn sounded anxious and stressed.

Finn stood and walked to the window. Damn, his friend had needed him, and he'd been in a meeting.

"Well," Ramirez pressed.

"He said he's in trouble." Finn decided not to reveal the entirety of the conversation to the detective.

"Did he say what kind of trouble?" Ramirez jotted down the details in a small, coiled notepad.

"No, he didn't give specifics," Finn lied.

"Did he say where he was?"

"No." Finn's back cramped. He stretched out his shoulders to relieve some of the pressure.

"Okay, so your buddy, David Quinn, rescues Marie Wilson from a home invasion and brings her here. I just heard from the fire marshal. The cabin on Deerborn Road, the one with the red roof, was burnt to the ground."

"What?" Finn spun around.

"Yeah, and it was definitely arson. It was sloppy, too. They found traces of gas splashed all over the area."

"Damn. David couldn't have done that."

"No, but he knows who did. I need to talk to him. Where does he live?"

"He has acreage out near Missoula."

"What does he do for a living?"

Finn thought about the dinner he'd had with his old friend at Christmas. "He's healing."

"Healing?"

"He was shot in the line of duty. Actually, a bullet grazed his face. He's adjusting to civilian life. He has ten acres of bush. He lives in an old camper and keeps bees."

"He's a beekeeper?" Ramirez's lips pressed into a thin line as he raised one eyebrow, which suggested he was skeptical of David's chosen profession.

"He seems to think there's a living to be made from renting out bee hives, and according to him, they're peaceful."

"Did he receive an honorable discharge?"

"As far as I know. The army was the only home he had. I can't imagine him doing anything to mess that up." This was beginning to feel like an interrogation. He glanced at Kennedy. She was leaning with her butt against his desk. Her coat was in a pile on his chair. Seemingly relaxed, she took a sip of her coffee, but her eyes were focused on Ramirez as he continued to ask questions.

"When you say the army was his only home…"

"He was a street kid. Actually, he lived on the streets of Granite City. He was taken in by a local charity. He got his GED and then joined up."

"The charity that took him in…could it be Marshall House?"

"Sounds familiar, but I can check."

"Check with whom?"

Yes, this was definitely an interrogation. "There was a small posse of them living rough, which included Sinclair, David's twin sister, Tim Morgan, and Michael Papin. They all went into the army together. They still keep in touch."

"When was the last time you saw Quinn?"

"Christmas dinner. It's not unusual for us to spend the holidays together." Mainly because none of them had anyone else so they'd become a family.

"Us?"

"Yes, they've included me in their group since basic training. We've known each other for fifteen years."

Ramirez narrowed his eyes. "But you didn't live on the street with them?"

"No. I grew up in Chicago." There was no way Finn would reveal his background unless it was absolutely necessary.

"You met in basic. How long ago was that?"

"As I said, fifteen years." Finn forced himself to relax. He hadn't done anything wrong, and as far as he could tell, neither had David. Mateo Ramirez was just doing what any good detective would do—ask questions.

"I think that's all I need to know." Ramirez tucked his notebook into his back pocket.

Finn took a deep breath. "Look, David's a friend, but I won't help him if he's committed a crime."

"That's good to know." The detective backed out of the room. "You'll let me know if he contacts you?"

"Of course." Another lie.

As soon as Ramirez was gone, Finn closed the door. He turned to Kennedy and then pointed to the chair across from his desk. "Take a seat."

She leveled her steady gaze on him. "What's going on?"

"I want you to listen to this." He tapped his smartphone.

David's strained voice rang out. "Finn, there's a lot going on. I heard Portman give the order to kill us. He owns the police so watch your back. I just put her on a flight to Seattle. I'll call again when I get settled."

An electronic beep indicated the end of the call.

Kennedy's eyes widened. "I assume he's talking about Dr. Wilson when he says 'her.'"

"There's more," Finn said and then pushed another button on his phone.

"They tried to grab Marie at the airport. I got her away, but...I don't know. These guys are good. I don't know what technology they have at their disposal. I really need your help. We're going to lay low. Check out Portman and the police. I'll call once we're safe."

"Dear God." Kennedy put a hand to her mouth. "Is he accusing Marshall Portman of public corruption?"

"Yes, let's talk this through. Last night Dr. Wilson was the victim of a home invasion."

"And your friend saved her."

"And brought her here to me." Finn's gut clenched. He

should've taken Marie's statement instead of passing it off to the Granite City-Elkhead police department. But at the time it seemed like a normal home invasion.

"Her cabin is torched," Kennedy added.

"Between the time David dropped Marie at the police station and left the first message, he heard something that scared him. I wonder where he went after he dropped Dr. Wilson off here? Oh, and I think he told Dr. Wilson that it was his first day on the job."

"Job? What Job?"

"I don't know. I don't think Wilson knew either."

"Do you think Ramirez knows?"

"It's hard to tell."

"Do you think we can trust him?"

"Ramirez? I don't know that either."

****

Finn scrubbed a hand over his face. He was supposed to be going over a case of domestic terrorism, which involved a militia group, The Sons of Freedom. The case would be going to trial soon, which was why his meeting with the federal attorney had gone long.

He glanced at the surveillance photo of Marie Wilson with David that he'd obtained from the desk sergeant. Quinn didn't look all that different from when he'd served. He'd worn long hair and a beard then, too. It had helped him blend into the Afghan population. But the scar deformed what would otherwise be a handsome face.

He should call Sinclair. If anyone knew the identity of David's employer, it would be his sister. She hadn't made it home for Christmas, which meant he hadn't seen her in over a year. She'd opted out of the army a few years ago and was now an investigator with Finders International, an organization that helped find victims of human trafficking. She traveled extensively in a job that had to be grueling and emotionally taxing.

If she didn't know what her brother was up to, then Finn would call Tim or Michael. One of them should know something. He already suspected his friend had been employed by PDE. That was the answer that made the most sense, but in an investigation, he couldn't assume.

The head of Granite-Elkhead Police Department, Chief Notley, strolled into Finn's office. His receding hairline and his paunch made him seem older than his thirty-nine years. "Heard you had a visitor this morning."

"Yes, a young woman named Marie Wilson was brought here by someone I knew in my military days." Finn wasn't about to go over the details again.

"A friend of yours?" He rubbed the back of his neck. There was something off in the chief's disposition. Finn's experience in interviewing subjects included picking up on non-verbal behavior. At this moment, Notley's body language showed he was distressed and needed a soothing mechanism, hence rubbing his neck.

"We were close once," Finn admitted.

"Why were they here?"

"You should talk to Detective Ramirez. He took the complaint." Finn didn't like this line of questioning. Something was wrong, and considering David's voicemail, he wasn't about to reveal anything.

"Does your friend have a name?"

"Quinn, David Quinn." Finn had a feeling the chief already knew that.

"I thought it might be. There's something you should see. Come to my office."

Finn shivered. The feeling of ants crawling down his back told him there was a big pile of trouble coming his way.

The police station floor plan was simple. Six desks for the detectives were crammed into the bullpen, with the coffee room and interview rooms around the edge. The cells were at the back of the building. Police Chief Notley's Office sat in one corner. It was spacious with large glass windows that allowed him to oversee his detectives.

The Chief shut the door as soon as Finn stepped

inside. "A man named David Quinn is wanted in connection with the kidnapping of Dr. Marie Wilson."

"No, that can't be—"

"How well do you know him?"

"We were in basic together. Then I joined the military police, and he became a member of the Special Forces." Finn wasn't about to reveal he'd had Christmas dinner with Quinn, which was stupid. Notley was bound to find out sooner or later because Finn had just told Ramirez.

"Special Forces?"

"Yes."

"And Dr. Wilson was in here at this police station on her own?"

"Yes, she said four guys burst into her cabin, one of them was David. They were looking for a prototype of a solar panel. She thought she was going to be raped and murdered, but David got her out of there and brought her here to me. As I said, ask Ramirez."

"Who the hell would want a solar panel?"

Finn shrugged. He didn't want to speculate.

"PDE emailed us a video this morning. Watch it with me." Notley sat at his desk and motioned for Finn to stand next to him.

Marie and a uniformed officer walked toward the PDE building. She reached the door as David walked out. He shoved the young policeman and dragged Marie away.

By Finn's estimation, the video was less than ten seconds long. He put a hand to his head. *Shit.* David must've been at PDE when he'd heard Portman.

"Your friend"—the chief hammered his fist on his desk—"just attacked Officer Calder and kidnapped a woman. He's a wanted man."

Finn stared at the blank screen. "Can you play that again?"

Notley hit the replay button. David shoved the policeman and then grabbed Marie by the arm. Marie was clearly surprised by Quinn's actions. The screen went blank.

"Is Officer Calder okay?" Finn tried to keep his tone impassive.

"Yes, he's fine. I sent him home for the day."

"Good," Finn said. David probably knew several ways to kill without using a weapon so he obviously hadn't wanted to hurt the young officer. Finn straightened away from the chief. "Where's the rest? There has to be more."

"No, that's all there is."

"Who gave you this video?"

"I told you, PDE."

Why had Marie been in front of the PDE building? He needed to figure out a way to ask without seeming suspicious.

"I want to make this clear. I'm only showing this to you as a courtesy because you know the suspect and can help us with our investigation. The kidnapping of an adult falls under the jurisdiction of the Granite City-Elkhead police department." Notley stood, resting a hand on the weapon at his side. To the untrained eye, it might seem like a casual gesture, but to Finn it was an obvious show of force, which was out of place considering they were both supposed to be on the same side.

"I have no intention of ignoring jurisdiction, but there's a chance our cases will overlap. Ramirez has begun an investigation into the home invasion. I'm also exploring a possible connection to the Sons of Freedom." That was an outright lie. There was absolutely no connection to the terrorist group, but Marie's cabin was on land adjacent to the Son's headquarters. He could work with that.

The chief took a step closer. "I'm not going to step on your toes when it comes to domestic terrorism, and you're not going to interfere with my kidnapping case. Do you understand what I'm telling you?"

Finn forced himself to relax. "Of course, I have no intention of getting in your way." He wanted to appear nonchalant, and indifferent. Notley had been in law enforcement long enough he knew how to read people, and Finn didn't want the chief to recognize his lie.

"I'm glad we understand each other. I'd hate to have to report you to your superiors."

Finn said nothing. He knew a direct threat when he heard one.

"You can leave the door open." The chief sat down and began typing on his keyboard, effectively dismissing him.

Finn slammed the door of his office. He was stunned, not just by the video, but also by his conversation with Notley. Normally in a kidnapping case, the local police would be happy to have FBI resources. They would not threaten their resident agent.

Every molecule in Finn's body screamed that something was wrong, and it wasn't just Notley's behavior. Something was off about that video. It was short—too short. It didn't show the whole scene.

He had to get out of here. There were too many implications to deal with: David accused of kidnapping, Marie and her solar panel, Notley's behavior, David's warning, and Marshall Portman. He needed to think through all the complexities.

He checked his Glock 27, shoved it back into his shoulder holster, and felt his belt to make sure he still had his cuff case. Then he grabbed his go-bag. It was packed with a water bottle, snack food, evidence bags, extra ammo for his Glock, flexi-cuffs, a flashlight, and a first-aid kit, along with all the other stuff he carried. He just never knew what was around the corner. His raid jacket and a box of latex gloves were already in his vehicle.

His cell phone played a funky jazz tune. "Agent Callaghan."

"What's going on with David?" An impatient voice barked down the line.

"Michael, is that you?" Michael Papin, ex-street kid and computer genius. He had become a cyber specialist and was now an agent specializing in cybercrime for the United States Army CID.

"I'm picking up a lot of buzz about David and some woman. Have you heard anything?"

Finn filled Michael in on everything he knew, leaving out his own questions and doubts. Papin possessed a unique mind and would make his own lines of inquiry. "This video is only ten seconds long?"

"If that."

"I'll look into it." Michael hung up without saying goodbye.

Finn stared at the phone. He still needed to call David's twin, Sinclair, and confirm the name of Quinn's employer. He scrolled through his contact list and then dialed the number. Her phone went straight to voicemail. "Hi, you've reached Sinclair—"

He hung up without leaving a message and then patted the pocket of his cargo pants to check his credentials were still there.

On his way to the stairs, he stopped in at Kennedy's office. "You busy?"

"Just finishing some paperwork." She pushed her keyboard aside.

"I need you to go to the airport and check out all the video recordings from this morning."

"You're kidding. All the video from all the cameras?"

"Yep. PDE gave Chief Notley a video that shows David taking Marie."

She leant forward. "Taking? As in kidnapping?"

"That's what they're saying."

"But you don't believe them?"

"No. In the first message, he said he'd put her on a flight to Seattle. The second time he called he said they'd tried to grab her at the airport."

"And if they tried to snatch her, one of the cameras would've caught it. Gotcha. I'll head over there now." She stood, snagging her coat from the back of her chair.

"Where are you going?"

"David struck a young officer by the name of Calder. I'm going to talk to him."

"Do you think he's involved?"

"I don't know." He walked toward the stairs. "See you back here after lunch."

The wind whipped at him as he walked across the parking lot, almost knocking him off his feet. Hopefully, he had enough time before the snowstorm to drop in on officer Rick Calder and see how he was doing. If the young man wanted to talk about his experience, then Finn wouldn't stop him. Then he'd call Sinclair, again, and try Tim. One of them should know what the hell was going on.

He scanned the sky where low, dark, ominous clouds now blocked out the sun. If he were unlucky, the blizzard would hit when he was on the road. He threw his gear onto the passenger seat of his standard-issue black Ford expedition then checked the emergency kit in the truck, making sure it contained flares, a candle, a foil blanket, and waterproof matches.

Common sense told him to wait until the weather conditions improved, but his instincts screamed, telling him he needed to figure this out—soon. Somehow David Quinn was enmeshed in something nasty that involved the possible corruption of the Granite City-Elkhead Police Department.

Finn drove out of the parking lot as the first flakes of snow hit the windshield. He shook his head. This was turning into a fucking wonderful day.

Chapter Thirteen

David loved Glacier Country. It was the wildest part of the state and was dominated by mountains, forests, and rivers. If he ever got his cabin built, he would make sure it had a view of the snow-capped Rockies. Today, a wall of clouds covered the peaks. Snow. Even with the acidic trace of diesel coming off the engine, he could smell the frigid dampness in the air.

Marie slept, curled in his lap. He stroked a long dark strand of hair away from her face. He shouldn't be attracted to her, and he most certainly shouldn't act on that attraction. Maybe he should rethink his plan to become involved with her. Any response from her would be marred by the gratitude she undoubtedly felt. As he saw it, his job was to protect her and keep her safe until the FBI could sort this mess out, not use their situation to take advantage of her. Besides, she probably wasn't interested in him, not with his scarred face.

She sighed in her sleep and exhaled into his chest, sending a frisson of pleasure to his groin. He smothered the urge to kiss her. She seemed to have no clue of her own appeal, which made her more tempting.

Jake had lapsed into silence a few miles back and had turned on the stereo to listen to some country music. David's butt bounced off the seat as the truck hit a rut. Marie's head snapped up and connected with his chin. He grunted and rubbed his face with his free hand.

Her eyes flickered open. "Are we there yet?"

"No, sweetheart, we've only been driving for twenty minutes. Go back to sleep." He wrapped his arms around her and hugged her tight so she wouldn't bump around.

Jake's smartphone gave an electronic trill. He placed it

on the dash and pressed a button, answering it on speaker.

"Jake this is Al. The police have asked us to get in touch with all our drivers. They want to know if you've seen a man and a woman? The man has long, shaggy hair, a beard, and a scar down the side of his face. His name is David Quinn. It's believed he kidnapped a woman by the name of Marie Wilson."

David's heart raced as his breathing hitched. Thank God he was seated because his knees had turned to spaghetti. *Kidnapping?* He stared at the phone and then at Jake. This couldn't be happening. Maybe they'd get lucky and Jake wouldn't put the pieces together. *Yeah, right.* He was never that lucky. He gently released Marie's legs, freeing his left hand.

The truck driver paled and glanced at David. "Is he talking about you?"

The voice on the phone said, "Who's with—"

David pressed the disconnect button. "I didn't take her. We're traveling together." He shook Marie. "Wake up."

Marie blinked and rubbed her eyes. "Is it time to go?"

"Yes." He straightened his left knee, which lowered her legs to the floor. The isolated highway lay between a stretch of forest on one side and a hill on the other. David was familiar with the area. They were still in Elkhead County. There was a turn off a few hundred yards ahead, a trail that curved north to the small town of Hopefalls. There were no other cars on the highway. Not surprising given the weather warnings.

Jake steered the rig onto the shoulder and applied the brakes. "Let's call the police and let them sort this out." He reached for the phone.

"That's not a good idea." David shoved Jake hard. The trucker jerked to the side, his face connecting with the driver's door.

"Why?" Jake held his arms up in a position of surrender.

"We're being chased." David slipped the phone into his coat pocket.

"Yeah, because you're a sick bastard who—"

"I did not take her, and I will not hurt her," Then he gave Marie a quick hug. "You need to get off my lap."

"You go. She stays with me." Jake dove for Marie, grabbing her wrist so she was bent over the center console.

She gaped at him. "No."

"Is he forcing you?" Jake yanked her closer.

Marie tugged back. "Forcing me to do what?"

"To go with him?"

She blinked, and frowned. "No, our car... We—"

"Why are you protecting him?" Jake jerked her arm again.

"Stop pulling on my wrist. I don't know what you're talking about." She scowled, and with her free hand grabbed at his fist, trying to release her arm.

Using the distraction, David sprang forward and punched the trucker hard on the shoulder knowing the blow would numb his arm. Jake released his grip. Then David stood, his head bent so it wouldn't hit the ceiling, and placed his body between Jake and Marie.

Marie tried to push David out of the way, but tripped on his foot and slammed against the passenger door. "Will someone tell me what's going on?" She pounded the window, clearly at the end of her patience.

David's pulse quickened as panic bubbled, threatening to overwhelm him. He inhaled a calming breath. Deal with the immediate, and form a plan later. That was how he'd coped in Afghanistan. He'd lived in the now. "While you were asleep, Jake got a call about a woman who was kidnapped."

The trucker clutched his injured appendage as his nostril's flared, and his lips curled into a sneer.

"That's not us. I trust David with my life. In fact, he has saved my life," Marie explained.

Jake lowered his other hand, reaching under the

driver's seat.

David sprang on the trucker, ramming him against the door, and then pinned his hands, restraining him. "Don't do it."

Jake shoved, trying to shake free. "Do what? I wasn't doing anything."

"You were reaching for the weapon under your chair."

The trucker's eyes widened, telling David his guess was on target. The cab of the truck was so small it was hard to imagine no one would get hurt if Jake managed to fire a round. "We're too close. You'll hurt—"

"I watch the news. I know what sick bastards like you do. You're going to murder her, aren't you?"

David straightened his elbows while holding Jake in place. He wanted to see the man's face. "No, it's not what you think."

"You bastard," Jake spat, his voice shrill.

"I'll let that one go because you believe you're doing the right thing, but trust me, I'm not kidnapping anyone."

"Then why would the police be looking for you?"

"I don't know, but I'm not going to hurt her." David made sure he had a good grip on Jake and then called over his shoulder. "Marie? Honey, are you all right?"

"Y-yes," she stuttered, her voice shaky. She sat in the passenger seat, curled in a protective ball.

"Was that your dispatcher on the phone?" he asked Jake.

"Yeah."

"Okay, so he's going to be looking for you." At that moment, Jake's phone rang again. They all seemed to hold their breath as the electronic trill continued. Finally it was silent.

"It doesn't matter where you dump my body, they will find you." Jake was pale, frightened, and desperate.

"Dump your—? I'm not going to kill you. I don't do that, not anymore."

"How very noble," Jake sneered.

"I try." David said dryly. "Marie, look around. See if you can find some rope. Check the bunk. There's bound to be some duct tape lying around."

Marie crawled between the seats, opened the curtains, and disappeared into the back.

David shoved Jake into the driver's seat. "Now listen carefully, as I said, I don't want to hurt you. You're a father, and you want to go home to your boys. I'm going to tie you up because we need a head start. I'll leave the truck running so you won't freeze to death. Do you understand?"

Jake nodded, his lips trembling.

"Is this truck LoJacked?"

Jake nodded again.

"Don't lie about this. I'm asking so people can find you. I don't want you dying out here."

"No, they'll be able to find me, but…"

David sat in the passenger seat and leant over the console so he was close enough to grab the trucker if necessary. "But what?"

"Why do you want them to find me?"

"I just explained, so you don't die."

Marie appeared with a roll of electrical tape and some string. "I don't think we should tie him up."

David ignored her. "Get behind him and throw the rope around his chest and pull it tight.

She didn't move. "No."

David couldn't believe his ears. "No?" He was trying to protect her, and she was arguing with him.

"We need to think this through. There's going to be a storm. What if no one finds him in time?"

"What if he calls the police?" David said.

"Of course, I'm going to call the police," Jake spluttered.

Marie slapped Jake's shoulder. "You know your attitude isn't making this easy."

Jake's mouth fell open. "My attitude?"

"Yes, now be quiet." She moved so she was standing behind the center console and retrieved the phone from David's pocket. "Call Agent Callaghan? Maybe he can help?"

David pointed at Jake. "I'm faster and stronger than you, and it'd be easy to hurt you. If you move, I will tie and gag you. Understand?"

Jake nodded and raised his arms.

The agent picked up on the first ring. "Hello."

The line crackled. "Hello. Finn, can you hear me?"

"Dav—" Electrical static crackled down the line.

"Finn can you hear me? Finn?" The line went dead.

"Damn, he must be in a dead zone. What's the point in having a Federal Bureau of Investigation if you can never get them on the phone?"

"The FBI? Why would you call them?" Jake tilted his head as his eyes narrowed.

"Cause we're the good guys." David locked his jaw. He needed help, the type of help that could only be provided by law enforcement. He hated the idea of leaving Jake stranded with a blizzard bearing down on them. Abandoning someone to die from the elements was worse than putting a bullet in their head.

"Maybe we should wait and try Agent Callaghan again," Marie said.

"I don't know that we can. Jake's dispatcher has probably called the police. They might have tracked us down, which means we don't have much time."

Her eyes shot to her backpack, which sat on the floor of the truck. She straightened, as if preparing for a fight. She glanced at Jake and then turned her gaze to him. "I want to call Portman. If I agree to hand over the prototype and the plans, he might call this whole thing off."

David didn't like the idea. The call would be traceable, especially for someone with Marshall's resources, but they were in an untenable position. The accusation of kidnapping upped the ante. It wasn't a case of leaving

Granite City and lying low until Finn could investigate. Now, police from all over the state, hell, all over the country, would be hunting them. Their odds of getting out of this alive had nosedived to zero because once they were captured, it would be easy to engineer their deaths. She was right. Negotiation was their only option. He passed her the phone. "Go ahead."

Marie placed the phone on the center console. "I'm going to put this on speaker. Jake, I need you to be quiet. I don't want him to know you're here."

"Why the hell should I be quiet?" Jake's hand lowered toward his weapon again.

David pointed at him. "Don't be stupid. Don't think because I'm in the passenger seat, I can't move fast enough to break your arm."

"Bastard."

"Yes, I am. I'm also trying to keep you alive. If Marshall Portman knows you're involved, he will kill you."

"How can I believe you?"

David groaned. How did he explain something he didn't understand? Marshall's reasoning was a mystery, his reaction so bizarre it bordered on the insane.

Marie cleared her throat. "Jake, the way I see it you have two choices. You can get out of the truck and walk away or you can stay and be quiet while we make this call. You're also free to take your gun out and have it handy. I just ask that you don't point it at anyone."

David heard the words, but could not believe she'd just told a frightened man that he could hold a weapon. He grabbed her collar, forcing her to stoop, until her face was just inches from his. "Have you gone insane? You can't make people—"

"Look, we both know that you're not going to hurt Jake. We can't tie him up and leave him here, so we need him to listen." She poked David's chest. "And he's not going to do that unless we give him some control."

"There's control, and then there's a freaking gun."

She inched closer so that her nose was a hair's breadth from his. "He's not going to shoot us."

"No, he's not going to shoot us. He's going to shoot me, sweetheart. I'm the one accused of kidnapping, remember?"

She cupped his face with one hand and kissed his nose. "Don't worry. We're the good guys. It'll work out."

He closed his eyes, unsure how to react. On the one hand, he enjoyed the comfort of her touch, but believing they would get out of this unscathed because they were the good guys was irrational. The world sucked, and he had the scars, emotional and physical, to prove it.

"Besides, if Jake shoots you, I'll kill him." She grinned. "And unlike you, I haven't sworn off killing."

He couldn't help but smile, despite his concern. He liked the idea she would kill for him, although his common sense told him they were just words. He was almost certain she had never taken a life, otherwise she would know that talking about it was a lot easier than actually doing it.

He leant back in the passenger seat and slanted his gaze to Jake. The trucker hadn't reached for his weapon. He'd had plenty of opportunity while they were arguing and he hadn't taken it. If their roles were reversed, David would've grabbed the sidearm and kicked them out of the truck.

Wind rocked the cab. The storm had picked up, blowing snow across the highway.

Jake nodded toward the phone. "Make your call."

David dialed the number. He knew it by heart, had known it since he was sixteen. Once again, his gut twisted with the memory of hearing Marshall order his death.

"Marshall Portman."

"This is Quinn."

"Hello David, I take it I'm on speaker phone. Who else is there?"

David ignored Marshall's question. "Why are you hunting me?" As soon as the words were out of his mouth, he knew it was the real reason he'd decided to call. He needed to know why his friend and mentor had turned on him.

"It wasn't personal. You were just in the wrong place at the right time. I had to blame someone for her death, and who better than a burned-out soldier who shot his own man?"

Jake gasped.

Marie put a hand over her mouth, her eyes wide with horror.

David's mind flew back to that cold, moonless night in Afghanistan, listening to the screams of his friends as they lay bleeding, dying. He was a monster, a freak who had reacted in the moment, and now he had to live with the consequences of his actions.

"I was given an honorable discharge." David's stomach rolled, and he suppressed the urge to vomit.

"You're grasping at straws, Portman," Marie snapped. It didn't seem to occur to her that there might be an element of truth to the allegations.

"Hello, Dr. Wilson," Portman said.

"We'll give you the solar panel if you call off your men, retract the statement about me being a kidnapper, and leave us alone." David guided the conversation back to the topic at hand, not wanting to be sidetracked by his background or the events that had ended his military career.

"Why would I want to do that?" Portman's tone was honey-smooth, controlled and calculating.

"Your men created quite a stink at the airport. Everyone has a smartphone these days. Someone is bound to have recorded them trying to snatch Marie and put it on YouTube. I wouldn't be surprised if it was all over the six o'clock news."

"Then you'd be wrong. I have someone in place who controls that kind of thing. Don't you know the man who runs the media commands the power? No one will ever hear about Dr. Wilson's little solar panel, and if they do, I'll make sure it's discredited."

Something didn't add up. They were missing a piece of information. "Then why kill us? We'll just walk away and pretend—"

"You should have done that last night."

"You mean when you planned to shoot us and call it a murder-suicide? I couldn't do that."

"Pity." Portman sounded amused.

"Why didn't you just buy her project and stop it from being developed? Isn't that what you industrialists do when someone invents a technology that threatens your monopoly?" How had it come to the point where the only option was to kill Marie?

"She's created an independent energy source. Within twenty years, the electrical grid will be obsolete. There are people, powerful people, who won't let that happen."

Marie frowned. "But—"

"People don't realize that without power and oil, there would be a domino effect. The loss of employment will cause homes to be repossessed, banks will fold, and global money markets will crash. The world as we know it will end."

Marie's eyes narrowed. "But my work isn't even well received."

"Yes, we managed to discredit you, but people are starting to listen."

Marie stared at the phone, her face pale. "You killed Professor Hargreaves."

"No, I wouldn't do a thing like that. He died in a car accident." Marshall's voice was steady with no indication that he was lying.

"Why did you offer to fund my research?" Marie asked.

"For control, of course. The minute you signed the papers, I would've shut you down."

"You can still do that. We'll give it to you, the prototype, the plans, everything," Marie choked.

"That was my first plan before I investigated you. How much do you know about her, David? Did she tell you she was a child prodigy? She's only twenty-six years old. She graduated from university at eighteen with two PhDs."

"She's smart, so what?"

"She's a brilliant scientist. Her focus has always been on solar energy, and she's independently wealthy."

"B-b-but I'm broke. I was coming to see you to ask you to—"

"Liar. You have eighty million dollars."

"We're getting off topic. Is there any chance of a resolution?" Whether or not Marie had money wasn't pertinent because she couldn't access it without disclosing her location.

"I don't think so. There are people, important men, who want her dead. Now they know she exists, there's no going back." Portman's voice had a cold, hard edge.

"Thanks for the head's up," David said.

"If it's any consolation, I'm sorry you're involved. It's just one of those things. I needed a patsy, and you were perfect for the role."

David disconnected the call. None of what they'd heard should surprise him, but it did. For most of his life, he'd believed that Marshall Portman was a good person. Yes, he was rich and powerful, but he was also generous. He had plucked David off the streets and given him a life, and a future.

David needed time to come to terms with this new reality. At his core, Marshall was a businessman, which meant his reactions were based on profit and loss. Shareholders were his concern, not people. Marshall judged David to be a throwaway, someone who was no longer a benefit and was therefore expendable.

And Marie... She had created something that threatened Portman's way of life, and apparently, there were other people who wanted her dead.

"Did I hear him right? Is this about a solar panel?" Jake

stared at Marie wide-eyed.

David nodded. "It's about more than a solar panel. It's about money."

"What do we do now?" Marie's voice trembled, her face pale.

"I don't know." He had no idea what their next move should be.

"In the meantime, you're wanted for kidnapping me." She slipped the back off Jake's phone, removed the SIM card and the battery. She wiggled into the front, positioning herself between his legs. She avoided his gaze, concentrating on fastening her backpack.

"What the hell are you doing?" David asked.

"I'm stopping them from following Jake. We need to get out of this truck." She delved into the purple backpack, retrieving a hat and a pair of mittens. Then she zipped her coat up so the collar was snug against her neck.

David assessed the conditions. Snow whipped across the valley, driven by strong winds, creating whiteout conditions. Walking anywhere in this would be hell even if they were prepared for it, which they weren't. "I know that was the original plan, but going out in this is suicide. We need better clothing, and we need provisions," David stated, hoping she would see the logic of his words.

"You're right. At least Jake can clear your name and tell the police and the FBI you didn't kidnap me." Her voice was steady and strong as she stuffed her bottle of water and some chocolate bars into her bag.

"I'm sure Jake will drop us off somewhere. Now give him back his phone. He probably can't afford to replace it."

"But what if they trace this?" She passed the pieces to David. "They'll kill him just like they killed the professor."

Thank God, he'd managed to talk her out of taking off. She was tense, her face pale. Undoubtedly it was a shock to discover someone wanted her dead, but these were unusual circumstances. In civilian life, if someone wanted to kill you, it was because they had reason to hate you. This seemed to be a question of greed and control rather than hate.

He handed the phone and battery to Jake. "Don't put this back together, buy a new SIM card. Better yet, I'll keep the SIM card so you won't be tempted." He pocketed the small piece of plastic.

Marie opened the passenger door, allowing a blast of cold air into the warm cab.

"What the—"

She jumped out of the truck before he could grab her and walked away.

"She's something else." Jake shook his head. "I can see why you're taken with her."

Taken with her. No. He was frustrated with her. She was the most unpredictable woman he had ever met. He had no idea what she was going to do next.

He watched her in the side mirror as she marched in the direction of Granite City. They had driven westward for about twenty minutes. It would take her hours on foot to cover the distance they'd traveled so far, but still it was the wrong direction. She bent her head, shielding herself from the battering wind, and within seconds she was out of sight, obliterated by snow. "Listen, I—we need a favor. Call FBI Special Agent Finn Callaghan. He's in Granite City."

"You're going after her?"

He shouldn't. He was in no shape to provide the type of protection she needed, but he couldn't just let her walk away, not in a storm. "I'm trained to survive, she isn't. I know this stretch of road, and I can find us shelter. Now, repeat the agent's name."

"Finn Callaghan."

"This is for Callaghan's ears only. Do not leave a message, especially not with the police. Tell him everything you heard Portman say. Tell him that I want to come in, but I can't go to the police."

"I will."

"Who are you going to give that message to?"

"Callaghan."

"What are you going to tell your dispatcher?"

"I'll just tell him my phone was stolen."

"And the police?

"My phone was stolen."

"Good man."

Soon the blizzard would hit. Then everything would shut down. Between the driving snow and the relentless wind, traveling would be impossible, not just for them, but also for their pursuers.

"Do you know how long the storm is predicted to last?" he asked.

"Overnight. The weather's supposed to move on by noon tomorrow."

He grabbed the purple backpack that held their provisions, gave Jake a final wave. Then he tensed, bracing himself against the blast of icy wind and slipped out of the truck, following Marie.

Chapter Fourteen

Finn parked the SUV in front of the small, suburban, ranch-style house that Officer Rick Calder called home. He plucked his phone from his pocket and stared at it, willing it to ring. Whatever cellphone plan the FBI used sucked because his coverage was nonexistent. He could not afford to be unreachable, not if David was trying to phone. Maybe the weather had caused an interruption in service.

The hammering wind piled snow against the houses on the east side of the street.

Finn pulled up his collar as he climbed out of the car and strolled up the stone pathway to Officer Calder's door. By the end of the day, there would be stranded motorists, downed power lines, highway closures and disruptions on all public services. In other words—chaos.

The overhead door to the attached garage opened, and Calder walked to the back of an SUV parked in the driveway.

"Rick," Finn called, making his presence known.

"I take it you heard?" He didn't look surprised to see Finn. He opened the trunk of the SUV.

Finn peeked inside, automatically checking for a weapon. There wasn't one, just cans of food and bottled water.

"I just came to see if you were all right."

"I'm fine." He crossed his arms over his chest as he stared at the interior of the vehicle.

There was something about Calder's body language that didn't fit with the video. If Marie Wilson had been taken, he might have been angry, or maybe guilty over the fact she'd been kidnapped while in his custody. His lack of eye contact, the way his lips pressed into a thin line, and his mannerisms suggested he was ashamed.

"Why don't you tell me what happened?" Finn said.

"I pulled a gun on the victim, that's what happened. They'll have my badge for this. Being a policeman is all I ever wanted to do, and now…" He grabbed a flat of water from the car, walked through the garage, and placed it on the steps leading to the house.

If all of Finn's suspects were as forthright as Officer Calder, then his job would be a lot easier. "Why don't you start from the beginning? Why did you take Dr. Wilson to the PDE building?"

"I was just her escort. I was supposed to take her to the airport, but she wanted to see Portman. She said she didn't have an appointment so she was going to leave a message." He paced to a woodpile in the corner of the garage.

Finn followed. "And if she got to see him?

"I don't know. I guess I would've left her there. I couldn't hang out all day."

"Then what happened?"

Calder stacked the logs, moving the pile a few feet closer to the door, still not looking Finn in the eye. "We'd reached the door of the building when this guy with a long beard comes flying out. He shoves me. I go flying down the steps. He grabs Dr. Wilson—"

"Did she seem scared?"

Rick straightened, his brow crinkling as he recalled the event. "No, but she didn't want to go. Then this PDE guy with a broken nose starts shooting at them."

"What?"

"Yeah, I pulled my gun, but then realized there was a good chance of hitting the victim. I screamed at the guy to stop, but he kept on. I aimed my weapon at him and forced him to relinquish his sidearm."

"Sorry, who did you scream at, the guy from PDE or Quinn?"

"The PDE guy. His name is Harper."

Finn took his notebook out and jotted down the name.

"By the time I managed to disarm him, Quinn had taken Dr. Wilson and driven away." Rick waved a log as he talked.

"Was Harper charged?"

"I don't know. I called it in."

"Then what happened?"

"Chief Notley arrived. Harper was talking about kidnapping and named Quinn as the perpetrator. The chief took my statement and sent me home. Told me there'd be an enquiry into my conduct."

"Notley's looking into your conduct?" Maybe there was justification, maybe not. To Finn, it sounded like a ruse to keep the young officer out of the picture.

Calder shrugged. "Yes."

"But you didn't actually shoot at the victim."

"No." He threw the wood into a heap, seeming to have given up on making a neat stack.

"What kind of vehicle was Quinn driving?"

"An old black Ford pickup. It was pretty rusted. I gave the chief the plate number. Do you need it?"

"No, he'll have dumped it by now." Finn should contact his head office in Utah and tell them about this development. But he'd wait until he had more than a hunch and the accusation of a wanted man. He needed something concrete if he was going to accuse the chief of the Granite City-Elkhead County Police department of corruption. Warning Finn off didn't mean anything. Sometimes police got territorial about their cases. It happened, not as much as was portrayed on TV, but it did happen. Had Portman bribed Notley? Finn had probable cause to get a warrant for their financial records, but this was the chief. He would have to tread lightly.

Calder finally turned and looked Finn in the eye. "Do you think I'll lose my job?"

"Not if I can help it. We need honest policemen like you," Finn said as he backed away, heading to his car. It was snowing hard, and the wind was so strong he had to fight to stand upright. He struggled to close the driver's door.

The jazz tune played on his phone. He answered before the jingle finished. "Agent Callaghan."

"This is Sinclair. What's going on?"

"David's been accused of kidnapping a scientist."

"What? You know he'd never hurt a civilian."

For some reason, he found her certainty in her brother reassuring. "What can you tell me about his relationship with Marshall Portman?"

"Portman? What's he—"

"Just answer the question."

"Portman rescued us from the street when we were sixteen."

"How did David get along at Marshall House?"

"At first, he didn't want to be there. He didn't trust Portman. He said do-gooders always wanted something in return, but you just didn't know what."

"Why'd he go?"

"I couldn't live on the street anymore. I had pneumonia. And Tim wanted a future that didn't involve stealing food."

"What about Michael?"

"He'd already left. He wasn't like us."

"What do you mean?"

"We were runaways. We had nowhere else to go. Michael had a home and a family."

"Then how'd he end up living on the street?"

"Michael graduated high school at fifteen. I think he wanted to see the world before heading to university. You know, experience how the other half lived."

Finn understood. Michael was the smartest man he had ever met.

"David never trusted Portman?"

"I didn't say that. For some reason, Marshall took an interest in my brother. Gave him books to read and stuff like that. He talked to David, encouraged him to go into the service and get a degree. They grew to be friends. At Least, David considered him a friend."

Finn recalled the video of Quinn supposedly kidnapping Marie. He'd talked to David at Christmas dinner. He had been a shadow of his former self. Gone was the vibrant man of action. The new David was quiet and withdrawn. He'd worn a long shaggy beard and had been pale with dark circles under his eyes. The only time he'd shown any enthusiasm was when he talked about his bees. "He looks haggard and disheveled. How's he been since he left the army?"

"Not good. Something happened that forced him to leave."

"He never mentioned anything. What happened?" Finn asked.

"I don't know. I asked, but he said it was classified."

"He was Special Forces. His sneezes were classified."

"He doesn't sleep."

Damn. Sleep deprivation was known to impair cognitive function, and mess with a person's ability to make decisions.

"He was drinking, but that stopped about six months ago," Sinclair added.

"What changed?"

"I told him he had to straighten himself out and get help. I threatened to kick his butt, and I reminded him of all the drunks we'd known when we were on the street. I don't know if that's why he turned things around, or if there were other factors, but he seemed to get better. He purchased some beehives and got into beekeeping in a big way. Talked about planting wildflowers and clover."

"Yeah, he mentioned the bees."

"He said they were peaceful and were helping him. Anyway, he had a business plan. Apparently, there's a market for honey products, and renting beehives out for pollination is big business."

"He was organized?"

"Yes, as far as I can tell the only thing he doesn't have is a house to live in."

"You mentioned a camper."

"It's about thirty years old, with no washroom or shower. David named it the Shithole."

"Delightful. Do you think he's mentally unstable?"

"No. Are you sure he kidnapped this scientist?"

"No."

"What has this got to do with Portman?"

He ignored her question. He didn't have any answers, and even if he did, he couldn't discuss the details of an ongoing investigation. "Where are you now? I may need you to help negotiate with David."

"I'm in Washington DC. All the flights to Granite City are canceled due to the blizzard, so I'm flying into Billings and renting an all-wheel-drive from there. I should arrive by tomorrow morning."

"Okay, call me when you get here."

"I will, and Finn…"

"Yes?"

"I'll want some answers by tomorrow." She hung up.

This kidnapping was not premeditated, at least not on David's part. None of this made sense. The man Finn knew was disciplined, loyal, and honest, but he was also a man in crisis. Up to six months ago, Quinn had been drinking, and his sister said he had insomnia. These were points that called into question his mental stability.

But whatever his psychological state, he had rescued Dr. Wilson from a home invasion and had brought her to see Finn. That was a fact, so whether he was having difficulties or not, something was still going on. His gut told him that Portman had chief Notley on the payroll, but it wasn't enough. All he had was Quinn's word. He needed proof.

He dialed Kennedy. She picked up on the first ring. "Where are you?"

"Heading back. You?"

"I'm at the office. The roads are getting nasty."

"I'm only a few blocks away. I'll be there soon. How did it go at the airport?"

"You'll never believe this, but the security cameras were out."

"What?"

"I know. Granite City is a small airport, but they have international flights. You'd think in these times of terrorism and drug smuggling they'd make sure their cameras were working. It's basic stuff."

"I doubt it's a coincidence."

"Good luck proving that."

Finn closed his eyes as he imagined what David would do when faced with an enemy like Marshall Portman. Where would he go? He was a trained Green Beret. He probably knew how to survive anywhere, in any conditions, and they were in Montana. There were forests and mountains. These were places where a survival specialist could hide indefinitely, but what about Marie Wilson? She didn't strike him as particularly athletic. He doubted she could survive outside in a blizzard. Wherever Quinn and Wilson were, he hoped they'd found a warm place where they could shelter the storm.

Chapter Fifteen

Marie had never been so miserable in her life. By her estimate, they had been marching for twenty minutes, wading through piles of shifting snow. David had directed them into some sort of valley. A line of trees lay to her left, protecting them from the merciless wind. Occasionally an errant gust would cause ice pellets to hammer her skin like shards of glass. Her cheeks and nose prickled with pain. She curled her free hand into a fist inside her mitt in order to protect her fingers.

She prayed David wouldn't release his grip on her hand. If he did, she would never find him again. He seemed to know where he was going as if guided by some inner compass.

He yanked on her hand, altering their direction so the bursts of wind hit the back of her neck. She tugged at her collar and hunched her shoulders in a futile attempt to shield her skin.

He pushed her against the eave of a building. How he'd known it was there was a mystery. A white swirl of snow had obliterated it from view. She'd been oblivious of its existence until her back touched the wall. To her right was a door, and to her left a window. From what little she could see, she guessed this was the back of a house, and they were at the kitchen door.

"If there's no one home, I'll break in," David shouted, straining to be heard above the roar of the storm.

He pummeled on the door. When there was no response, he drew a combat knife from a holster on his ankle and used it to attack the lock.

In any other circumstances, she might be surprised by the knife, or even by the break-in, but right now none of that mattered. If they didn't get inside, they would perish. That was all there was to it.

Within less than a minute, he stood, opened the door, and dragged her into a mudroom. The silence shocked her. She hadn't realized how loud a blizzard could be, but now that they were inside, the contrast was startling.

She stood, swaying on her feet. The house was dim. By her estimation, it was late afternoon. The storm had shortened the day, making dusk come early.

Coats hung on a line of hooks along one wall. Boots and shoes were strewn in a jumbled mess on the same side of the room. Against the opposite wall was a large bench seat. David sat down and kicked off his footwear. Marie slumped next to him. She tried to remove her boots, but she shook so wildly she couldn't get a good grip on her heel. Not that it mattered since her fingers were so cold they couldn't manage the job.

David tugged off her boots. "You stay here while I search the house."

"W-what are you l-looking for?" Her words were slurred.

"People," he whispered.

"Do-do you think they'd m-m-mind."

"Most people I know are pretty peaceful as long as you don't invade their territory. The minute we walked through that door, we illegally entered someone's home. There's a very good possibility we've pissed off the owners."

She glanced at his bare feet, his toes red with cold. *Oh, God.* He had given her his socks this morning. "Do-do you have f-f-frostbite?"

"No, I don't think so." Chunks of ice clung to his beard, and his cheeks were bright red. He still wore his hat, but had unzipped his coat to reveal a camouflage-green sweatshirt. "Wait here." He disappeared into the dim interior of the house.

Marie tugged off her hat and then struggled to her feet. She was exhausted, her legs so weak she could hardly stand upright, but she forced herself to the threshold that separated the mudroom from the kitchen.

The ground floor consisted of a large combined living room and kitchen. The space was divided by a staircase, which led to the upper level. Grey light filtered in through a huge living room window that ran the length of the far wall. She couldn't tell which direction it faced because the storm obscured the view.

David placed a hand on the wood stove situated beside the stairs. He didn't react or jerk his hand away so it was probably cold. He climbed to the second floor, disappearing from view.

The house was silent except for the muted roar of the storm outside. She edged into the kitchen and flicked on the light switch. No power. Honey-colored wooden beams covered the walls and the ceiling, giving the small house a rustic cabin feel. The kitchen cabinets were white with clean, sleek lines, which was odd given the assortment of cat figurines placed strategically on the countertops. A white table sat in the center of the kitchen. It had the same lines and design as the cabinets. On top of the table lay a lace doily with a ceramic cat in the middle. The contrast between the modern look of the cabinets, the old-lady-cat-and-lace theme, and the rustic cabin gave her the impression that the owners were engaging in a battle of decorative wills.

Within a few minutes, David returned. "The house is empty." He placed an arm around her waist and hauled her to the couch, which was against the back wall of the living room. Snow pounded the large window to her left, as if trying to gain entry. The sight of it made her cold, and yet she didn't shiver.

Without a word, he tugged off his sweatshirt so he was naked from the waist up, and then he unzipped her coat and pushed it down and off so it lay in a puddle on the floor. His actions were distant from her reality, as if she were watching everything rather than being part of it. He wrapped her in his arms and hauled her onto the sofa. Positioning her on top of him, he covered them with an afghan from the back of the couch.

She sucked in her breath at the searing heat that emanated from his body. She grabbed the side of his torso, enjoying the play of his muscles under her fingers. He was absolutely potent to an intoxicating degree. Lying on top of him, she could feel along the length of his body and knew he was as affected by their closeness as she was. That knowledge made her want to explore his body in detail. Maybe she'd do that later. Her eyes fluttered closed, and she laid her head on his shoulder, reveling in the feel of him. His scent flooded her senses, and she was consumed with an overwhelming lassitude. All she could do was lie in his embrace and allow her mind to drift, comforted by the fact that David was protecting her.

"If you ever do that again, I will kill you myself," he murmured, breaking the silence.

"Do what?" Her head shot up to look at him. Ten minutes—they couldn't have been lying on the sofa for more than ten minutes, and he had gone from being a gentleman to being a jerk.

"You dived out of Jake's truck with no thought of where we were going—"

"I was trying to protect Jake, a father with two children, and you. You weren't supposed to follow—"

"Bullshit."

"Don't use that tone with me." She jolted to a sitting position.

His hands covered his groin, protecting himself from her movement. "I'm wanted for kidnapping, and you're worried about my tone?" He yanked his legs from under her.

She toppled, almost falling off the couch, but righted herself. "We both know you didn't kidnap anybody. There must be a way to fix this. There must be some way—"

"Fix it? Like it's some big misunderstanding—a

mistake. Look lady, when I took the job with PDE, that was a mistake. When I took you to the airport, that was a mistake. What I should have done was drag you back to Finn, but you wanted to go home."

She slammed a fist into his chest. "Why are you so angry?"

His lips curled as he clenched his teeth. "I'm not angry. I'm-I'm…I'm livid. No, I'm—I'm… There are no words for how I feel. Jesus, Marie, they think I kidnapped you. My life is over. Everything I've worked for. I was just getting…" He slumped back, covering his eyes with the crook of his elbow.

"I'm sorry." She wanted to tell him it would be all right, but that would be a lie. Somehow, without meaning to, she'd done this to him, and there was no way to make it right.

She couldn't believe that her life's work could destroy someone so absolutely. She'd thought she was creating something the world needed, and that once she proved her research was sound, it would be well received. How had she been so blind she hadn't even considered the possibility that someone would object so violently to her solar panel? Tears gathered at the corners of her eyes. She blinked, trying to control her reaction, but it wouldn't go away, wouldn't be buried. She turned her back to him. Her shoulders shook as she tried to suppress the pain that flooded to the surface.

He rubbed her shoulder. "Hush, I'll be alright. We'll figure it out."

She scooted along the couch as a howl of despair escaped her throat. She wanted to get away, wanted the world to stop. She crumbled to the ground, unable to keep the fear, pain, confusion and hurt at bay any longer.

Without a word, David scooped her up and settled her in his lap.

She buried her face in his neck and sobbed. To tired and shattered for restraint, she cried until her throat hurt and her eyes were dry and sore. She cried until exhaustion claimed her and she fell into a deep, dreamless sleep.

****

David shifted out from under Marie and covered her with the throw he'd used earlier. He shouldn't have snapped at her, but damn it, she'd nearly killed them with that stunt of hers. She needed to listen to him when it came to their survival, and she had to understand they were in this together. Even in sleep, her eyes were swollen and her nose red. He would've liked to curl up next to her and get some rest, but he had things to do before it got too dark.

He rummaged through his backpack, selected a protein bar, and then downed it with some water. She needed food and water, too, but he'd let her nap for now. He wanted some time alone to process the last twenty-four hours. He wasn't over Portman's betrayal, but it wasn't such a kick in the teeth now, although it still pissed him off.

The space under the stairs was full of wood, a lot of wood, as if someone had stocked up before the storm. He grabbed some old newspaper and kindling from the firebox and lit a fire in the stove, then carefully added a few logs until he was satisfied they would catch. Almost immediately the chill dissipated and the cabin felt homey.

He doubted this house was on municipal water, which meant they would need electricity to pump water from the well. He tried the taps in the kitchen anyway. They gurgled and spluttered, but no water came out, so he grabbed a couple of pans and headed outside.

The house had not been designed with safety in mind. The door to the mudroom was the only exit, which troubled him. The kitchen window opened, as did the windows upstairs, but if the stove caught fire, there was no way out of the living room. It was also the warmest room in the house.

The temperature had dropped in the short time since they'd arrived. Being sure to stay under the eave, he filled two pots with snow and then used the moment of solitude to take care of his personal needs.

Marie's crying jag was a reminder of how sheltered her life was. For him, being in danger and vulnerable were second nature. Yes, he'd left that world behind, but he still knew how to handle himself. For her it must be terrifying. She was rich and had probably never had to deal with a perilous situation. For all that, he had to admire her sense of decency. She had walked away from the safety of the truck to protect a man she didn't know. Yes, it was a stupid thing to do, but he couldn't fault her intent.

Marshall Portman on the other hand was a bastard. David slammed the door as he stomped inside, and then remembered Marie. He crept into the living room and was relieved to find her still asleep.

He placed the pot of snow on the stove. It was dark now. Only the glow from the fire lit the room.

He felt his way to the kitchen. *Damn it*. He should've grabbed a flashlight at the gas station. He searched the drawers, looking for anything that would provide them with a light source and was grateful to find a small penlight. It wasn't ideal, but it was better than nothing. Then he explored the utility room behind the kitchen. There wasn't much there but a generator, a breaker box, a small tankless hot water heater, a furnace, some paint brushes, empty paint cans, and one big-ass flashlight.

He set the light on the kitchen counter. It was large enough to illuminate the whole room. Then he combed through the cupboards looking for food. The protein bar was fine in a pinch, but he needed something with more sustenance. He found a ton of canned foods. There were fruits, vegetables, assorted soups, chicken, tuna, and even canned bread. He selected three cans of beef stew and dumped the contents into a pot. Then he set it on top of the wood stove to warm.

He headed up the stairs and started his search in the larger of the two bedrooms, which held a king bed and dresser. There was no evidence of a woman living in the house, no clothes, make-up, hairbrushes, creams or lotions, and no trace of feminine hygiene products. The only thing that could be remotely considered effeminate were the cat figurines.

Marie was far too curvaceous to fit into men's pants, so he didn't bother looking, but did find a thick, black fleece. It would hang to her knees, but would provide a warm layer over her thermals. He continued to rummage through the drawers and was pleased to discover a new, sealed three-pack of men's underwear. He opened them and held them up. They would be tight on her, but they were stretchy so they might work.

He checked the smaller bedroom. It had two single beds and two dressers. There were boy's clothes of varying sizes thrown on the floor. He glanced at the pile, but didn't bother to look through it. He was filthy enough. He wasn't about to wear someone else's dirty clothing.

The house was a mystery. Given the stack of wood and the amount of canned food, he might conclude that it belonged to a survivalist. Although that assumption could be wrong since there were no weapons, unless they were hidden in an outbuilding. The survivalist theory was still valid.

He wasn't sure what to make of the pile of coats and boots in the mudroom and the state of the boy's room. Then there was the old lady cat theme and the straight clean lines of the kitchen cabinets. The whole house was a puzzle of contradictory elements.

With his search complete, David grabbed the clean pack of underwear, hoping they would fit Marie. His penis throbbed to life as he imagined her voluptuous body modeling the boxers with no bra. He had to stop thinking of her in that way. They were in a dangerous situation. He was accused of kidnapping. Sleeping with her would only muddy the truth and make it seem as if he had an ulterior motive.

The rational part of his mind told him to quit picturing her naked, but his body had free will. Once again his manhood jerked at the memory of her lying on top of him on the couch with her nipples pressing against his chest. He groaned, "Get it together."

Leaving the clothes in the bathroom, he went downstairs. His mouth watered at the wonderful meaty aroma as the stew bubbled.

The little stove had done a good job warming the room. Marie had kicked off the throw, her cheeks a pretty shade of pink. He'd checked her fingers for signs of frostbite when he'd warmed her earlier. He still needed to check her toes, but for now he'd let her sleep. Not only had she been in the early stages of hyperthermia, she was also overwhelmed and exhausted. Maybe he should have considered that before he'd lost it with her, but she could've killed them.

It surprised him that she characterized herself as timid, and it was disturbing her father would call her Mouse. Maybe that was a leftover from when she was young. He could see her being quiet and introverted, but that didn't mean she wasn't strong and determined. It seemed to him she had followed her own path and used resolve, strength, and discipline to achieve her goals. He was a little envious of that. He'd given very little thought for the future when he'd joined the army. Serving his country and proving his worth were his only goals. Once in the military, he had followed orders, doing the bidding of others. For the last year, he had struggled to find his way, and now, finally, when things were coming together, he was plunged into this…whatever it was.

He pushed that line of thought away. It would do no good to think of what the future might hold. He had to survive in the moment, and right now he had things to do.

Using a tea towel, he moved the stew to a cooler part of the stovetop away from the chimney stack. Then he replaced the pan of hot water with another pot of snow, setting it on the warmest part of the stove. Marie would want to bathe once she awoke.

He grabbed the purple backpack and carried the warm water upstairs to the bathroom. It was time to cut his hair and get rid of his beard.

Chapter Sixteen

Marie opened her eyes, sat up straight in one fluid movement, and then groaned, every tendon and every muscle hurting. She blinked. Even her eyes were sore. She rubbed her tongue along the roof of her mouth. It was as dry as sandpaper, and her throat ached. That would teach her to cry like a baby. She groaned again and covered her face with her hands.

David probably thought her a spoilt brat. He was already angry with her for leaving the safety of the truck, but he didn't have to deal with the fact that this was all her fault. She had caused this mess when she'd developed her solar panel, and now Professor Hargreaves had died because of her. And then there was David. He was accused of kidnapping, and his life was now in ruins. What would happen to Jake, a man who'd unwittingly given them a ride?

Wind battered the tiny house, howling, haunting and relentless. The only light in the room came from the fire burning in the small potbelly stove. David must be somewhere. He wouldn't have gone out in the storm. She stood, edged closer to the stove, and inhaled the scent of warm, rich meaty soup. Her stomach rumbled. The only thing she'd eaten today was the chocolate bar she'd had in the truck, and that was hours ago. David had obviously built a fire and organized dinner while she'd slept.

A creak sounded overhead. Feeling her way, she scrambled upstairs. As soon as she got to the top, she saw the light. He'd left the bathroom door open, and she stopped, motionless. She couldn't move, all she could do was stare at him as he splashed water on his face. He looked so different. She only recognized him by his stance and his taut economic movements. His shirtless torso revealed a slim, powerful body with muscled arms and shoulders and a flat waist. Her heart thudded in her chest as warmth flooded her veins. Her fingers ached to touch him and smooth her hand over his chest and down his belly.

She stepped closer, entering the bathroom. A flashlight cast long shadows as it bounced off the bathroom mirror. A pair of scissors and a pack of disposable razors lay on the counter.

"You shaved and cut your hair," she accused. But why she should feel put out by his grooming she couldn't say. Maybe it was because it was so unsettling. He looked so different, wholesome and yet deadly. The same intense green eyes stared back at her. In this light, she could see his irises had no striations. They were a flat, pale green encircled by a black ring. Strangely, without the beard, his scar was less noticeable. Perhaps when he wore a beard, the scar was made visible by the fact that no hair grew in the deep furrow. But now that he had shaved, all she could see was a thick white line that melded into his cheekbone.

His hair was cut into a short, thick, shiny pelt. It looked darker than it had before. That could be a trick of the light, or maybe the sun had bleached the ends.

He cleared his throat. "You need a haircut, too."

It was only after he spoke she realized she'd been staring at him for a considerable amount of time. "Now?"

"Yes, people don't really look at faces. They just take in the general outline, height, hair, weight, glasses or no glasses."

One glance in the mirror told her she was a wreck. Her normal dark brown waves were a tangled, disheveled mess, and her eyes were red and swollen from crying.

Even though her hair looked like a bird's nest, she didn't want to cut it, which was stupid. She'd never considered herself vain, and it wasn't as if it wouldn't grow back, but it was another loss of self, another piece of her stripped away in this frantic fight for survival. But he was right. It was necessary. She sighed. "Let's get this over with."

She turned her back to him and the mirror and closed her eyes so she wouldn't see her hair fall to the ground. When it came to her appearance, she was normally a rational person. She didn't wear high heels because they weren't practical, she wore warm clothes in the winter and cotton blends in the summer, and she'd always kept her hair long because it was easy. Most people thought short hair was practical, but in her experience, that was a misconception. Shorter styles needed tending everyday. And you had to trim your hair regularly to maintain the shape, whereas with longer hair you could just tie it up and forget about it. There was also the fact she wanted to look pretty for David, which was absolutely ridiculous. In her present condition, she looked like she had used a tornado to blow dry her hair, all the while burning her eyes with acid.

He stepped behind her, placing himself between her and the bathroom counter. And then dipping his fingers into the warm water, he wet her hair and lifted it away from her neck. Shivers tingled down her spine. She'd been fighting her attraction to him since the moment he'd checked her toes for frostbite. She licked her cracked lips. The contrast between his powerful body and gentle touch unsettled her. Her skin flushed as her breasts pressed against the fabric of her long johns. Her nipples were so sensitive, the soft cotton fabric chaffed.

He clasped the ends of her hair as he combed, careful not to pull on the tangles, and then held it taut. "Hold still."

Short strands brushed against her nape as he snipped off her waves. He repeated the process, his fingers gently grazing her neck each time he cut her hair. Maneuvering around her until he stood in front of her, he judged his handy work. "You look cute."

She shook her head, getting used to the shape and feel of it, but also shaking away the quivers that resonated through her body.

She reached up and touched his cheek, unable to hold back. He closed his eyes. A small tremor racked his body. She saw it, felt it, and was empowered by it. She ran her other hand down his neck, feeling his pulse under her fingertips. It was powerful and vigorous, proof of his compelling life force.

He coughed, clearing his throat. Without taking her hands away she stared into his eyes. His irises were enlarged, making them appear almost black, only the outer rim light green. His gaze flickered down away from her. He tried to turn his head, but she held his face, gently coercing him to look at her. She understood his reaction because she had experienced it herself. He was unsure, and somehow his vulnerability made him more appealing.

She tugged his head down until his lips met hers. He was soft, warm, and gentle. She snuggled closer, wanting him to wrap his arms about her, but he didn't.

Before she could stop herself, she threw her arms around his neck, deepening the kiss. He pulled back.

What was she doing? She'd just forced herself onto a man who had shown no interest in her. She placed her hands on his shoulders and shoved him away. "I'm sorry. I didn't mean—

"Why'd you stop?"

"I forced—"

"No, you didn't. It's just—"

"Just what?" If he said he didn't want her or wasn't attracted to her, she'd die of mortification.

"I don't want you to feel obligated."

"Obligated? Why should I feel—?"

"Because…ah shit. We had a moment, and I ruined it." His cheeks seared to a bright red. Only his scar was pale.

She poked his chest. "Tell me why you think I would owe you."

"You know, the whole saving you thing."

"You think I'm the type of woman who would have sex with you because I'm grateful?" She punched his shoulder, hard. "While I appreciate everything you've done for me, maybe you can tell me what it is about me that makes you think I'd repay you with my body rather than a hearty handshake."

He shrugged. "Well, you have to admit, I'm not exactly handsome."

"Yes, you are."

He gave her a quizzical look that suggested she'd gone blind.

"You have a scar. Big deal. Get over it. My father has plenty of friends who are successful and handsome, and they're not as good-looking as you, so don't tell me I can't be attracted to you, otherwise there's a good chance I'll punch you again, rather than—"

His lips touched hers, soft and demanding. He ran his tongue along her lips, sensually urging her to open her mouth to him. She complied, deepening the kiss. His hand splayed across her back, the heat of his touch melting her insides. His other hand cradled her head, his fingers kneading her scalp. She should push him away. Tell him she'd changed her mind. She was angry with him. She tugged him closer, rubbing her sensitive breasts against his naked chest. The cotton fabric of her underwear frustrated her. It was a barrier, a layer of clothing that prevented her from touching him and being touched in return. His tongue stroked hers, and a ball of light that started at her breasts flashed through her body, searing her. The feel of his hands on her hipbones made her want to rub herself against him. He grabbed her hips and lifted her so she sat on the counter.

She'd always considered herself logical, and yet in this moment, she couldn't form a coherent thought. It was as if her mind had shut down and her body had taken over, instinctively reacting to him. She wasn't sure how she felt about him emotionally, but physically, at least, she wanted him. She needed to feel his hands on her skin. He must've understood her urgency for he grabbed her legs and tucked them around his waist. In this position, she was open to him, vulnerable. He rubbed his erection against the apex of her thighs in a mimic of lovemaking. Oh god, it had been years since she'd been intimate, and she had never experienced sex with a testosterone-fueled man like David. The thought of him driving into her sent another wave of lightening through her body, and she arched again.

A click sounded, and David's head snapped up as he pushed away from her. "Shit."

In the doorway was a red-faced man, his moustache encrusted with ice. The hood of his dark winter coat was pushed back, revealing a black woolen hat. He pointed a long-barreled gun at David's head.

David disentangled himself from her legs and raised his hands.

It took a moment for Marie to grasp the fact that there was a man, a stranger with a gun in the house. She lifted her hands in the universal sign of surrender. "Please put the gun down." Marie slid from the bathroom counter and stepped toward David, planning to position herself between them.

David leveled his arm blocking her. "Marie…honey, why don't you do us both a favor and take a step back?"

"Listen to him. Move away. I don't want to accidently shoot you," the stranger said.

Marie straightened. "No."

David lent toward her. "Damn it. You are a pain in the butt."

"I'm a pain—"

"Step away from the woman, nice and slow." The stranger waved the weapon at David.

David took one step, but there was no room to maneuver in the small confines of the bathroom. "Who are you?"

"Someone who knows you're trespassing."

Marie wanted to explain. "We were caught in the storm—"

"Save it." He waved the weapon in her direction. "Okay, girl, I want you to grab the flashlight and lead the way down the stairs. Nice and slow. No funny business. I'm going to have this shotgun aimed at your boyfriend. If you make any sudden moves, I'll shoot him. Got it?"

She nodded, picked up the light, stepped in front of David, and started down the stairs.

A grunt sounded. She stopped and spun. David had one hand on the barrel, pointing the weapon at the ceiling. A deafening shot echoed through the house. Wood chipped from the wall at her side.

She ducked, her heart racing, while the men struggled for control of the gun. She switched positions so the flashlight shone in the stranger's eyes, blinding him. David took advantage and grabbed both ends of the weapon and used it to slam the older man against the wall. He pulled the stranger forward and then smashed him into the wall again and again. Marie flinched with every blow and groan. The man went limp. With the shotgun in hand, David backed away.

Chapter Seventeen

Marie watched as David pushed the stranger into the kitchen.

"Are you alone?" David barked.

"Go to hell."

The flashlight illuminated the kitchen, but not enough to see into the corners, and the fact she couldn't tell if anyone was hiding freaked her out.

David pointed the shotgun at him. "Yes, I probably will, but that doesn't answer my question. Stand with your arms wide, feet apart."

The stranger obeyed. "Your picture is all over the news."

David patted him down. He retrieved a cell phone from the man's coat pocket and held it to his ear. "No dial tone." He threw the phone onto the table. "Are you alone?"

The man nodded. "Of course, I am. No one would wait outside in this." Then he glanced at Marie. "Do you need rescuing? Or is this a lover's thing?"

"No." Marie and David snapped at the same time. For her, the answer was true of both questions. They weren't lovers and she didn't need rescuing, but David's vehement answer smarted. If the stranger hadn't interrupted, she might have had sex with him. She liked to think she would've shown some restraint eventually, although she wasn't sure.

Her head throbbed. She'd been absorbing metaphorical body blows all day. Everything was happening so fast. It was like flying a commercial jet through turbulence, except she didn't know where she was going and when the journey would end. It seemed that the woman who had arrived in Montana yesterday was a different person. Since then she'd survived a home invasion, a shooting, a kidnapping attempt, a blizzard, and an angry man had held a gun on them. It was a lot to deal with, and she wasn't sure she could cope.

It wasn't just the danger. David was different from every man she'd ever met. He was dark, cynical, hard, protective, and his kisses were intoxicating. One memory snapped into her mind and wouldn't budge. He thought she would sleep with him because she was grateful, which was a conceited, stupid thing to think, and idiot that he was, he'd said it aloud. That was a man-brain for you, too stupid to know when to shut up. Maybe her obsession with him was a result of stress. Yes, that was it. In order to function, she needed a distraction from the trauma of the last day, and her mind had compensated by fixating on David. She studied him as he finished searching the stranger, using swift, practiced movements. He was athletic, intelligent, and forceful. No wonder she was enamored.

"Sit." David used the gun to point to one of the kitchen chairs.

"I want you out of my house," the older man spat.

"You're lying. This isn't your house." How David knew that she couldn't imagine.

"You asshole." The stranger surged to his feet.

"Stop." David placed the flat of his hand on the man's chest and thrust him back into the chair. "I'm fit and trained. I will hurt you. Is that what you want? Now sit."

"Do you have a name?" Marie searched the cupboards looking for candles and found four in a drawer containing an assortment of bric-a-brac.

David pointed the shotgun away from them and slid the barrel back and forth, ejecting the cartridges. Shells fell about the floor.

"I'm Mac." Everything about him was coiled tight as though he were ready to spring out of his seat and attack.

David placed the unloaded gun on the kitchen counter and then picked up the shells and tucked them in the pocket of his cargo pants. "I'll keep these. That way you can't shoot us."

"Do you expect me to sit here and chat like we're having afternoon tea?" Mac growled.

David shrugged. "Talk or don't talk. You can do whatever you want, but you're stuck with us for the duration of the storm so you might as well make the most of it."

Mac glared at David. "You're one cool customer."

"Mac, what's your last name?" Marie lit each candle and tilted them so melted wax dripped onto a saucer. Then she plunged the unlit ends into the hot puddle, securing them.

"Klein."

"I'm Marie, and the scary man across from you is David." Marie smiled. There was no point in being hostile. There was a chance he was just taking shelter from the storm. "Well, Mac Klein, you look cold. Why don't I get us all a bowl of stew?"

Grabbing a tea towel, she escaped into the living room. She needed a moment alone to think. She eyed the couch where David had warmed her and held her while she wept. She never cried, not since her mother's death when she was five years old. When she considered everything that had happened, it wasn't surprising she'd chosen this place and time to have her breakdown. She decided in this instance she'd be kind and not beat herself up for her childish behavior. David hadn't seemed to mind. He'd been gentle and caring. Yes, he'd also been angry with her at first, but had looked after her anyway. She threw the tea towel on the coffee table as she folded the afghan. Then she placed the throw on the back of the couch. She sat on the couch, needing a few minutes peace, a chance to sort through her feelings.

She liked David, which was a revelation since she didn't

really know anything about him. She had no idea if he was a morning person, what his favorite foods were, or if he had a favorite color. But what she did know about him sat on the pro side of the chart. He was a good person, despite the fact he obviously knew some unsavory characters. He was solid, and he had put himself in harm's way to protect her. Plus, he'd been in the army for... She had no idea how long he'd served his country, nor did she know his age. Those were things a woman generally knew before she kissed a man in a bathroom.

Surprisingly, David didn't think her timid and had cited her behavior to prove his case. She wasn't sure what to make of that. Perhaps he had a point. She argued with him, freely, without fear of consequences, and wasn't emotionally intimidated by him. Whereas arguing with her father was devastating because he withheld his love as punishment. In fact, the reason he had refused to answer her calls for the last three months was because she'd asked him for funding, he had refused, and they had quarreled. She couldn't imagine David doing such a thing. He was too straightforward. He wouldn't stay silent for months, waiting for an apology. He'd tell her to her face why he was mad and then let it go.

Her coat lay in a crumpled heap on the floor. She glanced at her breasts. Her nipples were poking through the thin cotton fabric of her long johns. Great, she'd been virtually naked when she'd kissed David. Worse, Mac had snuck up on them and caught her wearing next to nothing. She shrugged into her coat and zipped it up, hiding her body from view.

Her stomach growled, reminding her that she hadn't eaten anything nutritious since yesterday. She wrapped the tea towel around the handle, and then using both hands, carried the pot into the kitchen.

David was hard and rough, but he was also generous, not in a I'll-buy-you-a-castle kind of way, but in all the ways that mattered. He made her feel strong. He'd had the opportunity to humiliate her and hadn't taken it. Even after the disaster at the airport, he hadn't scolded her. He'd told her they were doing things his way, and that was that. On the con side, he was high-handed, but she could live with that. Mac seemed calmer, less belligerent when she returned to the kitchen, making her wonder if David had said something when she was out of earshot.

She divided the food into three bowls while David laid the table.

Mac stared at his serving and then sighed. "You're right. This isn't my house. It belongs to my daughter, which means you're trespassing."

David gave a long slow blink and then nodded. "We needed to get out of the storm."

Mac scooped up a spoonful of stew and blew on it. "Understandable, I guess."

"As long as you leave us in peace, we won't hurt you." David stood and walked to the cabinet and retrieved a can.

"You didn't kidnap this young woman?" Mac yanked his knit hat from his head and placed it in his lap.

Using a can opener, David opened both ends of the tin. He pushed the cylindrical doughy substance onto a plate and placed it in the middle of the table.

"No, he didn't." She pointed at the latest addition to their meal. "What's that?"

"Canned bread." David placed three butter knives on the table. There were probably sharper knives in the drawer, but even she wouldn't put a weapon in front of Mac.

"That's not what they're saying on TV," Mac said, turning the conversation back to her "kidnapping." He seemed less tense, but not relaxed. "There's video of you forcing her into a car."

"On TV? We're on TV?" David's eyes widened as his voice rose.

"Yes." Mac pointed to David. "You're running out of a building. You push a cop and grab her. It's pretty incriminating."

David groaned. "That's not what happened."

"Why would the police say you took her?"

"It's a set up," David said.

"Why would I believe you when I know firsthand just how dangerous you are?"

"I served in Afghanistan." David pulled his bowl of stew closer and scooped a spoonful into his mouth.

"Are you still caught up in it, you know... What do they call it? P-P—"

"PTSD," Marie supplied.

"That's it." Mac smiled at Marie and then turned to David. "Do you have that?"

"No, sir."

"Then why would these people want to kill you?"

"That's a damn good question." David eyed Marie. "I would really like to know what's so different about your solar panel and why Portman is so threatened by you."

"It's just a...it's a prototype for a new—"

"You said that before. I need details." David threw his spoon into his bowl, splattering gravy over the table.

Mac twisted in his chair so he faced Marie. "Come on, tell us what this is all about."

"I can show you. It's in my backpack." She retrieved her bag from the mudroom floor and spread the gold plastic sheet on the table. "This is my prototype."

"It looks like a bit of shiny plastic to me." Mac fingered the edge.

She smiled. "I know." She held up the sheet, detangling a small black cord that attached the panel to the inverter. "Do you see how it's embossed with concentric squares? Those indents give it more surface area. And the gold coating is a special formula that absorbs energy from the sun. When I started this, I was just trying to make a small economical panel. I used recycled plastic in its construction. Normal panels are fragile and easily damaged, but mine shouldn't need special handling.

Actually, that's one of the reasons I came to Montana. I wanted to see how it would stand up physically to the cold. This one is intact despite everything that has happened."

Mac gave a small cough. "You have a highly portable solar panel. I don't see what all the fuss is about."

David leaned back and folded his arms across his chest. "What else is so special about this invention of yours?"

Marie licked her lips. "The energy output from my prototype is much greater than I expected."

"More than a regular solar panel?" Mac asked.

"Much more. Mine produces the equivalent of a hundred traditional solar panels."

"Why is yours so powerful?" Mac placed his spoon in his bowl and pushed it away.

"The earth and everything on our planet naturally creates energy. Most solar panels convert light into electricity. Mine uses both the naturally occurring radiant energy and light to create power." Marie knew she was babbling, but she couldn't stop.

Mac frowned. "I still—"

"Don't you get it? Once the panel warms your house in the winter, the heat it generates is recycled, creating more power. The more light and heat you have, the more energy you manufacture. It's self-sustaining. I came here because of the storm. I was supposed to test it in blizzard conditions and see if I could still power my cabin despite the lack of sunlight.

"How many of these sheets would be required to heat this house?" David asked.

"My tests indicate that a sheet this size could power a small office building, or maybe your house and an electric car."

"And it's made out of recycled plastic?" Mac scratched his jaw.

"Yes. The raw materials for this one only cost a few hundred dollars."

Mac smacked his knee. "My God, that's brilliant."

Marie blushed. "I don't know about that. I haven't completed my trials."

David Nodded. "I get it now. That's why they want to kill you. There are powerful people who can't afford for this to come out. It's a game-changer."

Marie put a hand to her cheeks. She was dizzy. He had to be wrong. "But it's only..." She dropped onto her seat. It was just a solar panel. Yes, it was very efficient, but it wasn't ready for mass production. "I-I don't understand."

David knelt down in front of her. "Because everyone will be off the grid. In fact, if this was ever sold commercially, there wouldn't even be a grid. There are men, powerful men, who want to keep things the way they are. There's no way they would allow you to develop this panel of yours, no matter how much it's needed. Portman wants to stop you because you are a direct threat to him, but he's not the only one."

"No, you're wrong. It won't affect them at all. Cars run on gas. Yes, I know there are electric cars, but there are a limited number of fueling stations—"

Mac pointed to the gold plastic sheet. "This will change all that. This is a mobile form of power. You could park, put this on the dash, and power your car."

"Even if it did change things, how many people could afford to buy a new car? It would take years to affect that kind of change. It's the same with houses. Not everyone can afford to buy the panel and do the wiring work to convert their house." Even as she said the words, she knew they were hollow. She could deny it all she wanted, but the truth was clear. She had deluded herself into thinking the world needed her solar panel. A cheap, efficient source of electricity, and she had been so caught up in her work, she hadn't stopped to consider the big picture. She hadn't seen the obvious—the most important men in the country would do anything to stop her from succeeding, including murder.

David took her hand in his. "How many years? Ten?

The fact is that once this solar panel goes into production, it'll be the beginning of the end for the power grid and oil production."

Marie bit her lip. "I never meant. I just wanted—"

"Wanted what?" David whispered.

"There are places in the world that don't have electricity to pump and purify water. There are catastrophes like earthquakes, tsunamis, and landslides. This could make a difference to people in those disaster areas."

David brushed her hair away from her face and rubbed his thumb over her cheek. "I understand. Field hospitals rely on generators. Doctors can't perform modern surgery without some form of power."

"Yes, that's the kind of application I had in mind." She broke eye contact, blinking away the tears. She refused to weep, especially after her earlier crying jag. She was a strong, sensible woman who was not given to emotional outbursts. All she needed to do was stay calm and think logically.

Mac strode to the cabinets, and then opened the cupboards, searching them. "These things are invented all the time, but they're normally shut down by large corporations." He found a large bottle of Scotch and three glasses, and then returned to the table. "Moments like these call for a splash of the good stuff." He dispensed a generous amount of the amber liquid into his glass.

David returned to his seat. "You've heard of this happening before?"

Mac passed the scotch to David. "Not to my knowledge, but I'm hardly an expert."

"What do you do?" David didn't pour himself a drink. Instead he re-screwed the top on to the bottle and placed it in the middle of the table.

"I was a state trooper for twenty-five years. Some people loved me, lots hated me, but I did the best job I could." Mac swept his arm in a wide arc. "My daughter and son-in-law are in Florida. I live in a small cabin near Livingston, in the Yellowstone River Valley. There's just me. My wife, Haley, died ten years ago, may she rest in peace. I live off the grid. I have a propane-powered generator, a wood stove, and an outhouse."

"Sounds like my place, except without the cabin." David smiled, but it didn't reach his eyes. "How'd you end up here on a night like this?"

"I was visiting a lady friend in Granite City. Blizzard hit. I thought I'd wait it out here. You know, I was tracking a company a few years back. They developed a water-powered generator. Now that would be a handy item. I was all set to buy, too, but the company shut their doors."

"Did they go bust?" David asked.

"No, they were acquired by some large corporation…Global…Global something or other, can't remember the name. Anyway, instead of developing the technology, they shut it down. It seems to me there are a lot of powerful people who want us to keep buying their gas and electricity. My theory is that when anything like this is concocted"—he pointed to the prototype—"some company sponsor comes along and buys it so they can shut it down."

David's cold, dead gaze was back. Was he angry over her solar panel and Portman's actions? Or was it something else?

"Seems that's normal business practice. They buy out anyone who creates something that threatens their lead in the global energy market." Mac splashed more scotch into his glass.

David eyed Marie. "You said earlier that you own the patent." He was anything but relaxed. His questions and the tension in the way he held himself suggested he was on edge.

"Yes, Father wouldn't allow me to give my ideas away again." She remembered her father's anger when he discovered she'd been gullible enough to trust her lover.

David leant back in his chair. "Portman can't stop you by having someone else claim it's theirs and tying your hands legally."

"Ironically, the jokes on him." Marie refolded the gold sheet.

"What do you mean?"

"I'm out of funds. I've spent every penny. I was hoping Professor Hargreaves would validate my work so that I could get funding from the Department of Energy."

"You've spent eighty million dollars?" David's eyes widened.

"You're rich," Mac added.

Marie answered Mac's question first. "No, I'm not rich, not anymore. And I never had eighty million dollars. My grandfather left me two million, which I've spent. I have about eighteen hundred dollars left."

"How did you spend two million?" David rested on his elbows, obviously interested.

"It was easy. I purchased and maintained a house. I converted the garage to a workshop. I paid for my supplies and food. Oh, and I paid my bills.

"If you were trying to get the Department of Energy to sponsor you, why were you at the PDE building?"

"The professor was going to recommend my work to the DOE, and now that he's dead…" She shrugged because some things really didn't need saying. "Portman had expressed an interest, so I thought I'd ask him to invest."

"Your work was over? He didn't have to do anything…son of a b—gun." David pointed to the prototype. "Any chance you can hook that thing up so we have power?"

She was surprised she hadn't thought of connecting her sheet to the house grid. It was just another example of how distracted she was. But the idea of doing a live trial lifted her spirits. This was her territory, where she was most at home. It was the place where scientific theory met practical application. And it might be the only time she had a chance to see her work in action. "What kind of a set up do they have? Are we on the grid?"

"A generator only. It's in the utility room. Come on Mac, don't you want to see how it works?" David grabbed the flashlight.

Mac's gaze flickered to David, and then he stood and followed them. There was something going on between the two men, an unpleasant undercurrent. If she had to give it a word, she would've said distrust. Yes, that was it. They didn't trust each other, but then, why should they? Mac had pointed a gun at David's head and they, in turn, had broken into Mac's daughter's house.

David stood at the door to the utility room, shining the light inside.

Marie unplugged the generator and then checked the breaker box. "I wouldn't be able to do this if they were hooked up to the power grid."

"Why not?" David asked.

"Because grid-tied systems have a safety switch that prevents the use of outside power during a blackout."

"I don't understand." David aimed the light at the electrical panel.

"Electricity flows both ways down the line. If someone is working on a downed power line and we're feeding voltage along that line, they could be electrocuted."

She pulled the small black box from her backpack. "The inverter was the hardest component to make. It converts the power produced by the panel into usable electricity. There's no way to tell if today's events have caused any damage."

"What are you going to do?" David asked.

"Plug it in and see. I should also mention that none of this is legal."

"Legal?" David's eyes widened.

"Yes, all off-grid systems are strictly regulated to ensure

they can't cause electrocutions and house fires. I haven't got to that stage in product development."

"Maybe we should just use the generator." Mac stood behind David, peeking over his shoulder.

"We can't unless we put it outside. The fumes from the engine will suffocate us. Besides, I'm not sure if there's any gas in it," David pointed out.

"You're just going to plug that thing into the breaker box? Don't you have to rewire anything?" Mac asked.

"What's the point of inventing a mobile unit if you have to take an electrician with you to make it work? If you were going to have this as your main source of power for a house and run your washing machine, dishwasher and stove, then I'd recommend you get a qualified expert to install it and wire it through the fuse box, but this should work in a pinch.

"Plug it in," David urged.

"If there's a loud pop or a sizzle, then I've just fried the lines, and this test is a bust." Marie held her breath as she inserted the plug into the outlet on the fuse box, which was designed for the generator. Nothing happened. No noises, no lights, no power.

"I guess there's no reason for anyone to want me dead. It doesn't work." Her heart sank. All her hard work was for nothing. Maybe the inverter was damaged. She'd need to take it apart and check.

"Hold on." David flipped on the light switch.

The overhead light flickered on. They had power.

"It works." Her prototype was producing electricity in a storm, without sunlight. Laughing, Marie jumped into David's arms. He held her up, spun her around, and then hugged her.

Mac inspected the set up. "Amazing. You could throw this in your bag and have electricity anywhere. I wouldn't have believed it if I hadn't seen it with my own eyes."

The years of hard work, loneliness, and single-minded determination were all worth it. She had created something that had the ability to make a real difference.

David put an arm over her shoulder and hugged her to his side. "And that's the reason people want to kill you."

Chapter Eighteen

Finn struggled through the heavy snow toward the coffee shop. Peggy, the owner of the Dumb Luck Café, had decided it was safer and more profitable to keep her business open during the storm. Many people were forced to camp at work. They needed food, and although the roads were closed, the city buildings lessened the effects of the wind, making walking possible, if unwise.

Cell service had gone out an hour ago, meaning there would be no call from David tonight.

Finn pulled his hood down over his face and zipped his collar past his mouth as he struggled to stay upright in the driving gusts. Finally, he made it across the street to the north end of the square and was grateful to reach the buildings that shielded him from the impact of the wind.

The eatery was an assault on his senses. The place was crowded with stranded office workers, city employees, a few cops, and civilians of all walks of life.

Detective Ramirez approached Finn as he made his way through the crowd. "Agent Callaghan, any news on the kidnapping?"

Finn shrugged. "I'm not on the case."

Ramirez frowned. "That's weird. I wanted to join forces with the investigator. I figured the home invasion and abduction were connected. When I spoke to the chief, I was told that the FBI had muscled in and taken over the case."

"We can't investigate, we don't have jurisdiction, but I did offer our help. Chief Notley basically told me to back off."

"He said that?"

"Not in so many words, but it was implied. For what

it's worth, I think you're right. The home invasion and the kidnapping have to be connected."

Ramirez leant closer, lowering his voice. "Oh, by the way, I checked your friend out. He has an impressive military record."

"I know."

"He's a decorated soldier. It seems he was injured by one of our own, according to the eyewitnesses. This guy, a private, went nuts. He was hallucinating and started shooting at his own guys."

"Shit." David hadn't mentioned any of this.

"Quinn took him out, but not before a bullet grazed his face. There was an enquiry. The survivors all claimed David saved them. He was awarded a purple heart. I'll forward the file onto you."

"That'd be great." Most men would have been proud. According to Ramirez, David was a hero, so why was he holed up on his land? "Maybe he got sick of fighting."

"What?"

"Oh, nothing." Finn changed the subject. He didn't want to discuss David, Portman, or Chief Notley. "How come you get to sit in here when every other policeman in the department is out saving marooned motorists?"

"I'm heading out now." Ramirez held up a disposable tray that contained four large-lidded cups. "Can't go without supplies."

Ramirez flipped up the hood of his coat as he headed out, struggling to hold onto his drinks in the driving wind. Finn stepped up to the counter and ordered a coffee and a Reuben sandwich. He smiled and nodded to the owner, Peggy, as she toasted sandwiches on the grill. She waved and turned back to her work. Normally, she stopped to chat, but this evening she was busy in her element making money.

She was a slim, attractive woman with a shock of spiky, thick, white hair and large brown eyes. The Dumb Luck Café was her dream, purchased with insurance money she'd received when her husband had met his death in an untimely fishing accident. They didn't have children, and she'd always dreamed of owning a coffee shop.

After paying for his Rueben sandwich, he leant against the counter, sipping his coffee as he waited for Peggy to make his order. A young man in a baseball cap caught his eye. He had a baby face with the intent look of an adult. He was either a young man who had seen a lot of life or an older man who looked like a kid. Finn decided it was the second option. He sat on a high stool near the window, nursing a large disposable cup. He stared at Finn, long and hard, and then turned back to look out of the window.

"There you go handsome." With a wink, Peggy placed the Rueben sandwich on the counter. Finn winked back, grabbed his food, and made his way to the door. Initially, he'd wanted to stay in the shop, but it was too noisy and crowded. He needed to sit down and rest, and there weren't any seats available. David, Dr. Wilson, the blizzard, and being warned off the case by the chief, all festered.

He flipped up his hood and took a deep breath, mentally preparing himself for the cold, wind, and snow. He'd only gone a few steps when he became aware of someone behind him.

Finn dropped his food and spun around as his hand went to his Glock.

The baby-faced man from the café put his arms up, surrendering. "Are you the FBI? I heard that cop call you Agent Callaghan."

"Yes, that's me."

"Can I see your badge?" he shouted, straining to be heard above the storm.

"And you are?" With his left hand, Finn took his credentials from his pocket and flipped them open. His right hand still rested on his weapon.

"I'm Jake." He moved closer, studying Finn's ID, holding it up to the small stream of light that filtered from the coffee shop window. Then he nodded as if satisfied with what he saw.

"What can I do for you?" Finn put his identification back in his pocket and stepped closer to the wall out of the wind.

"David sent me." Jake blew on his exposed fingers.

"David—David Quinn?"

"Jake nodded."

"Where is he? He needs to come in and straighten this mess out. Let's go inside and talk about this." Finn nodded toward the Dumb Luck Café.

Jake stared into the coffee shop and shook his head. "No. I'll talk to you alone and then I'm leaving."

"But I need a state—"

'No, it's too dangerous. I have a family—"

"What's too dangerous?"

"A man named Marshall Portman wants him and the woman dead. I heard…" Jake gulped.

"What?"

"I heard that Portman guy on the phone. He said Marie was dangerous. He plans to kill them."

Finn sucked in a breath. "You heard this."

"Yes, I thought he'd kidnapped her, but he didn't."

So this corroborated David's earlier accusation. Portman was trying to kill them. "Anything else?"

"David said he wants to come in, but he can't go to the police. That's all I know." Jake backed away.

"Wait, you're my witness. I need you to—"

"No, I said I'd deliver the message and I have."

Finn desperately wanted Jake to stay. "Do you realize you're the only person who can prove David's innocence? Come on, I'll buy you a coffee and we can talk."

"No."

"Where are you headed?"

"Away from here. I want to see my kids again." Jake retreated, fighting the wind as he trudged through the snow.

Finn watched until he disappeared from sight. He could have forced Jake to stay, but that wasn't practical. If David was right and the police were compromised, then he had no one to watch Jake while he investigated. Peggy had security cameras. The whole thing would've been caught on tape. If need be, he could track Jake down later.

Portman had enough money to do a lot of damage, but the widespread corruption of multiple forces would take organizing. All he really needed to do was bribe those at the top of the ladder. Chief Notley's behavior indicated he was shady, but that didn't mean the officers in his charge were. Ramirez had come to him, wanting to share information on the home invasion, and coordinate with the kidnapping investigation. Or was the detective only asking to throw Finn off balance?

He rolled his eyes. Things were bad enough without becoming paranoid. He scanned the deserted city square. The blizzard obliterated the PDE building from view. A shiver inched down his spine that had nothing to do with the weather.

He needed to talk to Kennedy and contact his superiors in Salt Lake City as soon as the phones were back. A large vice tightened around his chest. Once the blizzard was over and the roads were cleared, they could get backup, but until then, he and Kennedy were isolated and alone. They couldn't rely on anyone but themselves. He tried to inhale a deep lungful of frozen air, but his ribcage wouldn't expand. He leant against the wall of the coffee shop and stared at the snow, allowing the hurling flakes to calm him. Finally, he relaxed enough to breathe.

He plucked his Rueben sandwich from where it had landed in the snowdrift. It was still in its brown paper bag, but his coffee was gone. He stepped away from the shelter of the building. Almost immediately, a gust of wind propelled him sideways, throwing him off balance. He'd wait out the storm. Then he would do what he always did—work the case.

Chapter Nineteen

Marie leant against the bathroom sink, washing her face, marveling at the healing power of hot water. It was such a simple thing and yet it lifted her spirits. But did they really have any chance of getting out of this? She'd developed a solar panel she believed would benefit mankind and help her gain the recognition of the scientific community. Instead, they were embroiled in a terrifying situation.

Using a towel from the rack, she rubbed her face dry. At least she looked better than she had when she'd first entered the bathroom. But there were still dark circles under her eyes, and her cheeks and ears were pink from exposure. She brushed her teeth, using one of the toothbrushes purchased at the gas station.

David might as well have used a hatchet to hack off her hair. Long chunks hung over her eyes, while the back was cropped an inch shorter than the front. She dampened her hands and then ran the water through her untidy mane. Frizzy curls formed immediately. She sucked in a breath as she studied her reflection. She was a scientist, so it was only fitting that she now looked like the female version of Albert Einstein.

David had found a new pack of men's underwear and a big sweatshirt, but no bra. *Damn.* She tugged on the white boxers, wishing they were a size larger. She wasn't exactly a pear shape since her chest and her hips were roughly in equal proportion. If she were being kind, she might describe her figure as Rubenesque. Whereas, men weren't known for their wide hips so the waistband of the underwear dug into her flesh. She grabbed the scissors off the counter and snipped the elastic so they fit.

While she appreciated the fresh, clean undergarments and the sweatshirt, she really would have liked to wear a bra. Her breasts actually hurt from the lack of adequate support. Using her hands, she held her bust up for a few minutes, enjoying the much-needed relief to her chest muscles.

She cringed as she climbed into her pink long johns. They needed to be boiled. No, once this was over, she would burn them. She thought about looking for some pants but decided against it. They would probably be a worse fit than the underwear, and she was too tired to fuss. She tugged the black sweatshirt over her long johns and left the bathroom.

She found David and Mac in the living room.

"How did you find this place in the storm?" David lounged on the couch. He seemed to have relaxed as he stared out the window, watching the windblown snow as it accumulated into large overhanging mounds on the eave.

"It was tough. I thought I'd missed my turn. Everything's white, but the snow was higher on either side of the driveway, and the lane itself formed a straight line. That's how I knew I wasn't driving into a field or creek. How did you find it?" Opposite David, Mac was reclined with his feet up, his back resting against the wing of the loveseat.

"Same. It was the lay of the land that gave this place away." David glanced at her as she reached the bottom step and patted the empty spot next to him.

"If it's all the same to you, I'll use the facilities and then bed down for the night." Mac stood and headed for the stairs. His footsteps creaked through the house as he made his way to the bathroom.

A pile of assorted comforters and blankets were stacked on the coffee table. As Marie sat, David unfolded a large comforter and stretched it over her. Then he threw an arm over her shoulders and tugged her against his side. He smelled of soap and man. Once again she was captivated by the allure of his scent. She tried to dismiss her attraction to him, not because she wanted to ignore it, but because he was so much more than a handsome, rugged man. He was annoying, flawed, intelligent, and protective. He had put himself in the line of fire for her and deserved her gratitude and respect, not just her lust.

She let out a sigh, and then relaxed against him as her eyes blinked shut. She was beyond tired. All her energy left her body, making her feel like a deflated balloon. This day hadn't just been long and arduous. It had been a nightmare of dangerous situations and revelations, the most irritating of which was David assuming she wanted to thank him with sex. She elbowed him to show her displeasure.

"Ouch. What was that for?" He sounded put out, but she knew she hadn't hurt him because he hadn't moved.

"Thank-you sex," she growled.

"Still miffed about that, huh?"

"Of course, I am. You thought I'd—I'd—"

"Look, I'm a guy. I can run five miles in an hour carrying a fifty-pound rucksack. I can do a hundred pushups in two minutes, and I can swim a hundred meters wearing military issue boots and fatigues, but don't ask me about how I feel, how you feel, or any of that shit, because I haven't got a clue."

"You're oblivious."

"Yeah, can you let this go? I messed up. It's been a long time since I've kissed a pretty woman, and I'm a little low on finesse."

"I don't think this is a day for finesse."

"You got that right, but on the bright side, the fire will die down in the night so we'll need to snuggle to stay warm." He waggled his eyebrows.

She giggled at his obvious attempt to lighten the conversation and then gave a prolonged yawn.

"Get some sleep." He pulled the blanket higher around her neck.

She wanted rest, but there were questions she needed

to ask before she could relax. "Why are you helping me? Why haven't you left me behind?"

"I did…twice. I left you with the FBI and I left you at the airport. It didn't take either time." He made light of her questions when she needed answers.

"But why do you keep saving me?" If there was ever going to be anything between them, she needed to know more than his name and that he was a Special Forces soldier.

"It's my job."

"No, it isn't."

"Ok, not technically, but…" His voice trailed, and he stared out at the blowing snow. "I'll explain later."

She closed her eyes and listened to the wind as it howled around the house. She was adrift. It was as if her whole world had tilted and what she had thought was the truth was in fact a lie. She'd believed the world would welcome her brainchild, and that no one would object to a cheap, clean source of power, but she'd been wrong.

It wasn't like the criticism of her colleagues, one of which had described her hypotheses as unsubstantiated hogwash. These men wanted the absolute obliteration of not only her work, but also her very being.

"Stop thinking." David tapped her forehead. "I can feel the cogs turning."

She sucked in a deep breath. "I want to know why you're helping me."

"Why I'm helping you? Because…because you're a pain in my butt who keeps getting into trouble."

She said nothing, refusing to acknowledge his glib answer. It wasn't just a question of trust. She didn't know anything about him, and yet she was becoming emotionally involved. She wanted to understand the man who could disarm an assailant in the morning, but at the end of the day kiss her senseless.

Finally he sighed and said, "What kind of a person would I be if I just let them hurt you?"

"A normal one."

He held three fingers in front of her face. "Three times I've saved you, and you still don't believe in me."

"I do, it's just—"

"Just what?"

"I need to know how you're involved in this and why you helped me when it would've been easier to walk away."

"Because you're in trouble, and I may be a bastard, but I'm not that big a bastard. And I'm involved in this because I let my guard down."

"How?"

"Marshall kept calling me, insisting I take this job. I thought he was a friend and trying to help me get back on my feet, but—"

"How do you know him?"

"He saved me."

"You're Special Forces. How did a business man in Montana save you?"

"When I was fourteen, I caught my stepfather trying to rape my sister."

"Oh…"

"I killed him."

It was a bald statement with no embellishments, no justification. She swallowed, not knowing which shocking fact she should react to first, the knowledge that David had taken a life to protect his sister, or that his fourteen-year-old sister had been assaulted. She tried to imagine the scene, but that left her with more questions than answers. "What about your parents, your real parents?"

"Dad died when I was eight. Mom remarried when I was twelve. She died a year later."

"I'm so sorry." She placed her hand over his.

"Anyway, after I killed Russell, that was his name, Sinclair and I ran away. We made it from Denver, Colorado to Granite City before we ran out of money."

"What did you do then?"

"We lived on the street." He spoke as if they were having an everyday conversation over a cup of coffee and not talking about what had to be the most devastating event of his life.

"How did you survive?

"Begging and charity. Anyway, one cold night in January, the three of us were huddled in a doorway when Portman walked up to us—"

"Three of you? I thought it was just you and Sinclair." She struggled to keep a tight grip on her emotions. As a child, he had lived off the charity of others and begged for food. She wanted to cry for him but knew he wasn't revealing his past to gain her sympathy.

"At first, then we met Tim and Mike. They were runaways, too. We watched each other's backs. Took care of each other. On the street, there's safety in numbers."

"Portman walks up to you and?"

"He offered us a place to sleep and a spot in his program."

"What program?"

"Marshall House. I wasn't too keen on it at first, but Sinclair was sick and needed off the street, and Tim wanted a future where he wouldn't have to steal. Me, Sinclair, and Tim went to Marshall House. Michael had already gone home to his family."

"Tell me about Tim and Michael."

"Tim's pretty straightforward. His parent's own a ranch in Elkhead County, just north of here. As a teen, he got into some trouble and ran away from home. He's charismatic. Sinclair says he just pretends to be charming. It's the face he shows the world."

"What do you think?"

"I think she's right. Not that it matters. He's family."

"And Michael. What's he like?"

"Michael is complicated."

"How?"

"He's like you."

"Me?"

"He's smart, except with him it's computers and cyber stuff. He's a cyber specialist with Army CID."

"Were they good to you at Marshall House?" She already knew the answer. Why else would he consider Portman a friend?

"Yeah, really good. We had onsite schooling to help us catch up. They even sorted out our legal problems."

"What legal problems?"

"I'd killed a man, remember, and Tim had some issues, too. Anyway, Marshall House helped us get our high school diplomas, and with a clean record, we were able to join the army."

"Was that what you wanted?"

"I never thought about it. The program is about giving back to the community. We were encouraged to get a job that benefited others in some way. The army wasn't a bad way for me to go. I'm tough, fit, a good fighter, and I'm good with languages. In return, I got three meals a day, a bed to sleep in, a post-secondary education through distance learning, and a place where I belonged."

"What did you do for a post-secondary?"

"Entrepreneurship."

"Why a business degree?" She couldn't imagine him in a suit.

"I like working with numbers and the idea of being my own boss. I figured when I was ready, I could put something together, and if a small business didn't work out, I still had the qualifications to get a decent job."

"How does this lead to you breaking into my cabin and rescuing me?"

"I have a ten-acre parcel of land west of Missoula. It's peaceful, but there are no structures on the property. I live in an old camper. I was hoping to build a small cabin." He looked around. "Smaller than this place. I wasn't planning to hook it up to utilities, just a wood fire for heat and an outhouse."

She glanced at the potbelly stove. "Sounds cozy, except for the outhouse."

"It would be. Anyway, I burned through most of my savings buying the land and paying for food and sh—stuff. I have some left, but I'm saving that to purchase more hives."

"Bees?" That was unexpected. She hadn't pictured him in an agrarian environment. Hunting, sure. Beekeeping—never.

"Products made from beeswax are in demand, and I can also rent out the hives for pollination. It's a growing industry, and I like bees. They keep it simple."

She tried to imagine him in the protective gear worn by beekeepers, but couldn't. He was just too energetic and dynamic. "I think we're getting off topic."

"Marshall offered me a lot of money to help retrieve a solar panel. He told me it was stolen. In fact, he insisted that my help was needed to intimidate the suspect—you, but once we broke through your door, I knew I'd made an error in judgment. Plus, it was all a lie. I should have realized when I met the others on the team that I wasn't needed. I believed criminals weren't in Portman's sphere of expertise. I was so blind."

The memory of David, a terrifying scarred man with shaggy hair, a long beard, and intense, pale eyes coming through her door, sprang to mind. She had been so scared of him she hadn't paid attention to the men who were the real threat.

David continued, "Even if the job was legit, I could never be a part of it. I'm not a thug. But Marshall kept calling. He needed a favor. He wanted my help. And I owed him…everything. I couldn't refuse." He scrubbed a hand over his face. "The charge of kidnapping, that's something else. We really need Finn's help. In the morning we'll form a plan with the goal being to contact the FBI."

"Good idea." She snuggled closer. The sound of his heartbeat echoing through his chest was like a drug coaxing her to sleep.

"I have no intention of running and giving up my acreage and my future. I want to be left in peace, on my land, just me and my beehives."

Marie's throat tightened. It didn't matter how much she liked him or how attracted she was to him. Even if they got through this mess, there was no future for them because he wanted to be left alone.

****

David listened to the even rhythm of Marie's breathing. His pulse quickened as an image of her escaping the Paxtons at the airport flashed into his mind. He'd been so close to losing her. It was foolish, but since that moment, he held her hand at every opportunity, unable to let her out of his sight. She seemed comfortable with his touch, which was good because he had no intention of stopping. He'd read somewhere that deeper emotional bonds developed between people who touched each other. He wasn't sure if that was true, but he'd enjoy trying. He had no right to want her as much as he did. She was beautiful, brilliant, and surprisingly passionate. He'd been shocked when she'd kissed him and had responded by acting like a teen. Despite that, she'd welcomed his desire and matched it with her own.

He'd like to show her his land, and maybe he could persuade her to live with him. Then again, that might not be a good idea. He was still pretty messed up and had no right to drag her into his bleak world.

She shifted in her sleep, wriggling closer. He rubbed his shaved chin across her head, reveling in the silky texture of her hair. Being clean-shaven felt strange and familiar at the same time. There were times in his career when he had grown his hair and beard long. It made it easier to infiltrate other cultures. But when he'd been in basic and in Special Forces training, he'd had a traditional military haircut. Getting rid of the beard had been a pain. After not shaving for a year, he was out of practice, and his skin was tender.

It had felt good to share a little bit of his past with Marie, as if he were finally releasing a weight that was tied around his ankles, pulling him under.

"She asleep?" Mac asked as he settled onto the loveseat opposite. He arranged a blanket so it covered him from his feet to his chest. His head rested on the arm of the chair, while his feet dangled off the other end.

There were contradictions in the old man's story. How had he seen David and Marie on the news if he lived in an off-the-grid house? Although he said he'd just come from his lady friend's house, so maybe he had seen them there. He had also recognized David immediately despite the fact that he had shaved his beard and cut his hair. But then again, Mac did claim to be an ex-cop so maybe he was more observant than the average person.

Not that any of the speculation mattered because he was still a lying son of a bitch. This place didn't belong to his daughter. There was no evidence of a woman living here, despite the God-awful cat and lace theme. The old man would've been bound to a chair if it weren't for the fact there was no ammunition or weapons in the house. This was a dangerous enough situation without having to worry about getting shot in the back. Perhaps he should have called Mac out, but he hadn't because Marie had been through enough for one day. She needed rest, and he figured he could handle one out of shape old man without causing her more stress. He'd let her sleep. The morning would be here soon enough.

David's mind flooded with questions. Was Klein connected with PDE, or was he only lying because he was scared? It was the second possibility that had stopped David from taking action and tying him up. The average person didn't realize how much nerve damage could be inflicted by tight restraints, and he was reluctant to do that to a man who was just frightened. But he'd insisted they all sleep in the living room on the pretext that this room was warmer so they wouldn't have to worry about freezing to death. That way he could keep an eye on Mac and make sure he didn't try anything stupid. The phones were out, and he would know if Klein went for the kitchen knives.

There was nothing else to be done while the blizzard raged. In this moment, they were safe and warm. He would watch Mac and make a decision at sunrise.

Chapter Twenty

Marshall Portman slammed the smoked glass door of the conference room, not caring if it shattered. He wanted the computer nerd sitting at the oval table to know he was serious. Door slamming was juvenile, but it was also an effective way to communicate a subliminal show of force.

It was hard to believe the scrawny Native American was one of the world's best hackers. Unlike most of the geeks Marshall employed, who were normally a disheveled mess, this one was stylishly dressed in expensive but informal attire. His hair was cropped short, and he wore a new, clean pair of blue jeans.

PDE investigators had discovered his real name, Michael Phillips, but he preferred to use his street name, Spider. He came highly recommended. It was rumored he had hacked into Homeland's personnel files, apparently bypassing their multi-billion-dollar detection system. He was a fugitive, demanding a six-figure payday in return for his services, not that Marshall cared about his background, as long as he got the job done.

"Spider, I haven't had a chance to talk to you since your arrival, but I wanted to welcome you to Public Domain Energy. I've heard good things about you."

The hacker stopped typing on the two laptops that formed a vee on the tabletop in front of him and sat up straight. His black eyes blinked behind gold-rimmed glasses, but he said nothing.

Marshall continued. "You'll work in this conference room. It's across the hall from my office, and I'll be able to keep an eye on you." Then he turned his back and walked to the fifth-floor window.

The darkness of night coupled with snow obliterated

the view of the square so that all he could see was his mirror image staring back at him. He'd always been a man comfortable with his own reflection, until now. He'd sacrificed David Quinn because he was the best candidate for a setup. He was a wounded vet, a loner, and there were questions about why he'd left the service. All that added up to a man on the edge, a man who would break into a woman's cabin and kill her. That was the story Marshal had wanted to sell, and as much as he hated to sacrifice a good man, it was necessary. He'd been left with no choice. The Syndicate had assigned this task to him, and if he failed, they would kill him. They had made that very clear. Members were expected to do their part to maintain the status quo. This was his assignment because it was in his territory. It was as simple as kill or be killed.

"What progress have you made?" He needed David and the woman caught.

Using his index finger, Spider pushed his drooping glasses higher on his nose. "The tracking device your man attached to her backpack at the airport traveled west on highway two, but I lost it. It's probably blocked by interference from the storm."

"Can you pick it up again?"

He tilted his head to one side, thinking. "If it's the blizzard—no problem. If the signal's damaged—that'll be a little trickier, but, with luck, I should be able to get it back once the snow stops."

"It's imperative we hunt them down. I have two men tracking them. Their names are Brad Harper and Mac Klein. Use the company directory to get their phone numbers. Mac called to say he had Quinn and Wilson cornered and was moving in. I've lost touch with him since then. Brad figures he will reach Mac's last known location some time in the night. I want a situation report on both men as soon as possible." He'd offered both Mac and Brad a substantial bonus to finish the job.

"I'm on it." Spider focused on the screens in front of

him, his fingers tapping the keys. "Do you know what kind of tracking device they are using?"

I had my men attach it in case she managed to ditch her backpack. It's new technology, a microscopic tracker, as small as the head of a pin, almost invisible. All they had to do was press against her and presto." He waved his hands like a magician. "We can follow her."

"Wow. Head of a pin?" Spider's eyes widened.

Marshall was gratified to see that he was suitably impressed. "I also want you to control the media on this. I took out the airport cameras, but there are several personal videos of my men trying to grab Wilson at the airport. My people have managed to shut most of them down, but I need an absolute blackout."

Spider leant back in his chair. His dark eyes glittered. "Shutting down social media will cost more."

"Money is not a problem.

"What if they split up?"

"Follow Wilson. She's the most important target. She is smart and rich, but she's a loner. Quinn is just the distraction. I want you to plaster his name over the media."

"I thought you wanted me to shut down—"

"Media can be a useful tool. We are going to spread the story that Quinn has PTSD. There's been some question about his discharge from the army. We're going to add that to the mix and let the media focus on him. Dr. Wilson will be the victim of his deranged mind."

"That way we'll keep the story off her and her achievements and have the news vultures concentrate on him."

"That's right. I want everyone in the country hunting him. I want to make it impossible for them to leave Elkhead County. Once the police have him, we can arrange to have them killed."

Marshall pictured David as a skinny teen. He had taken the young man under his wing, hoping one day he would be ready for a trusted position at PDE. Quinn was intelligent, good with languages, and honest. Unfortunately, he'd returned to Montana a burned-out shell, shattered by his own actions in combat. That had made him perfect for one last mission.

"You won't be disturbed here, but be aware I have technicians checking on you."

Spider smiled, revealing a set of perfect white teeth. "I wouldn't expect anything less."

Marshall glanced at his watch, an extremely rare Rolex chronograph. For a Rolex, it was understated with a leather strap and cream face. At first glance, it didn't look like a one-of-a-kind, million-dollar timepiece, and that suited him perfectly. Flaunting his wealth in the faces of the people of Granite City was not productive. The slim, solid gold hands told him it was approaching nine o'clock. He wouldn't go home tonight. There was no point, not with the blizzard raging outside.

He dialed his wife's number as he strolled to his office.

Lucy picked up on the first ring. "Hello, sweetheart."

He ground his teeth at the sound of her sickly-sweet voice. "I won't be able to make it home tonight, not with the blizzard."

"I heard there was a problem."

"Yes, your man, Harper, failed."

"He's not my man. He's the Syndicate's."

He wasn't going to argue with her. He suspected Harper was one of her lovers, and she had arranged his recommendation so she could keep him close.

"I have to stay and deal with the issue." That was the truth, but he would also enjoy a night away from her scrutiny.

"I'll be in as soon as the roads are cleared." On the outside, Lucy Portman seemed demure, maybe even a little uptight, but in reality, she was a she-devil who used her body to manipulate men and women alike. He'd met her two years ago. She'd hooked him with a mind-blowing mix of kinky sex and business acumen. They'd married within six months. There were those who said he was a fool who was too old to satisfy his young, attractive wife. They were right. Although in truth, her infidelities didn't bother him. He hoped and prayed for the day she would leave him. He would give her anything she wanted, his home, his business, even his money, if she would just get out of his life. But she refused to go, and he couldn't leave her. She came from money and had connections to the most powerful people in the world. Just the thought of the Syndicate made him shudder. They were a collection of powerful men with enough influence to control the distribution of wealth and the future of the country. They were the ones who decided what products were on the shelves in the supermarkets, what cars were available, how the nation used their energy reserves, and which stories appeared in the media.

After their wedding, Lucy arranged for him to join their ranks. At first, he'd been flattered. He enjoyed the benefits that came with being part of the elite group. They impeded all developments that threatened their success. In theory, he didn't have a problem with that. He himself had purchased and dismantled a number of new inventions that could jeopardize his monopoly, but murder was a new game. He wasn't opposed to it morally. He just didn't like the idea of being on the losing end.

Chapter Twenty-One

Marie stumbled down the stairs, following the aroma of coffee. She had dampened down her waves as best she could in the bathroom, but one curl insisted on standing straight up on end. Her short hair wasn't like the shock and fear of yesterday, nor the disbelief of discovering someone wanted her dead. But it was another blow, a reminder when she looked in the mirror that everything had changed and she could never go back.

A good night's sleep would've helped, but nightmares had punctuated her dreams. She'd awoken several times and been aware of the chill in the air, the glow from the woodstove, and David. Leaning against his warm, hard body was reassuring and arousing at the same time.

The blizzard had stopped sometime in the night. The howling wind and driving snow were gone, leaving behind a landscape that was covered in a clean, white blanket.

Her breath caught at the view from the large living room window. Stretched out before them was a magnificent landscape that encompassed forests, rivers, and a flat snow-covered prairie in the distance. The cabin was situated on the side of a hill. At the bottom of the valley was a small ice-covered creek. Pine trees peppered the property, each one covered with distorted mounds of snow. The effect was breathtaking.

David smiled as she entered the kitchen, making her heart do a little flip.

"Mac has offered us the use of his cabin." He looked relaxed, one foot crossed over the other as he leant against the counter, drinking coffee from a mug that declared *Truth fears no questions.*

She was all too aware of his masculinity and her

physical response to him. Just one glance, and her breathing hitched and pulse quickened.

"I'm not sure that's a good idea." She turned to Mac. "Won't you get in trouble with the police for helping us?"

Mac Shrugged. "I figure you need a place to lie low for a few days and decide what to do next. I made flapjacks. Why don't you sit and eat?" He headed for the stairs. "I'll just use the facilities, and then we'll go."

Marie nodded and sat at the table. She wasn't particularly hungry, but the idea of pancakes with syrup cheered her up. As far as she was concerned, the road to happiness was paved with carbs and sugar.

David sat beside her, pointed a finger toward the ceiling, and whispered, "Listen."

She stopped eating and strained, paying attention to every sound. The world was still; there were no birdcalls, no cars, and no people—nothing. Then she heard the faint murmur of someone talking. She smiled. "Is Mac talking to himself?"

"The son of a bitch must've pocketed the cell phone. He's been lying. This isn't his daughter's cabin."

"How do you know?"

There are no women's clothes or female products of any kind."

"Why would he lie?"

"I can't think of a good reason. I'm even more worried about who he's calling."

They sat in silence, struggling to hear. The low tone of Mac's voice suggested deception. She shoved her plate away, her appetite gone, as her stomach twisted in a nauseating knot. Once again, she was reminded of her poor judgment when it came to people. She'd believed Mac was a nice old man who'd needed shelter from the storm, but David had seen something else, something that made him suspicious.

"Whatever happens, stay close to me." David grabbed the shotgun off the kitchen counter and loaded it. "Go pack up the panel and then put on your coat and boots."

She did as he asked and then slung her backpack over her shoulders. She rummaged around the floor of the mudroom until she found their hats and mitts. She passed David his and then slipped hers on.

Once David was dressed for the cold, he shrugged into the purple backpack and squeezed her hand. "Remember, stay close."

She nodded, straightened her shoulders, and controlled her breathing. *Be strong.*

Mac's footsteps sounded on the stairs.

****

If he hadn't sworn off killing, David would have happily choked Mac. It was bad enough that the older man had lied to them, but his duplicity hurt Marie. She would never be a master poker player, or even a competent liar. Her expressive face revealed every emotion, thought, and feeling. The color had drained from her cheeks, and her lips were pressed into a thin, colorless line. They were small nuances, but were as obvious to him as neon signs.

"Shall we go?" Mac walked to the mudroom and stuffed his feet into his snow boots. "Are you going to give me my gun?"

"No, I'm keeping it." David stood at the threshold between the kitchen and mudroom, holding the weapon.

Mac's eyes widened. "I thought—"

"Who did you call?"

"My lady friend—"

"Save it. You lied about this being your daughter's house. Now I'd really like you to tell us the truth. Who did you call?"

Mac's jaw clamped tight as he narrowed his eyes. "I thought I had you."

"You should never have claimed to know the people who live here. That was your first mistake."

Mac shrugged and reached into his pocket.

David cocked the weapon. "Careful."

Mac held a hand up. "It's a piece of paper." Using two fingers he withdrew a folded sheet from his pocket and handed it to David. "There's a reward for you two. A hundred thousand dollars. I called for backup, but they said they're waiting for the highway to be cleared. I'm supposed to stall you."

It had to be another lie. Portman had probably triangulated their position when they'd called him from the truck. They hadn't been able to cover much ground after they parted ways with Jake. Marshall's men would've branched out, searching from the last known location. Mac probably wasn't working alone, which meant they needed to leave. David cursed.

"We have time to get away." Marie opened the paper. "There's just a picture of us. No mention of a reward. Mac, how could you? You know they'll kill us."

Mac shrugged. "It's a hundred thousand. I could do a lot with that money."

"A hundred thousand? That's what Portman is paying you?"

"It was two hundred thousand split four ways—fifty thousand each. But you took the twins out so I got a pay raise."

"You were in on this from the start?"

"Yep."

"Where the hell where you when I was with the others?"

"I followed in your truck. We were supposed to leave it behind otherwise there would've been questions about how you got there."

"Then you returned it to PDE."

Mac shrugged. "We needed a vehicle after you shot the tires."

"Son of a bitch." David had the sense of being a leaf, blowing in the breeze. He had no control over his destination or how he would get there. He was reacting to whatever obstacles Portman could throw at him. In his mind, he was fourteen again and his stepfather was lying on the floor dead. He hadn't been able to protect Sinclair from Russell's advances. He hadn't even known what was happening, but this was different. He was different. He was older, stronger, and trained to survive. He would protect Marie, and he would find a way through this ordeal. "This is what we'll do. Mac, you're going to come with us."

"Why can't we take his truck, destroy his phone, and leave him here?" Marie asked.

"We could, but he must've given Portman his location. What will happen once his associates arrive?"

Marie shrugged.

"Mac will be able to give them a description of us. I want to get into Canada before our new look is flashed all over the media."

Marie touched her hair. "I didn't think of that."

"Plus, he might be able to give a description of our vehicle. If we take him with us and dump him in the middle of nowhere, then he'll have to walk to the nearest phone, and that will give us some time."

"I suppose it's that or kill him."

David nodded. "We might only get a few hours' head start, but by that time we'll be close to the Canadian border." He had no intention of heading north to Canada. They would go west into Idaho. Once they were across the state line he would call Finn and go to the police. *Wait.* They could use Mac's phone to call Finn.

David waved the Shotgun at Mac." I want you to toss your phone into the living room."

Mac's eyes narrowed as his nostrils flared and his body tensed. Hate oozed from every pore.

"Two fingers." David reminded him.

The phone bounced off the window and landed in a shattered heap of plastic.

"Damn it. You did that on purpose."

Mac shrugged.

"Why would he destroy his phone?" Marie's voice raised as she shook her head.

"So we can't use it. Have you ever driven in the snow?"

"Yesterday was my first time." Her lips trembled. He couldn't say if she was reacting to the idea of driving on the icy roads or the fact that Mac had a photocopy with their faces on it, and he wasn't about to ask. There was nothing he could do to change their current predicament so they might as well get on with it. "You'll do fine. Just remember to gun it through the snowdrifts and slow down for the turns, and don't use the brake."

She frowned at his explanation.

If their situation wasn't so dire, he might have smiled. He'd just told her to speed up, go slow, and not use the brakes. Oh yeah, he was a real genius.

Holding the shotgun on Mac, David motioned for Mac to open the door. A gust of cold air hit him as Mac stepped outside. Snow had drifted so the right side of the yard was almost bare, whereas the snow on the left stood in deep mounds.

David froze at the threshold. The hairs on the back of his neck stood on end. He knew that feeling. It was a gut reaction, an instinct that had kept him alive in Afghanistan. *Ambush.*

He studied the landscape. The house was situated on the side of a hill. To his left, the land dropped away to reveal a stunning view of the valley below. On his right was a steep incline where the topography included a densely-forested rise. It was the perfect place for a sniper.

Mac stood knee deep in snow, a few feet ahead, the good-old-boy persona was back in place. "I guess we'll have to shovel this to get—"

A crack sounded in the cold still air.

He flinched as Mac's body slumped to the ground. A pool of red sprang from the side of his head and spread, staining the pure white snow.

"Get back!" David slammed the door, and then hurled

himself at Marie, sending them flying through the mudroom and across the kitchen.

Bullets punctured the kitchen door, sending pieces of floor and wall flying in all directions. He forced her to the ground and covered her with his body, trying to protect her from the shrapnel.

The shots hit the house at an angle, telling him there was one shooter stationed on the rise. The sniper would move soon, repositioning for a clearer shot. That would be their opening, the only chance they would have to get out without being killed.

First, they needed a way out of the house. There were no other doors or exits. They were trapped.

Chapter Twenty-Two

Marie's heart slammed against her ribcage as she gulped for air and struggled to make sense of what had happened. One minute she'd been walking out behind David, and the next...bullets, blood, and snow.

David pinned her to the floor, squashing her. More pops sounded. He grabbed her around the waist and rolled them to the stairs.

She fought, shoving at his shoulders, trying to escape his vice-like grip. "We need to help him."

"He's gone."

She pounded his arms. They couldn't leave Mac behind. He needed help.

"Marie, he's gone. There's nothing you can do."

The meaning of David's words sank into her mind. "Gone? He can't—"

"We're trapped. Right now, we're out of range, but soon the shooter will move closer." He put his hands on either side of her face so she was forced to listen. "That'll be our only chance to get out of here."

She gasped at the futility of their situation. More shots rang out in the cold morning air. Holes punctured the walls, causing chunks of floor to splinter.

David sprang to his feet and darted to the line of hooks near the door to the mudroom. He grabbed all the keys and then threw himself across the room. Splinters of floor, glass, and crockery flew as bullets trailed a path behind him. He landed in a heap at her feet.

Marie grabbed his shoulder, guiding him to the safety of the stairs. "Why'd you do that?"

"We're not going to be able to escape on foot. We need a vehicle. The bastard has an assault rifle."

"Does that matter?"

"Yeah, the one I used in combat shot six hundred rounds per minute and was accurate to two hundred feet. Our only option is to go through that window." He pointed to the large picture window that ran along the side of the house.

"I don't know if that's possible. It's not like the movies. You can't just jump through glass. When I replaced the windows in my house, I learned about their construction. There's a good chance it won't break, and you'd bounce off and land on the floor. If that doesn't happen and you went through, it would cut you to ribbons, or worse, hanging pieces could guillotine you," she shouted to be heard as bullets peppered the house.

He winced at the thought. "What do you suggest? That window is our best way out."

"What about upstairs?"

"No good. The drop is too steep on that side, or we'd come out on the same side as the sniper."

"If we can punch a whole into the corner, then it might shatter and we can knock out the rest." Modern panes were layers of glass and plastic, making it almost impossible to break.

"How long will it take?"

"Longer than we want, and smashing the window would be loud, too."

"Okay, we'll have to do it while he's still shooting." He glanced around the wrecked house. "I don't see any other choice." He aimed the shotgun at the window and fired. A small hole appeared in the corner surrounded by a series of tiny holes. The rest fractured into tiny pieces, but remained in the frame. "Damn." He crouched low and crawled to the stack of wood under the stairs, grabbed some logs, and then crawled to the back of the room. Once he was in position, he stood and hurled a log at the window. The glass disintegrated, allowing frigid air to blast in, but the hole wasn't big enough. He threw another two logs, aiming for the remaining glass.

The shooting stopped.

David put his finger to his lips, telling her to be quiet. The gunman must be moving closer.

"Time to go," he whispered. "I'll jump down first. You follow. I'll catch you. Okay?" He leapt, curling into a ball, with his knees to his chest. She didn't have a chance to stop him. It wasn't safe. There were still pieces of glass hanging from the frame.

The idea that a shard could decapitate her made her hesitate. But David was down there, exposed, waiting for her to jump. She rolled her shoulders and then ran. Coiling her body as tight as she could, she jumped, clearing the window. She hit the ground hard and bounced, her mouth filling with snow. So much for him catching her.

Before she could find her footing, he grabbed her hand, dragged her against the cement blocks that supported the house. "Do you see how there's a dip in the land?" he whispered.

She nodded. The owners had built a retaining wall to keep the ground from sliding down the hill. They stood in its shadow. The footing on this side was uneven and sloped as it gave way to a sharp incline. One misstep, and they would fall into the ravine below.

He leaned close and whispered, "We're going to use it as cover, and it'll lead us to the back of the barn. I just hope that's where they keep the vehicles. Stay low. Do not poke your head up to take a look. You'll give away our position. We also need to move silently. It's important that he doesn't find us. You got that?"

She nodded and followed his lead, mimicking his movements. The snow had the consistency of fluffy sand that blew into her face.

Finally, he stopped. He pushed her against the wall and waited. Everything was quiet and still. There wasn't even any wind to rustle the trees. She craned her neck to see his face. When he didn't make eye contact, she realized he was listening. The shooting had stopped. A crack of splintering wood echoed through the frozen air, and then the shooting resumed.

"He's in the house. Let's go." Without waiting, he grabbed her around the waist and shoved her to the top of the retaining wall. They were only a yard from the back door of the barn. David scrambled up behind her and then twisted the door handle, careful not to make a sound.

"Stay behind me." He passed her the bundle of keys.

Her fingers fumbled, sorting three sets, a Jeep, a Ford, and a Chevrolet.

"We'll take the Ford. It's too old to have Bluetooth, in-car navigation, or computerized components. It's the blue one. Climb in and start her up." He breathed the words into her ear. The cars were lined up in the barn. The Chevy pickup was on the right, the brand-new jeep in the middle and the dented, old blue ford on the left.

"Are you coming?" She kept her face close to his so she didn't have to raise her voice.

"No, I'm going to draw his fire while you get a head start."

She pulled back, staring at him. "I'm not leaving you behind." After all they'd been through together, he thought her so selfish she would abandon him to face a sniper alone.

"Yes, you will." He gave her his cold, intense stare.

She wasn't intimidated. "No, I won't."

"You will, and that's an order." He moved closer, bending his head so he towered over her.

"I'm not one of your soldiers. You can't order me around. If you're staying, I'm staying." She clenched her teeth, straining with the effort to control her voice and not shout at him.

"Be quiet. You'll give away our position," he whispered.

That gave her an idea. "I'll scream if you don't come with me."

"You are a pain in the ass." He smiled, but why he should smile at a moment like this was beyond her.

She poked his chest. "So are you. Come up with a better plan because we are staying together. You know as well as I do that I won't make it without you." She hoped that last bit of logic would sway the argument in her favor.

He kissed her lightly on the lips, stunning her into silence. Then he rocked back on his heels. "As far as I can tell, there's only one shooter. If I had to guess, I'd say he's discovered the broken window and is heading for us. He's positioned somewhere between the house and the barn, which means he's on our right. I could be wrong, but since this shotgun is no match for an assault rifle I'm not going to stick my head out to see."

"Okay." She had no idea where he was going with this. Maybe he was just talking aloud while he thought things through.

He moved to the back of the other truck, put his hands on the side, and pushed, creating a sloshing sound. "There's gas in the tank."

"I told you we're—"

"Don't worry, sweetheart, I'm not going to drive it. I'm going to blow it up."

****

David wasn't sure if his plan would work, but they were backed into a corner. The snow was too deep for them to escape on foot through the wilderness. Not only would they become mired in the snow, but there was a chance they could suffer serious frostbite or worse.

"How are you going to explode a truck?" Marie was pale and shaky, probably a little shocked, too. Not surprising given the circumstances, but he could only deal with one situation at a time, and getting them out of this barn and away from the gunman had to be his priority.

"These old Chevy's have sidesaddle fuel tanks that sit outside the frame. I'm going to put the truck in neutral. Hopefully it will roll down this incline." He pointed to the cement floor of the barn.

"I didn't notice the slope. What about the doors?" The big barn doors at the front of the structure were closed.

"I think they're controlled by that panel." He pointed to a switch near the back door. "Then I'll push the truck to get it to roll down the slope."

"Then what?"

"Hopefully it'll stop at the door of the barn, between us and the gunman. You're going to turn onto the driveway, away from the house. Stay to the left of the Chevy. I'll shoot the gas tank. That will put a burning truck between us and the gunman."

"I don't understand how shooting the gas tank will help us."

"The smoke and fire will provide cover so the shooter won't be able to get a good shot."

"Wouldn't it be better to rig the tank to explode and then start the truck and wedge the gas pedal with something to——"

"No, it'll probably blow us up, too, and I've seen enough bodies blown apart to know not to get too close."

Her eyes darkened as she nodded. "Okay, what do you want me to do?"

"First we have to make sure the Ford runs, so go start her up and be ready to drive when I give the order."

"I won't go with——"

"I know. The moment I'm in the truck, you drive. You'll have to step on the gas to make it through the snow. We can't afford to get stuck. If we do, we're dead."

She nodded, climbed into the vehicle, and shifted the driver's seat forward so her feet reached the pedals.

He was relieved when she revved the engine. He strode to the passenger door and stood, waiting as she reached over and unlocked it.

"How much gas does it have?" He placed the shotgun on the back seat.

"Half a tank."

He nodded and jogged to the back of the barn and pressed the button that opened the overhead door. Shots rang out as he pushed the Chevy toward the entrance.

The sniper kept up a constant fire, his automatic weapon shooting large holes through the barn wall. The front of the Chevy took continuous hits. Finally, it gathered enough momentum and rolled on its own. He ran for the Ford. "Go, go go."

He scrambled onto the back seat and slid open the rear window, steadying the shotgun, preparing to fire. The Chevy came to rest in a deep pile of snow just outside the barn.

Marie turned onto the driveway, steering to the left of the Chevy, blasting through the snow.

Bullets peppered the Chevy as the gunman moved toward them.

They passed the truck. David aimed and fired. The pickup exploded on the first hit.

Marie sped up. Snow had drifted to the left of the driveway. She steered to the right. The Ford skidded, but she regained control and kept the vehicle on the trail.

Pretty Boy Brad ran around the edge of the smoke cloud, strips of white bandage across his broken nose. He had an assault rifle with a scope but didn't aim his weapon. They were probably out of range. They turned onto the highway, heading north.

Chapter Twenty-Three

Finn pulled on his wool-lined leather gloves as he made his way across the square toward the elegant headquarters of Public Domain Energy. He was tired and a touch irritable, mainly because he'd slept in his chair. Maybe he should have stayed with Kennedy in her downtown apartment. Fraternization between agents wasn't exactly frowned upon. They were allowed to date, but they weren't allowed to work in the same unit if they were involved, and he didn't want anyone to misinterpret his intentions.

Now, in the stark light of day, he had to wonder if he'd imagined last night's conversation with Jake. The idea the whole police department was corrupt seemed implausible. He could believe there were one or two crooked cops, but the department consisted of almost a hundred men and women.

He pictured Officer Calder with his earnest, young face. He was a likeable, open man with two young children. No, they weren't all bad. At first glance, Calder had believed David was a threat, which was understandable considering Quinn had instigated a confrontation by shoving him. And when PDE security had opened fire, he had drawn his weapon, but he had not shot at the victim. Once it was over, he questioned his responses.

The square was almost empty. There were a few city workers plowing sidewalks, an old lady feeding sparrows, and a group of children from a local playschool making snow Angels. Their teacher struggled to keep the kids contained in one small area.

Finn doubted Portman had made it home last night not

if, as he suspected, he was hunting Dr. Wilson and David Quinn. Hopefully, the president of Public Domain Energy was in his office. It was a risk, and he had no idea what he hoped to accomplish with this interview.

The jazz tune played on his phone. He answered before the melody could finish. "Callaghan."

"It's me, Kennedy. I have coffee."

The thought of coffee made Finn's mouth water. "Meet me in the square by the fountain."

She was already sitting at an outside table when he arrived, two to-go cups in hand.

"We need to talk." Finn took a drink from her hand.

"That's mine," she snapped, passing him the coffee in her other hand and taking hers back.

"I had a visit last night."

"From whom?" She leant back, taking a long sip.

"A man named Jake. He had a message from David." Finn filled her in on everything Jake had told him.

"You believe Marshall Portman is behind the home invasion, and he set up David to take the fall for Dr. Wilson's murder. You also think the police are corrupt and doing Portman's bidding."

"Yes, I do. It's the only explanation that fits. If David thought Marshall Portman controlled the Granite City-Elkhead County Police Department, that would account for his actions. He had come barreling out of the PDE building and run into Marie accompanied by a cop. His first instinct would have been to save her."

"But you only have David's word. Your witness left. Where's your proof? For all we know, he's lying to throw you off the trail."

"Why would he bother? I'm not on the case."

"He might not know that."

"He brought her to us—to me—because she was in trouble, and he trusted me. That has to count for something."

She narrowed her eyes, considering him.

He sighed. "I suppose it comes down to trust. I trust Quinn. You have to decide if you trust me."

She stared into the distance for a moment and then nodded. "Okay boss, what's our next move?"

"Let's go." He stood and walked toward the PDE building.

"Where are we going?" She tossed her coffee cup into the garbage as she jogged to keep up.

"To see Marshall Portman."

****

Finn was struck by how sophisticated the furnishings were in the Public Domain Energy headquarters. The orange and brown color scheme added a simple elegance that indicated class and wealth without being ostentatious.

A receptionist, who could've easily made a living as a model, ushered him and Kennedy in to Portman's office. The president of PDE stood as they entered and extended his hand.

"Agent Callaghan, it's good to meet you."

"Hello." Finn shook his hand, noticing the faint traces of a New England accent. "This is my partner, Special Agent Norris."

"Is this a friendly visit?" Portman made himself comfortable in a very expensive-looking leather chair and picked a piece of lint from his lapel, which registered with Finn as a subconscious sign of annoyance.

"Unfortunately no, I'm here about the kidnapping." Finn sat opposite Portman, while Kennedy roamed the room. Disclosing he was here about Quinn was risky and provocative, but that was the point of the interview. He was shaking the tree, hoping something would fall out.

"Ah, bad business. My security personnel tried to protect her. We've cooperated with the police."

"I see." Finn kept his response vague, hoping that Portman would fill in the blanks.

"I don't know if there's anything new I can tell you." Portman struck him as one of those people who wanted to seem ordinary, but when push came to shove, would insist on preferential treatment.

"Can you give us the details again?"

"Well, to start, I have no idea why Quinn was here. I don't know his mental state, but I can speculate."

"Speculate?" Finn wanted to hear this hypothesis. It had probably been carefully planned, researched, and rehearsed.

"Yes, it is known that his military career finished under a cloud. Maybe he's having a breakdown."

Quinn's career *had* finished abruptly, and it was obvious he'd experienced some kind of traumatic event, but he'd received an honorable discharge. "And you think he took her?"

"There's no doubt in my mind. I saw the video."

That damn ten second video.

"Is there any chance of seeing the whole film?" Kennedy studied the porcelain figurines that adorned an antique, dark wood dresser on the far side of the room.

"What do you mean the whole—"

"It's only ten seconds long. There must be more," Finn said.

"We gave everything to the police. You'll have to take it up with them."

Finn decided to take a chance and ask about the only other subject Portman and David had in common. "Tell me about Marshall House."

"What about it?" Portman leant back in his leather chair, distancing himself from Finn and the conversation. He was uncomfortable with the line of questioning.

"Was David one of the street kids who went through your program?"

"Yes, he and his sister, Sinclair. Did you know he has a twin sister?"

"Yes, but we haven't been able to locate her." It was a lie. Finn knew damn well that Sinclair was on her way here, but he wasn't about to tell Portman that.

"Neither have I." He leant forward, obviously more at ease talking about Sinclair.

"Why are you trying to find her?"

"I feel responsible. I took the twins off the streets and put them back into society. I've helped many children and have a ninety-five percent success rate. That's something I'm very proud of. This kidnapping puts the whole program in a bad light. If there's anything I can do to help, just let me know." Portman relaxed, interlocking his fingers.

"I've read Quinn's file. I have a hard time believing a decorated soldier would kidnap anyone," Kennedy said as she examined personal photos that hung on the wall.

Marshall placed his coffee mug in the middle of the table and leant back to put a barrier between them. Portman wanted them to believe in David's guilt and was uncomfortable with Kennedy's last statement. "I've told you everything I know, which I admit isn't much—"

"What can you tell us about Dr. Marie Wilson?" Finn asked, once again changing the subject.

He shrugged. "Nothing. I have no connection to her."

"Oh, I'm surprised. She told me you were interested in sponsoring her research."

Portman's eyes widened. "I-I don't personally deal with all the projects we sponsor, but I can have my assistant find the relevant department head if you want." He momentarily squinted and then relaxed his features. A negative response, covering what Finn knew to be a lie.

Finn stood and walked to the window. "You have a great view."

"Thanks." Portman rose and placed his leather office chair between himself and Finn. It was another barrier, and another attempt to put some space between them.

"Do you know anything about Dr. Wilson's solar panel?" Finn paced around the room as Kennedy took Finn's vacant seat.

A framed photo of Portman with a bunch of kids

standing in front of a grand brick house caught his attention. Marshall House. He examined the children's faces, searching for David.

"I know nothing about her portable solar panel, but as I said, I can put you in touch with—

"No, that's fine." He pointed to the photograph. "Is David in this picture?"

Portman glanced at the photo, squinted again, and then smiled. "No, that was taken at least eight years before David's time in the program."

"How long have you been operating Marshall House?"

"Nineteen years. It never occurred to me when I started it that it would be a long-term project, but there seems to be an endless supply of homeless children. It's so sad."

Finn nodded and walked back to the window, staring at the snow-covered town square. He couldn't very well accuse the President of PDE of trying to kill David and Dr. Wilson, not without proof.

"To be honest, I'm surprised to see you."

"Oh, why's that?" Kennedy asked.

"I'm no lawyer, but I thought the kidnapping of an adult fell under local, not federal jurisdiction. Isn't that breaking the rules?" And there it was—a veiled threat.

"There might be a connection to a local terrorist group, the Sons of Freedom. We have to investigate all leads. Thank you for your time. You've been most helpful." Finn headed for the door.

"Anytime. You can see yourselves out?"

Finn and Kennedy waited for the elevator in silence. Portman's response to the photo of Marshall House had been the hardest to read. He had squinted and then smiled. The squint showed an adverse reaction. Initially, Marshall hadn't liked him looking at the image. Then he had smiled and relaxed when Finn asked about David. What was in the picture that Portman hadn't wanted him to see?

The elevator pinged and then doors opened. A tall, slim

man with cropped dark hair and glasses walked out. There was something in the man's gait, a familiarity. He knocked Finn's elbow as he passed, mumbled an apology, and then ducked his head and carried on as if nothing had happened.

What the hell? That was Michael Papin, the same Michael who had called him yesterday morning demanding to know what was going on with David. What was he doing in the PDE building? Had he inserted himself into the investigation? Of course, he had. Michael, David, Tim, and Sinclair were family. Finn gathered his thoughts and followed Kennedy in as the doors slid closed.

Finn stuffed his hands in his pockets and was surprised to find a crumpled piece of paper, probably a note from Michael. He had gone old school. Bumping into someone and slipping them a message was a trick from a bygone era.

Finn waited until they were in the middle of the square before taking the paper out of his pocket. "Keep your phone on. Evidence forthcoming."

He passed the note to Kennedy, who glanced at it and then said, "What am I supposed to do with this, eat it?"

A laugh bubbled up from his throat, which had nothing to do with humor and everything to do with relieving tension.

Chapter Twenty-Four

Marie struggled to control her tears, which was silly because she'd known Mac for less than a day. He'd lied about everything and was not a very nice man, but to see his life snuffed out was…was…devastating. She wanted to pretend it had never happened, or hide her face in her hands and weep. If David had stepped through that door first, it would've been him lying there on the ground. Her pulse thumped against her temple, and she put a shaky hand to her head. The idea that David might have died caused a crushing pain in her chest so real her heart felt like it was being compressed. She stared at the trees, trying to banish that image from her mind. It didn't work. Pain and guilt overwhelmed her. David continued to place himself between her and danger because he couldn't turn his back. It was an important clue to his true nature. Beneath the scar, the intensity, and his cynicism was an honorable, decent man. She'd only known two men well, her father and her former lover, both were unreliable at best and deceitful at worst. David was rough, ready, supremely capable, and despite the fact she had known him for less than two days, she sensed that every man she met from now on would be compared to him.

They'd been driving for an hour, heading north. The snow-capped mountains were on their left, visible through the gaps in the trees. Snowplows hadn't worked this back road yet, but David managed to steer the pickup through deep grooves in the snow.

His warm hand clasped hers, lending her his strength and comfort. "Try not to think about it."

He let go of her hand to negotiate a snaking curve in the road. A large black pickup overtook them and swerved in front of them. David struggled to control their truck as the back wheels swung wide, coming to a stop sideways on the narrow road. The black truck did a U-turn, stopping ten feet in front of them.

Without glancing at her David said, "Do you have your seatbelt on?"

"What is it? Didn't he lose control on the ice?"

"I don't think so. I want you to duck when I give the signal."

"What's the signal?"

He didn't answer, but kept his gaze trained on the newer vehicle.

"What's the signal?"

A tall athletic man with a rifle climbed out and marched toward them, his eyes shadowed by the wide brim of his cowboy hat.

"Put it in reverse," Marie ordered. Everything about this man screamed military, from his square shoulders to his ramrod straight back.

A slow smile curved his mouth as David stared at the stranger.

"What are you waiting for? He has a gun." Marie yanked on David's elbow to get his attention.

"Well, I'll be damned. What's he doing here?" He opened the door.

"He? You know him?"

David didn't answer. He tugged his arm out of her grip and walked toward the newcomer.

The man grinned, placed his rifle on the hood of their truck, and took David's hand, embracing him in a short hug.

David seemed to relax, the tension easing out of his spine as he waved for Marie to join him. "Marie, this reprobate is Tim."

Tim was a head taller than David. He took her hand and placed it palm down against his chest. "It's a pleasure to meet you." Tim gave her a wide, warm smile, and she found herself staring into a pair of hazel eyes, trimmed with long black lashes that would be the envy of any woman.

"Let go of her," David growled.

"But we just met. I want to get to know her a little better." Then turning to Marie, he said, "Would you like to come back to my place?"

"Tim." David stepped closer.

"We'll get to know each other later." Tim winked and released her hand.

She couldn't be sure if he was flirting with her or just being nice, but then she had limited experience with men. She'd only been fourteen when she'd started college, so she'd been too young to go out to bars and to interest the boys in her classes. By the time she was old enough to date, she'd already experienced heartbreak and had walled herself off. She wasn't good at reading social cues, but she didn't want any confusion about where her affection lay. She took a step back and grabbed David's hand.

Tim's smile grew wider. He nodded as if answering a question. His grin disappeared, and he pointed to David. "You have a problem."

"No kidding. Portman—"

"Yeah, I know all about that. Michael kept me updated and sent me to find you. He said you've picked up a tracker—"

"Michael? What the hell has he got to do with it?"

"He said—"

"Fuck it. He's conducting his own investigation, isn't he?"

Tim shrugged. "You're not our protector anymore. We can make up our own minds. If we want to get involved, we will. There's nothing you can do to stop us." Tim smiled at Marie. "Michael is working as a computer expert for Portman. He's conducting his own lines of inquiry."

"That sounds dangerous." Marie pictured Mac lying on the ground, bleeding. What would they do to someone who'd infiltrated their ranks?

David poked Tim in the shoulder. "You need to contact him and tell him to get out of there. These people will kill him—"

Tim shoved David back. "What do you think he does for a living?"

"Computer stuff—hacking."

"He works for Army CID. I get the impression he does more than sit at a computer."

"How would you know?"

"He's never said anything definite, but I can read between the lines. I wouldn't be surprised if he routinely worked undercover."

"Really?" David's brow creased.

"Why are you surprised?"

David shrugged. "I'm not sure. I haven't seen him much in the last five years. I guess I've lost touch, but I'd feel better if he hadn't put himself in danger."

"I get it, but you're in trouble, and you're our friend, so let us help."

David nodded and clapped a hand on Tim's shoulder. Something inside Marie softened. This was what it was like to have friends and be loved. No matter what trouble came their way, they stood together. The fact that David had friends who would put themselves on the line for him touched her. He was so lucky, but maybe luck had nothing to do with it. She could easily picture him, placing himself in harm's way to protect them. He had earned their friendship and loyalty just as he'd earned hers. And one day she would find a way to repay them.

"Let's see if we can find that tracker." Tim headed toward his truck.

"Is it on the Ford?" David asked.

"No, Michael thinks they tagged you at the airport." Tim produced a small black box from the passenger seat of his truck. "I have a scanner."

David shrugged. "That would make sense. We were in

close quarters,"

Tim smiled at Marie. "I'm going to have to scan you."

She gulped. "Me?"

David shoved Tim, forcing him to step back. "No, he's not. If anyone's going to search you, it'll be me."

That was better, but only marginally. "You mean a search like at the airport where they look through your pockets and bag and stuff."

"Honey, it'll be thorough." David waggled his eyebrows.

"What?" She stared at him. On one hand, the thought of him frisking her was somewhat arousing, but they were in the middle of a snow-covered road.

David grinned. "I'm just kidding. Trackers are tiny, almost invisible, so I'll use the scanner. Tim." He held his arms, wide. "Do me first, and then I'll scan Marie."

Tim flicked a button on the top of the black box. A row of red lights immediately lit up. "You've definitely picked up a bug. Marie, honey, go stand by my truck so I can get a clear reading."

David stood still, his arms wide, as Tim ran the device down his body. His gaze locked with hers. She couldn't look away. She licked her lips, wanting to kiss him again. Good lord, they were in the middle of a deserted icy road, in the company of his friend, they were being tracked, and all she could think about was kissing. It was official—she'd lost her mind.

That idea made her smile.

"If you keep smiling like that I might be forced to kiss you," David said as he strolled toward her, scanner in hand.

"Would that be so bad?" she whispered, tilting her face up.

His eyes widened, and he groaned. "As much as I'd like to drag you into the truck and enjoy a session of mutual pleasure, we need to get rid of the chip and get away from here."

She inhaled, stared straight ahead, and held her arms wide. "Go ahead."

He passed the black box over her arms and down her body. "Take off your coat and sweatshirt and place them on the truck."

Without a word, she shucked off the garments, leaving her wearing nothing but her pink long johns. A breeze blew across the road, shifting icy pellets from a nearby snow bank. She shivered, but resisted the urge to pull her arms across her body. The cold made her nipples hard, erect and sensitive, or maybe that was a reaction to his closeness. He didn't touch her, just ran the little black box across her breasts and down her ribcage.

"D-did you find the tracker?" Marie asked. Without waiting for an answer, she jerked her sweatshirt over her head and shrugged on her coat.

"No, where's your backpack?"

Tim joined them as she retrieved her bag from their truck and threw it on the hood. The lights on the scanner intensified as all the little strobes blinked.

"We have it," David announced.

"Just leave the bag." Tim said as he headed to his truck.

"No." Marie's spine stiffened.

Tim turned. "No?"

"No. I'll move my stuff into something else."

"Are you kidding?" He turned to David. "Is she kidding?"

She clutched the bag to her chest. "We are being hunted because of this solar panel. It is our only bargaining chip and could provide us with a way to prove your innocence. I'm not leaving it behind."

David gave a small nod and then addressed Tim. "She's right. It's important. Do you have a plastic bag or something?"

"I have a cardboard box."

David grabbed her bag and turned it upside-down emptying the contents into a box with the words *Layer*

Mash Organic Feed printed along the side. Then he threw her backpack into the trees at the side of the road. "We need to go." He placed the box onto the floor of Tim's truck.

Marie clambered into the back and settled on the bench seat.

David strode to the blue Ford, climbed in, and started the ignition.

"Where's he going?" She was not leaving him behind.

"Don't worry. He's just pulling it off the road. It won't raise any alarms if it's parked because a passing policeman might think a hunter parked it there while he trekked into the woods.

"Oh." Why hadn't she thought of that? It was obvious they couldn't leave a truck sitting in the middle of the road. She might not be worldly when it came to street smarts, but since meeting David, her brain had shrunk to the size of a peanut.

David climbed into the passenger seat. "Where to?"

"My place. You can have a meal and a shower. Then you can borrow a truck and head up to a cabin on the mountain."

"Whose cabin?"

"One of my father's friends. He died a few months ago. It's isolated, and there's no running water or electricity so you'll be roughing it, but no one will notice you using it in the winter. It'll buy us some time while we get you fake ID so you can head north into Canada."

Marie sat in the back without commenting. She was relieved they were no longer being tracked. They would finally be safe, but the idea of David leaving behind everything he'd worked for, his land, his bees, and all his dreams, gnawed at her. He wanted to return to the life he'd planned, and it wasn't fair he should lose everything because of her. Somehow she would find a way to make it right.

Chapter Twenty-Five

"The FBI has just left." Marshall Portman popped an antacid into his mouth, resisting the urge to verbally assault Chief Notley. He'd asked for one favor—just one—let PDE deal with the kidnapping of Marie Wilson. He'd told the useless idiot the same crap he'd told the FBI, that he felt responsible for Quinn's actions.

"I told them this is a police matter," Notley whined.

"Can't you complain to their superiors?"

"I don't know if that's a good idea. If I complain, they will send someone to investigate. Let Callaghan look into this connection with the Sons of Freedom. He'll get nothing. There is no connection, is there?"

"Of course, there isn't. Just keep Callaghan away from my office. You owe me. I saved you from a life of prostitution, or do you want everyone to know you were a rent boy?" This was the first time he'd resorted to blackmail and had to admit there was a certain amount of satisfaction in having the power to manipulate others to do your bidding.

"I can't believe you—"

"I'm responsible for Quinn being on the street. Look at it as a family matter. A member of my family is acting up, and I have to bring them into line."

"Okay, I'll see what I can do about the FBI."

Portman hung up the phone and walked to the window, staring out over the snow -covered city square. He loved the square. It was the accumulation of everything he had worked for. Maybe he'd made a mistake in threatening Notley. The man wasn't Mensa material, but up until now he'd been a competent chief, and one never knew when an honest man would grow a backbone. He could easily decide being shady was harder to live with than the shame of everyone knowing he'd been a whore. Still, under the law, private security had the right to use necessary force to protect the lives of others. It wasn't their fault poor Dr. Wilson had gotten caught in the crossfire.

His cell phone buzzed. Harper's number flashed up on the screen. Hopefully the deed was done and this whole mess would be over. "Tell me they're dead."

There was silence for a moment. "No."

"You fucking useless asshole," Marshall screamed down the phone. "I thought you were some sort of decorated sniper."

"Yes sir, International Sniper of the Year three years in a row."

"Then get the job done, or do I have to report your stupidity to our superiors?"

"No. I'll get it done," Harper promised.

"What about your partner, Mac?"

"Dead."

"Dead? Are you telling me Quinn killed him? Fuck. He put the Paxton brothers in the hospital and killed Mac Klein. How did you escape?"

Harper hesitated. Maybe he needed time to organize his thoughts. "Mac's job was to smoke them out. My job was to shoot them. Quinn used Mac as a shield."

"You shot your own man, and Wilson and Quinn still escaped." What a fucking idiot.

"It wasn't—"

"I want you to track them down and kill them. There's no room for failure."

There was a pause, then Harper said, "They've gone dark."

"Dark?"

"Yes, I'm at the location of the last transmission. The truck's abandoned, and there's no sign of them. They must've carjacked another vehicle."

"I thought you said Paxton attached a GPS to her bag."

"I found the backpack in the ditch."

"And the prototype?"

"Gone."

Marshall stared at the phone. *Fuck.* He picked up one of the humanitarian awards that sat on his desk and hurled it across the room. "Now listen to me. If you fail, we're both dead. Do you understand?"

"Y-yes. It's that Special Forces asshole, Quinn. He thinks he's hot shit, but he forgot about the tire tracks in the snow. I can follow them, and I'll find him."

Marshall pressed the disconnect button on his phone and threw it on the table. He slumped into his soft leather chair, closed his eyes, and massaged his temples.

Things were spiraling into an uncontrollable mess. There was no way Harper could follow tire tracks to Quinn's location. The man was an idiot with an ego the size of Montana.

Marshall had made his fortune because he understood timing, and their time was running out. From his recent conversation with the FBI, he knew they suspected his involvement. They were not going to take things on face value. When the authorities moved in, there would be arrests. The Syndicate would not take the chance their existence might come to light. They'd probably suicide him. He shuddered as he pictured his body hanging from his bunk in his jail cell.

A cold sweat leeched down his spine. He needed an exit strategy, a way to get away without his wife or Harper suspecting. All he had to do was keep both of them occupied while he escaped.

He opened his eyes, inhaled one last deep, calming breath, and then unlocked the safe that was attached to the underside of his desk. He flicked through the fake passport and credit cards and stuffed them into his inside breast pocket. He might need to move at a moment's notice, and he didn't want to have to come back to his office.

The lump that had burned a hole in the pit of his stomach lightened. He would use this God-awful situation to his advantage. He'd have to leave behind everything he had worked for, but that was a price he would happily pay for his freedom.

He pressed the button on the intercom. "Send in Spider."

The hacker shuffled into the office.

"Have you managed to block all personal videos of our couple? I don't want the media running with any story except what we've told them."

"No problem. The biggest story on the news is the storm. The rest of the time the news channels are just repeating our storyline." The hacker's eyes sparkled with delight.

"Harper has lost his prey—"

"Yes, the signal's gone dead."

"Can you access a satellite and help him?"

"I can try. Hacking in is not a problem. But if there are no satellites over the area with the ability to take high resolution pictures, it might take hours to move one into position."

"Do what you have to do." Marshall was about to dismiss him when Lucy barged in. The fact that his wife hadn't bothered to knock didn't surprise him. Her lack of respect had become more pronounced of late.

"I hear there's a problem."

He discharged Spider with a wave before he acknowledged her. "Yes, your man Harper has made a mess of things."

She put her hands on her slim hips. He remembered the days when they were first together. She would visit him for lunch, hitch up her skirt and—

"What kind of mess?"

"Dr. Wilson escaped the first attempt. She's running."

"I invited you to join our circle because I thought you shared our resolve and single-minded determination."

"I've sent Harper after them, but this thing could go sideways fast." He stared into her shrewd, green eyes. She was attractive rather than pretty. She worked out everyday to maintain her size-four figure. Her hair was dyed with the perfect blend of color so that it wasn't a brassy blond. She always wore business suits with stylish low-heeled shoes when at work, but under her clothes she modeled the sluttiest collection of underwear he had ever seen.

It had been a long time since she'd turned him on. Maybe because he knew what a heartless bitch she was. Perhaps he could get her selfishness to work in his favor. "The FBI were here asking questions."

"What did you tell them?"

"Nothing, but they have their suspicions."

"What will you do if they persist?"

"Don't worry, I'll protect you and the Syndicate. I'll take the fall if necessary." He was amazed he had managed to tell the lie with a straight face. "Perhaps it might be a good idea for you to distance yourself. I hear Mauritius is lovely."

"Mauritius?"

"They have no extradition treaty with us, and its nicer than Kuwait."

"I don't know." She bit her lip as she frowned.

He didn't want to overplay his hand. "You're right. Maybe you should stay. The Syndicate will want to talk to you before me. After all, you've been a member for much longer than I have."

"No, I'll go." She graced him with a wide smile. She hadn't smiled at him like that since their wedding.

"Hopefully, I can sort this mess out and join you soon." That was the biggest whopper he'd told all day. "Do you have an offshore account?"

"Yes, in the Cayman Islands."

"Text me the number. I'll put ten million in an account for you."

"That's very generous." She tapped on her phone.

"You're my wife. I'm supposed to look after you." His cell pinged, and he glanced at her incoming text.

"Oh, Marshall, I do love you." She pounced, straddling him, and then placed his hand on her stocking top.

"I love you, too," he lied.

She kissed him as she unzipped his fly. His arousal surprised him. The evil soul-sucking bitch was seducing him, and he loved it.

Chapter Twenty-Six

Marie closed her eyes. The sensation of hot water cascading over her skin felt like a long overdue indulgence. David had taken his shower first while she sat and enjoyed the view. Tim's ranch, situated in the foothills of the Rockies, was magnificent, if a little run down. The dated furnishings, peeling wallpaper and empty corrals gave the impression he had fallen on hard times. She just hoped their presence wouldn't make things worse.

She tipped her head upside-down under the spray of water, ridding her hair of excess suds. Not used to the shorter length, she'd used way too much shampoo, which gave her an excuse to stay in the shower a little longer.

A firm knock at the door dragged her back to reality.

"Do you want me to wash your clothes for you?" David stepped into the steam-filled bathroom and closed the door behind him.

She peeked around the curtain. He wore his cargo pants and a clean T-shirt. *Damn.* He looked fine.

She climbed out of the shower and then grabbed a towel off the rack, "Will they be dry?"

He grinned, making him appear even sexier, which she hadn't thought possible. "Sure, he has a drier. The load won't be big, so it shouldn't take too long."

"The thought of having clean clothes is so enticing I've decided to forgive you for entering uninvited, and I refuse to be embarrassed by the fact that I'm wearing nothing but a towel. You're the one who should be embarrassed."

He laughed, which made her stomach do a little flip. She hadn't thought he was beautiful when they'd first met, but now she considered him breathtaking.

He stepped closer. "You've got that look again."

"Look?" Her voice squeaked.

"If you don't want this, all you have to do is say the word, and I'll back off."

Her heart hammered in her chest. He was so close she could feel the heat that radiated off his body. "This?"

He bent his head. "Yeah, this." He placed his hands under her butt, and picked her up. His movements so swift she gasped and grabbed his shoulders. Then he sat her on the bathroom counter.

His mouth crashed down on hers, hard and tender. Their tongues dueled. He tasted of toothpaste and honey. She became vaguely aware her towel had slipped to the floor. One of his hands circled the base of her spine, causing shivers to surge through her body.

His mouth moved to her neck, and he placed small bites below her ear. Her hands trailed down his spine and then traveled up until they cupped his face. She arched back and tilted her head to give him greater access. Positioning himself between her legs, he kissed the pulse at the base of her throat and then laid small kisses in a path toward her breasts. Every molecule in her body throbbed with need. She wanted more, wanted to feel the weight of him pressed against her, to touch his hard chest and feel his warm, firm flesh.

He continued his sensual onslaught. She gripped his head, holding him closer, until he sucked her nipple into his mouth. She arched again as another flash of desire wracked her body, sending shockwaves through her nervous system and down into her core. The hard ridge of his penis pressed against the apex of her thighs. She wrapped her legs around his waist and rocked against him. He was still dressed, and the bulge at the groin of his cargo pants rubbed her sensitive folds. His mouth on her breasts and the intense pressure on her clitoris sent a violent surge of desire threading through her. But it wasn't enough. She wanted him, all of him. She tugged at his clothing. He let go of her breast long enough to shuck his T-shirt. Then his mouth clamped onto her breast again and she was lost.

A loud knock sounded on the bathroom door.

"David, you've got to come see this. You're on the news," Tim shouted through the door and then stomped down the stairs.

They stopped. It was like being doused in cold water.

David leant his head against hers "We cannot catch a break."

He backed away, disentangling himself from her legs as he tugged his shirt over his head.

She tried to smile as she plucked her towel from where it had fallen on the floor. "We don't have any luck when it comes to bathrooms—that's for sure."

He grabbed her clothes off the floor where she'd left them. "You can use the robe on the back of the door for now."

"I don't suppose Tim has a bra?"

He smiled, looked at her breasts, and then winked. "Not a chance."

Her face heated, and she yanked the towel across her body, struggling to cover herself.

He hooked her chin with his free hand and gave her a peck on the lips. "When the time is right, you won't be embarrassed, we will both be naked, and we won't be in a bathroom.

Then he left, closing the door behind him.

****

David smiled. Marie's boldness in the face of their mutual attraction was a pleasant surprise. He got the impression she was sheltered and a touch naïve. Her innocence could work in his favor. She might see their attraction as special, which it was, as far as he was concerned. She was also a scientist, so she might think it was just a new experience, something to be explored and examined. He growled at that thought. For him, this was more than physical. She filled his mind. He had an almost overpowering need to kiss her, touch her and, most of all, protect her.

"What are you making?" David asked as he entered the kitchen in time to see his friend place two large flat dishes in the oven.

"Roasted chicken with vegetables. He set the timer on the stove and then headed for the living room. You have to see this."

A large, older television sat on top of a cabinet in the corner of the room. When Tim pressed the remote, it flickered to life.

"There are no new updates on Dr. Marie Wilson, the scientist who was kidnapped yesterday from Granite City. It's believed she was taken by this man, David Quinn." A photo of him in his dress uniform flashed onto the screen.

The commentator, continued. "There's a possibility that Quinn, an ex-Green Beret, is suffering from PTSD. Understandably, most of his military service is classified, but we have managed to uncover some details that forced his resignation. While on a mission in Afghanistan, Quinn shot and killed one of the soldiers he had been sent to rescue."

David's stomach lurched, and bile burned his throat. His worst nightmare and private shame were now on public view. Everyone would know. Sinclair, Tim, Michael, and Finn would all know…and Marie. What would she think of him? He squeezed his eyes shut, trying to block out the memories of that awful, cold night. Then he pictured Marie, her face flushed with desire, and his gut twisted again. That would be gone, too, now that she knew who he was and what he was capable of.

Marie slipped her hand in his. He hadn't even known she was in the room. She held on tight even as he tried to pull away. He couldn't look at her. He wanted to explain, to somehow justify his actions. He opened his mouth, but he didn't know what to say. The words lodged in his throat. He should, at least, let go of her hand, but instead he gripped it tighter.

Tim changed the channel to the next newscast where a middle-aged man with a round face said, "This is Cruz MacDonald, owner of Big Sky News. At this station, we pride ourselves on getting it right. We've checked the reports on this kidnapping. My sources at the Granite City-Elkhead police department have told me David Quinn actually brought Marie Wilson to them after she was the victim of a home invasion. Now, I'm no lawyer, but to me that's reasonable doubt. What's going on here? Are they lovers? Friends? Or did he kidnap her?"

He leaned in close to the camera. "We won't know until they are found or they come forward. If David Quinn or Marie Wilson are watching this broadcast, I urge you to contact us and sort out this mess."

Then he backed away and read the papers in his hand for a moment. "Another thing about this case... It has been reported by some of the other channels that Quinn shot one of his own men while on a mission. If that's the case, why did he receive an honorable discharge? We're supposed to be reporting the news, not spreading rumors. When I served in the first Gulf War, all that Special Forces information was classified, so where the heck are these so-called reporters getting their material?" He took a moment to catch his breath. "Okay, now to road closures—"

Tim switched off the television. "Cruz MacDonald from Big Sky News may be eccentric, but at least he's honest."

****

Marie had never been so angry in her life. "They can't slander you like that."

David didn't acknowledge her. He released her hand and walked outside, slamming the backdoor behind him.

If he thought she wouldn't go outside in the cold, wearing nothing but a robe, then he was wrong. Tim stopped her as she reached the door. "Here." He wrapped a blanket around her shoulders and gave her a hesitant smile. "David's used to his own company. He's never been comfortable talking about his feelings. Hell, I don't know many men who are, but don't back down." He glanced outside and then at her. "You need to understand, David was always the strong one. He's used to that role. It's hard for him to ask for help and even harder for him to accept it."

She nodded, grateful for Tim's advice and support.

She found David leaning against a weathered porch post on the wrap-around deck, staring out at the panoramic view of the snow-capped mountains.

She strode to his side and rested against the railing. Wafts of moisture escaped her mouth as she breathed. Damn, it was cold. She pulled the blanket over her head in an attempt to stop her wet hair from freezing. She wanted to stay out here to talk, but she couldn't do that if she froze to death.

They stood there in silence until she couldn't take it any longer. "We have to do something."

"No." He didn't look at her.

"But it's not true."

Once again, he fell silent and stared at the mountains.

"What happened?" She held her breath, trying to control her temper.

"I can't talk about it."

"Can't or won't," she snapped.

"Can't."

The significance of his answer calmed her and made her feel less combative. It wasn't that he didn't want to talk about his experiences, he couldn't. He had made an oath and was keeping it, in spite of the fact that honoring his promise meant he couldn't refute the allegations levied against him. It was more proof of his integrity, honor, and the depth of his character. But the news people had used the classified nature of his work to say whatever they wanted, knowing he couldn't disprove their slander.

"I'm so angry right now I could spit," she yelled, reaching the limit of her patience.

"You should be angry. But you have to believe me. I didn't mean to deceive you." His voice cracked.

Her heart ached for him. "You—"

"I should've told you—"

"Tell me what? Details of classified missions that you aren't allowed to talk about? I don't need to hear that stuff. I know exactly who you are."

His gaze slanted to her. "And who am I?"

"You're the man who saved me. When I was in trouble at the airport, I knew if I called your name loud enough you would come to my rescue. Actually, I'm angry for two reasons. First, that MacDonald man was right. They shouldn't be allowed to smear your good name without proof. Once this is over, we're going to sue the pants off that news station for reporting those lies."

"And second?"

She grabbed his arm in an attempt to get him to look at her, but he continued to stare out at the landscape. "You're shutting me out, and I don't like it." Now that she'd said the words aloud, she realized that was the real source of her anger. It might be silly, especially since they'd known each other for less than two days, but it was the truth. If he couldn't confide in her, then they were just two people who'd been thrown together by circumstance, but she wanted more. She wanted to matter, to be more than a woman he kissed in bathrooms. She wanted a future with him, which seemed ridiculous because they didn't have a future. Even if they managed to escape the mess they were in, he wanted to go back to his land and his bees—alone.

Whatever happened, it came down to feelings. She couldn't be involved with someone physically if there was no emotional connection. If they couldn't share their feelings, then she couldn't get involved. She poked him in the shoulder. "You listen to me. We're in this nightmare together, and that means something. You've earned my friendship and loyalty whether you like it or not."

He blinked, which was the only sign he'd heard her.

She sucked in a breath. She'd never been a fan of tough love. In her experience, it involved her father saying mean things to manipulate her, but David wouldn't want her pity. Something terrible had happened to him, and she couldn't allow all that hurt to fester inside him. Even if they parted ways tomorrow, he needed to talk to someone, if not her, then a professional. "Look at you. You might as well be lying on the ground, curled in a ball."

"What do you want me to do? I can't talk about it."

"You can't talk about the event, but you can discuss how you feel. You think you're alone, and you're not. You have friends, people, who care about you. Your sister, Agent Callaghan, Tim, and the mysterious Michael have all stuck their necks out for you. Some of us don't have that."

"Do you have that?" He turned to face her, his pale green eyes as intense as ever. She hesitated. Her personal situation was not something she liked to talk about, mainly because she didn't want to be tagged as the poor little rich girl. But this was a pivotal moment. If she wanted him to share his pain, then she had to trust him with hers. "No, all I have is a father who ignores me. My mother committed suicide. She didn't even love me enough to stay alive."

He put his arms around her, embracing her. "I'm sorry. I don't know the circumstances, but maybe you had nothing to do with it. Perhaps she was sick and she didn't know what she was doing. I can't imagine anyone not loving you. What about your friends?"

"I lied. I lost touch with them after they had their baby. Our lives changed, and we drifted apart."

"Would your father have been there to meet you at the airport?"

"I doubt it."

Using his thumb, he tilted her chin up. "That makes him an asshole, and it means you have daddy issues."

"Great big daddy issues, the size of the moon." She shrugged. "Everyone has issues, including you." In a flash of inspiration, she said, "Is this incident the reason you don't kill?"

"What makes you think that?"

"It's what you told Jake, and you've discarded every weapon you've come across."

"Yeah, the truth is I've always hated killing. I hated it when I was fourteen, and here I am nineteen years later still hating it." He turned towards the mountains, staring into the distance.

She thought he wasn't going to say anymore, but then he cleared his throat. "It's not classified. I just don't talk about it because the guy has a family."

"What happened?"

"It was nighttime. We were in this dugout, hiding. We'd rescued these fobbits, they're guys who normally don't leave the base. They'd gotten themselves into some trouble. One of them started to hallucinate, a guy name Louis Heffermint. He thought we were the enemy. We tried to talk him down, but I guess he was too out of it to listen. He fired wildly. Jose and Cameron were killed. Jose was supposed to retire in two months. Once he was out, he planned to work with his brother-in-law at a Volvo dealership in Texas. Cameron had a family in LA. All he wanted to do was get home and make love to his wife and hug his children. If he had ideas beyond that, he didn't say."

He paused as if giving a moment of silence in memory of his friends. "I shot Heffermint."

"Good."

He carried on as if he hadn't heard her, and maybe he hadn't. "It was instinct, a gut reaction. He shot at us, and I shot him. I didn't think about it until after it was done. I've killed many men and could justify my actions because they were the enemy and I'm a soldier. For me, this was overwhelming. I don't know why. Maybe I just had enough."

"You had no choice." For another type of person, this awful episode wouldn't be so devastating, but for David, a man who hated killing, it was soul-destroying. Despite the way he looked and his death stare, at his core, he was a good, kind man. She could see how he would have buried the gentle side of his nature to survive on the streets, and then continued to bury it when he'd joined the army. Being forced to shoot one of his own men had been the last straw. It had become too much for him, and he'd quit.

"There was an enquiry. They concluded Heffermint had a psychotic break. It seems that he'd become withdrawn, and he'd said a few things that didn't make sense. There were also pages and pages of incoherent writing in his journal. I was cleared. I asked for my discharge, which was granted."

He'd given her the bare bones of the story in its simplest form. He hadn't mentioned if the enemy had attacked or if there were injuries. "Is that how you injured your face?"

"Yeah, I was grazed by a bullet."

The scar on his cheek was part of him. She hadn't registered that it had been caused by a bullet. An inch closer, and he could have been killed. A cold chill arrowed through her at the thought of how close he'd come to death. He had changed her reality. He brought vibrancy and energy to her world, and the idea of life without him made her hurt.

In a flash of awareness, she realized the truth, her truth. She'd been half in love with him since the airport, and now it was too late to turn back. It didn't matter if he wanted nothing more than a casual relationship. She was hooked. It was that simple. She would take what she could get, because every minute spent with him was a moment to treasure.

She ran a finger along his scar. "I'm sorry you were forced to shoot Heffermint. There's nothing I can do to change that, but I will not let you push me away. You have to come in and get ready. We're heading to Tim's hiding place. I want to be alone with you."

He stared at her for a moment as if deciding something and then said, "Yes ma'am."

Chapter Twenty-Seven

Finn wondered if the coffee he'd purchased on the way back to his office was burning a hole in his stomach.

Kennedy sat opposite eating a brownie while she flicked through the messages on her phone. "You know we should share this office."

"Don't you like having your own?"

"What's the point when I spend half my time in here, sitting in this hard chair with no cushion? I don't have my computer, so I can't check files, and I don't have my notes. Besides, my butt's starting to hurt." She yanked her chair closer and placed her half-eaten treat on the edge of his desk.

For a second, he pictured her butt, but then forced his mind back to the case. "Let's talk about the interview."

Kennedy fidgeted in the cheap seat as she tucked her phone in her pocket. "Portman didn't like you looking at the photograph."

"You saw that? Yes, but once I asked if David was one of the kids in the picture, he relaxed."

Her brow crinkled. "That's right, he did. What was in that image that he didn't want us to see?"

"There were a few things that made him uncomfortable."

"Yeah, and he out and out lied when he said he didn't know about Dr. Wilson." She took a last bite of her brownie and threw the wrapper in the bin.

"You picked up on that, too. I'm surprised he let it show. In fact, for someone in his position, he wasn't very good at concealing his body language."

"His position?"

"Come on, he's the president of a power company. He

must've told some whoppers to achieve his position." Finn took a sip of his coffee and then immediately regretted it as the drink corroded more of his insides.

She pinned him with a glare. "What's your friend doing there?"

"Michael?"

"Yeah, he's one of the street kids, isn't he?

"Yes, but he's not like the others." Finn visualized Michael slipping the note into his pocket.

"How so?"

"They ended up on the streets because they had nowhere else to go."

"How was Michael different?"

"He's smart, and I mean high IQ smart. He's Cree. I think he'd heard about street kids and wanted to see what it was all about."

"Seriously?" She shook her head.

"His first night out, he met David and the others. In them he found friends that didn't need anything from him. There were no expectations, no preconceived ideas about who he should become and what he should do. They didn't care how intelligent he was. They're his friends, and they watch his back."

She nodded. "I get that."

"Michael's pretty quiet. Doesn't say much, but he told me he didn't go to Marshall House with the others. He went home to his family."

"Did he have a falling out with the street kids?" She leaned forward, putting her elbows on the desk.

"No, he just said it was time. Then he joined the army. We were all in basic together."

"That's where you met them?"

Finn flashed to David, Michael, and Tim. They'd been thinner than they were now, but were still basically the same people. "Yep."

"And you've been friends ever since? I can understand. I still keep in touch with the people I met when I joined the marines." She tilted her head. "What's he doing at PDE?"

"He's doing exactly what he said, gathering evidence." He didn't like the idea of Michael working behind the scenes at PDE. It was too dangerous, plus there were legal ramifications, especially in the area of evidence collection procedures.

"And what makes him qualified to do that?"

"I'm not sure that he is. He's with the U.S. Army CID Computer Crime Investigative Unit. His work is classified, but I think if you want to uncover hidden computer files, he'd be the man to find them."

A knock sounded at the door.

"Can you get that? You're closer." He grinned, knowing the request would annoy her.

"I'm moving my desk in here tomorrow, and I'm putting it over there." She pointed to the window farthest away from the door, and then gave him a look that suggested he was a pile of dung.

"We have a problem," Detective Ramirez marched in before Kennedy had a chance to open the door. He slammed the door behind him.

"What's wrong?" Finn asked, but he knew it was about Quinn. There were no other cases where their paths crossed.

He held a manila folder in his hand. "No one's been assigned to the Wilson kidnapping."

"Are you sure?" Kennedy returned to her seat.

"There's no file, and I've asked every detective on the force."

Finn wasn't surprised. It leant further weight to David's allegations. "There's a lot of media coverage. Who instigated that?"

"As far as I can tell, that's all been done by PDE." Ramirez stood next to Kennedy, placing a hand on the back of her chair, crowding her personal space.

"You think PDE are working the case?" There had to

be a reason behind Chief Notley warning him off.

"That's how it seems, and there's more," Ramirez threw the Manila folder on Finn's desk. "I contacted Seattle PD to see if they had any info on Wilson. It seems they've been trying to get in touch with her. Her house burned down yesterday, and it's arson."

"No, shit." Finn shouldn't be surprised, but he was.

"And I got Wilson's and Quinn's financials. There's nothing in Quinn's. He doesn't have any income, but his living expenses are minimal. He owns his land outright, and by my estimation, he has enough in the bank to support himself for another year."

"And Wilson?" Kennedy stood and paced to the window.

Ramirez slumped into the newly vacated chair. "Hers were a little more complicated. She told us she was out of money, that's why she was here, to get Professor Hargreaves to validate her research so the DOE would give her funding."

"That's right." Finn wondered if the detective had crowded Kennedy's space because he wanted to sit down.

"That's where it doesn't add up. She's a multi-millionaire."

"You're kidding." Finn leant back, considering the ramifications. Did her wealth have anything to do with the events of the last two days?

Ramirez opened his folder. "The account she uses for everyday expenses has been completely drained. There's only eighteen hundred dollars in it, but there's a trust registered in her name. She was legally allowed access to it when she turned twenty-one."

"Do you think she knows about this account?" Kennedy asked as she stared out of the window that overlooked the square.

"How could she not know she has millions sitting in an account?" Ramirez asked.

"You'd be surprised what a trustee will do for their

percentage." Kennedy didn't turn around, but there was something in her demeanor. Her expression was guarded, her features blank, which served to remind Finn she came from money. There was a story there. Something had happened in Kennedy's past, and although it didn't have a bearing on the case, it gave her a unique insight into how the wealthy operated.

Finn forced himself to concentrate on Ramirez. "Who's the trustee?"

"That position was held by her father, but now she's over twenty-one, the money is hers."

"Do you think he's involved?" Kennedy said as she took her phone out and scrolled through the screen.

"I'm not sure what his deal is. I called him and asked if he'd heard from his daughter."

"What did he say?" Finn asked.

"It seems that Quinn took Dr. Wilson to the airport. He was supposed to put her on a flight to Seattle. The dad sent people to meet her, but she didn't show. Mr. Wilson, who's a lawyer by the way, thinks his daughter is trying to obtain money from him."

Finn stared at Ramirez and then at Kennedy. "Has there been a ransom demand?"

"No, but sometimes families don't come forward in these cases because they're trying to protect the victim."

Finn pictured Marie. She seemed quiet, shy, polite and, in many ways, innocent. "I could be wrong, but Dr. Wilson didn't seem the type for extortion. And why would she go to those lengths if she has access to millions? I think Kennedy's right. She doesn't know she has money, and I think the dad wants to keep it that way. But that's all supposition."

"I agree. I didn't get that vibe from her, and there's another thing."

Finn sighed. This case was getting more complicated by the minute. "More?"

"Mr. Wilson spoke to Quinn."

"What?" Finn couldn't hide his surprise.

"Yeah, he instructed Wilson to go to Seattle airport and meet his daughter personally. He also said she was in trouble because of her solar panel. Now I ask you"— Ramirez thumped the desk—"what kind of a kidnapper doesn't ask for any money and takes his victim to the airport?"

Finn glanced at Kennedy, who nodded, silently agreeing to share what they knew with Ramirez. "We don't think Quinn kidnapped her. We think he's protecting her."

"From whom?" The detective frowned.

"The police and Public Domain Energy, specifically Marshall Portman." He placed his phone on his desk and played the messages Quinn had left on his voicemail.

"Damn it." Ramirez scrubbed a hand across his face.

"We're investigating an allegation of public corruption against the Granite City-Elkhead police department," Finn stated.

"Do you know who in the department it is?"

Kennedy stood next to Finn. "No, and even if we did, we couldn't tell you."

"But everything leads to Marshall Portman being behind it," Ramirez said, stating the obvious.

"Do you have proof?" Finn asked. "This isn't about what we know. It's about what we can prove."

Ramirez didn't answer, but his unseeing eyes stared at Finn's desk as his mind seemed to work through the details of the case.

"Right now I have the testimony of a man who's been accused of kidnapping," Finn said, comfortable sharing a fact the detective already knew.

Kennedy grabbed the remote control on the desk. "There's more." She turned on the small television that sat on top of a filing cabinet.

Finn cringed as a photo of Quinn in his dress uniform flashed on the screen, alongside a picture of him with long hair and a beard, grabbing Marie. The reporter told of

David's exploits in Afghanistan and the incident that ended his career.

"But that's not true," Ramirez said.

"And the Department of Defense isn't in the habit of sharing that type of information. It seems to me that someone's working hard to destroy Quinn."

"Maybe there's more in his records. I'll see what I can dig up," Ramirez offered.

"Good idea, but this doesn't have anything to do with him, does it?" Kennedy said, while pacing the length of the room.

"What do you mean?" Ramirez swiveled in his chair, giving her his full attention.

She stared at Finn. "Well, the professor who was supposed to validate her research is dead. There was a home invasion, and the perpetrators were after her solar panel. Quinn saved her and got her away. I think he told the truth when he said he took her to the airport. I think they tried to grab her again—"

"You think they're using Quinn's history as a distraction to stop people from asking questions about Wilson." Finn finished her train of thought. "My guess is that her solar panel doesn't just work. It works really well."

Chapter Twenty-Eight

It was snowing by the time David parked the old jeep, burying the front end in snow. Tim had leant them the only spare vehicle at the ranch that still worked, but unfortunately it was painted bright blue. The color made it almost impossible to hide. It would be clearly visible to any passerby, but judging by the condition of the road, which was knee deep in snow, he doubted anyone had come this way in a while.

He glanced at the sky. With the cloud cover, it was hard to tell the time of day, but he estimated it would be dark in an hour, maybe less.

He left Marie in the truck while he scouted the small, A-frame cabin. It was a log construction with a green corrugated roof.

There were no tracks in the fresh snow around the house except his. He strained to hear, listening for any sounds in the frozen, still air. A raven took flight, screeching into the evening sky, and then there was silence.

The blizzard had covered one side of the roof and piled snow four feet high against the front of the house. Which told him no one had used the building in the last twenty-four hours. Using his boots, he kicked away as much snow as he could and opened the door.

From the corner of his eye, he caught a movement. Marie stood at the edge of the clearing, waiting for him. Damn it, he should've known she wouldn't remain in the car. She seemed determined to stay close to him, probably because she felt safer by his side.

The long day had caught up to him. He'd had long days when he lived on the streets, and then when he'd been in Special Forces. There were days when he was so hungry he'd eaten snow just to have something in his stomach. Nights when he was so cold he was scared he'd freeze to death in his sleep. But today had kicked him in the teeth. It was the emotional upheaval. The stress of their situation had worn him down and affected his critical thinking. On a logical level, he understood the psychology. Fighting it was something else entirely. He was so tired that every footstep was a hard-fought battle. He wanted to lie down where he stood and sleep. The fact that he couldn't see any way to resolve their situation added to his malaise.

He sniffed the interior. A small critter could leave a strong odor, but a large one, like a bear or a cougar, would stink the place out. Surprisingly, the cabin had a lemon scent. He smiled as he spotted a car air freshener hanging above the sink.

The little house was dark with the only light coming from the open door and a small window, but it was cleaner than he expected. There was a loft, which hopefully held a bed. A log wall ran the length of the main floor with a stone fireplace at the center. A couch sat facing the fire. The rear of the living space was divided. One side held a small bathroom with a sink and a composting toilet. The other side opened into a kitchenette, with a hotplate, a sink, and a propane-powered fridge. Everything was neat and orderly.

He signaled for Marie, letting her know it was safe. She'd been quiet on the way up, having turned in on herself. She'd been supportive at Tim's, but now that the reality of who he was had sunk in, she probably had doubts about spending time with him. At least his past was out in the open and she understood it was in his nature to survive no matter what the cost.

Marie stood at the door holding the heavy tray of food Tim had cooked for them.

"You could've left that in the jeep. I would've carried it in."

She kicked off her snow-covered boots and placed the

dish on the table near the kitchen. "It's chicken and vegetables with rosemary, basil, and oregano." She lifted the lid and sniffed, "I think there's balsamic vinegar in here, too. I'm going to eat it. If you want some, you have to hurry."

Maybe he was wrong, and she wasn't concerned about him. He had no clue what she was thinking or how her mind worked. She was unpredictable in the most disarming way.

She finished munching on a piece of mushroom. "I'm serious. This meal is too delicious to wait. If we don't eat soon, I might rebel."

Despite his mood, his lips curved in a smile. "Rebel how?"

"Instead of allowing you to be all silent and moody, I might insist you tell me all your secrets."

"And how are you going to get me to talk?"

She crossed her arms and raised one eyebrow. "I'm going to seduce you."

"Damn, that's despicable."

"I know. Let's do what needs to be done so we can sit and eat." She grinned, and his breath caught. God, she was gorgeous. Her short wavy hair curled around her ears, making her seem even younger.

He considered going to her and unzipping her coat, but then shook away any thoughts of sex. They were hungry, tired, and on the verge of collapse. When he made love to her, he wanted to please her, and he had serious doubts about his ability to do that at the moment. "Do you know how to set up a fire?"

"I'll manage."

He smiled. She would, too. He had no doubt she could accomplish anything once she set her mind to it. "I have to check the propane tank at the side of the house. Then I'm going to take some time to scope out the area. I'll be a while, okay?

She nodded. "Don't take too long. I meant what I said

about eating without you."

He waded through the knee-high snow to the side of the house. Crouching, he tapped the gauge on the industrial-sized tank—half full.

He stood listening. Everything was still, silent. He made his way to the back of the cabin. There were no tracks, not even from a deer. He continued walking, circling the clearing. The news story had done a number on him, and he wasn't sure how to react. He'd gone over that night in Afghanistan a thousand times, wondering if he could have done things differently, and he still didn't have any answers. The man he'd become sickened him.

It wasn't so much the killing. Once again his logical mind kicked in. Heffermint had not only killed two of his brother's-in-arms, he had also given away their position, and another four men had been injured in the ensuing firefight. What sickened David was the fact he had acted without thinking. His survival instinct was so strong that his first reaction had been to shoot to kill. It wasn't that he was wrong. It was that he wasn't the man he wanted to be. He wasn't husband and father material. He lived in fear that one day he would react with deadly force and hurt someone he loved. That was why he'd sworn off weapons. It wasn't that he couldn't kill. He just didn't want to.

He finished checking the perimeter and headed for the truck to gather the rest of their stuff.

****

Marie set the logs in a crisscross pattern in the fireplace and shoved some kindling in the cracks.

David had retrieved their meager supplies from the Jeep, including the box with her prototype. She'd told both David and Tim that she needed to keep it as proof. Now she wondered if that was a lie she told herself so she could rationalize lugging around her life's work. *Her life's work?* It was just a solar panel. It had caused the death of two men and had also cost David his good name, his life, and future.

When her ex-professor and lover, Daniel, had claimed her work as his own, he had destroyed her reputation as a scientist and made her a pariah. She'd worked to prove her theories and reestablish her standing in the scientific community. Now, two men were dead and lives destroyed because she wanted to restore her status.

David had been tense since they'd left Tim's, and she wondered if he was still thinking about the news story. The reporter's version of David's service festered in her stomach, making her want to call her father and demand he sue the network. She pictured her only relative. If he knew she was in love, he'd remind her of her past mistakes and that all men had ulterior motives. But then her father was a remote and manipulative man who assumed everyone was like him. She understood David's reserve was the result of trauma, and not an attempt to control her.

It was strange how comfortable she was in his company. She'd been on her own for a long time. Being with him had changed all that; she didn't want to be alone anymore. She wanted him, not just his body. That was a lie. She wanted to touch, feel, and explore every inch of him. She wanted to know him on a very intimate level, but for her, that intimacy could only come with an emotional bond. She wasn't experienced when it came to men, but she knew herself. The reason Daniel's betrayal had cut her so deeply was because she'd been in love with him. For her, sex and love went hand in hand. It was hard to believe she had known David for less than two days, and she was already thinking in terms of love, but as things stood, they really didn't have time to waste. They could've been killed in the attack this morning, and if they died tomorrow, she'd be sorry if she squandered a second of her time with him.

She lit the fire as he kicked off his boots and threw his coat over a chair. "We have half a tank of Propane. It's a good size, not huge, but bigger than you'd use for your barbeque. Which means we can cook on the stove and heat water for washing." He rubbed his hands together to warm them. "Have you started eating yet?"

"No, I waited for you." She couldn't muster a smile. The events of the last two days had conspired to rob her of her energy.

"Tired?" He sat at the table.

She nodded as an overwhelming weariness smothered her.

"Me, too."

Her fatigue had come out of nowhere. She struggled to lift her hand to put food in her mouth, and what had seemed delicious a moment ago was just too much work. They sat at the table and ate in silence, not because they had nothing to say, but because speaking was too much effort.

"You need some rack time before you fall face first into your dinner." David stood. "Do you need help to climb the ladder?"

"No, thanks."

The A-frame structure of the house meant that the walls of the loft slanted, the high point being above the center of the Queen-sized bed. She was pleased to see a window opposite the ladder, an exit. She'd never considered her surroundings in terms of escape routes, but she did after this morning.

The bed was made up with a patchwork quilt in pretty red and white fabric. There were two plain cotton pillows, one a neon green and one a muddy brown.

She climbed under the comforter grateful she still wore her long johns and sweatshirt so changing for bed wasn't an issue. Surprisingly, she didn't fall asleep straightaway. Instead she listened as David moved around the room. Finally, the bed sagged as he lay next to her, and then he put an arm around her waist and hugged her close. She lay still, enjoying his warmth, and finally allowed herself to drift off to sleep.

Chapter Twenty-Nine

Marie jogged along a sandy beach. The sun warmed her skin, and the swirl of the waves as they crashed against the sand calmed her. David stood ahead, his pant legs rolled up to his shins as he waded in the surf. He smiled and waved, and she increased her speed, anxious to be by his side. Suddenly, a loud pop sounded. She ducked and searched the headland for whoever had fired the shot, but there was no one there. Her heart stopped as she spotted David, lying face down in the sand. She screamed and tried to run for him, but her feet were mired, and she couldn't move. Blood leached from his head into the sea. The harder she struggled, the more her feet sank. Waves continued to crash against his body as more blood poured from his head. She needed to stop the bleeding. If only she could get to him...

She woke when David swung his legs over the side of the bed. Cold sweat dribbled down her back. She gasped for air and forced herself to regulate her breathing.

David's feet thumped against the rails as he climbed down the ladder, using a flashlight to guide his way. He stirred the coals in the fireplace and then added another log.

She sat up and ran her hand through her hair, once again surprised by the short length. It was hard to let go of the dream, it had seemed so real, which wasn't so odd when she considered how strange and foreign her reality had become: the thugs, the cold, tracking devices, the fear, and then there was David. Her desire for him was all consuming and solid. She loved him. That was why her nightmare had been so disturbing. She was scared something awful would happen to him, and given their current circumstance, it was a real possibility. He had already been shot once and survived. This time was different because he put himself in harm's way for her.

The only way to keep him safe was for them to part ways. Tears misted her vision.

He maneuvered up the ladder. The beam from the flashlight made her squint and turn away. He wore only his pants and T-shirt.

"Hey, what's wrong?" He switched off the light and climbed into bed.

The dark gave her a measure of protection against his scrutiny. He couldn't see her expression as she spoke.

"Why are you crying?" he whispered.

"I-I-I'm not. I guess I'm tired, and that makes me overly emotional. It's silly." She purposely made her words strong.

"No, it's not. Lie down. I'll let you sleep." He would, too, and then he'd lie awake and guard her. It was in his nature to protect, but it was time for her to protect him. Sometime tomorrow she would form a plan and then slip away. No matter what happened, he would be safe. He might not be able to return to his land, but he would still be in one piece, and that was all she could hope for.

Tonight she would make love to him, trace every line of his face, and enjoy her time with him. "Every time I close my eyes, I see blood and death. What I need is a distraction."

"I can think of only one way to do that."

"Me, too." She tugged her sweatshirt over her head and then climbed on top of him, straddling his legs. Then she leant down and ran her tongue across his lips, coaxing him to kiss her.

He drew her closer, deepening the kiss. Tingles of pleasure danced along her veins at the feel of his hard body under her, but soon that wasn't enough. She wanted to feel his skin against hers, run her hands over his warm, hard flesh.

She drew back, jerking his T-shirt over his head. He submitted to her, allowing her to explore his body. She took her time, running her fingers along his muscled torso.

Puckered, raised skin told her there were scars, one near his right shoulder, another near his waist. She undid his pants and slid them down his hips, planning to continue her exploration, but he had other ideas. He grabbed her around the waist and flipped them so she lay beneath him.

He kissed her deeply until she was wild with need. She ran a hand across his scalp wanting to grasp his hair, but it was too short. Using his tongue, he stoked an intense hunger that burned her soul.

He trailed small kisses beneath her ear and then traveled lower, along the cord of her neck. She hummed as a warm coil of yearning started in her belly.

He undid the top snap at the neck of her long johns and then kissed the spot where it had been. He inched lower as he unfastened the button at her cleavage and kissed her again. She writhed, wanting him to stroke her, to build the untamed craving she knew lay within her. When he reached her sensitive folds, he stopped. She arched, offering herself to him. He didn't caress her. Instead, he worked his way up her body, laying small kisses and licks along the way. He levered her long johns down her arms, gradually easing them lower. She raised her bottom to assist him as he slipped them off.

He positioned himself between her thighs. She couldn't lie still, couldn't wait to feel his long length within her. She sat up, finding him in the darkness. She kissed him, hoping to communicate her need with actions instead of words. He wrapped her in his embrace and lowered her to the bed. The crisp hairs of his chest grazed her breasts. She groaned and rubbed against him like a cat. He deposited small nips and licks along her lips, and then he deepened the kiss, plunging his tongue into her mouth. The back and forth between a low, soft caress and deep, sensual kiss heightened her pleasure.

His hand moved to her chest, and then his thumb brushed her nipple. She pressed her breast against his palm, reacting to the sheer pleasure of skin on skin. She grasped the warm flesh of his penis. He grabbed her wrist, and in one smooth movement, pressed her against the mattress. He snared her other hand and pinned both above her head. "If you continue, it'll all be over."

"I can't stroke you while you can drive me nuts. That hardly seems fair."

"I just want you to catch up."

She wrapped her legs around his waist so his erection pressed the entrance to her vagina and lifted her hips. The sensation sent shock waves of pleasure coursing through her body, her nerve endings electrified.

"Oh, God." He plunged into her, and then stopped.

She cried out at his entry, overwhelmed, as if every fiber of her being was overextended, coiled and wanting. It had been years since she'd experienced sex, and she had never felt this all-consuming heat that started at her core and cascaded through every molecule. She needed more. She wanted completion. She wanted to feel him pumping within her. She was so close, so near.

He hadn't released her hands. They were still pinned above her head. She was stretched beneath him, primed, and ready to shatter. If only he would move. She arched. The action drove him deeper within her.

"Don't." He held himself taught.

"I need you. Hard and fast." She heard the plea in her voice but didn't care.

"Listen, it's been a while, so fast is what you'll get."

She arched again, driving him deeper still, not able to wait.

He cried out as his control broke. He pumped, pounding into her. In a blinding flash, her body responded, matching his thrusts as her need drove her to the edge. She rode the wave of fevered pleasure as a white ball of light exploded behind her eyes. Her orgasm seemed to go on forever until it gave way to the darkness of the room and the gentle warmth of the man lying on top of her.

****

Marie had no idea how David managed to maneuver up the ladder, carrying the leftover dish of chicken and vegetables.

"I thought I'd feed you. You need to keep your strength up." He grinned as he sat on the bed and placed the food between them.

The only light came from the flashlight, which sat on his nightstand. It illuminated his naked body, casting stark shadows across his muscled chest. She popped a piece of zucchini into her mouth. "You need the fuel more than I do."

"I do?"

"Yes, for the rest of the night, you're doing the heavy lifting." She waggled her eyebrows and was delighted when he laughed.

His light-hearted mood only lasted a second. "I need to find a way to get in touch with Finn."

"Won't your friends—"

"I don't want to bring them into this. If there are charges, then they'll be seen as accessories. As it stands, we can tell the police I knew about this place from my visits to the area. We can keep Tim and Michael out of it."

She should have known he'd want to shield his friends. He would die to safeguard them just as he'd put himself in the line of fire for her.

"But Tim said they were working on a way to get you to Canada."

"Running's a last resort."

If they ran, he could never return to his land and the life he had planned for himself.

"You're right, so how are you going to contact Finn?"

"There's a gas station in Hopefalls."

"Where's that?"

"It's a small town about twenty miles east of Tim's ranch. They should have a payphone there."

She estimated they'd traveled about ten miles from

Tim's place, so that meant he would have to travel thirty miles to get to the phone. Given the winding mountain trail they'd navigated to get here and the condition of the road, he'd probably be gone at least an hour. That gave her a window, but she needed a plan…

"What are you thinking about?"

She shook her head. "Nothing."

"Your face was scrunched. If you think any harder, you might set fire to your head."

"I was just thinking about everything that has happened in the last two days," she fibbed.

"It's a lot to deal with."

She nodded, surprised at how easily she'd lied. She should feel guilty, but in her heart, she knew it was the right thing to do.

"Maybe I can help you forget." The glint in his eyes and the smile on his lips made her heart do a little flip. Oh God, she would miss him.

Leaning over him, she put the food on the floor and then knelt beside him. "Let's leave the flashlight on this time."

"Whatever makes you happy."

She ran a hand down his chest, feeling his muscled ribcage and abdomen. Then her hand moved lower. He sucked in a breath and closed his eyes as he gave himself up to her exploration.

Chapter Thirty

Marie opened her eyes to find herself lying across David's chest. She eased away from him. It had been seven years since she'd experienced the rigors of lovemaking, and her thighs screamed in protest as her feet hit the floor. Her breasts were sensitive and sore, probably from where his stubble had rubbed her delicate skin. His five o'clock shadow could also be blamed for her chapped face, chin, and lips.

The cabin was dim. The bleak light shining through the window told her it was nearly dawn. The fire had died sometime in the night when they'd been too busy enjoying each other to care about the frigid temperature.

David rolled on his side, his chest rising and falling in the rhythm of sleep. She held her breath, praying he wouldn't wake.

It took a while to find her clothing, most of which was scattered about the loft, but how her sweatshirt had managed to land on the couch was beyond her. She climbed down the ladder, wincing at every creak. She needed some alone time. Moisture vapor escaped her mouth as she breathed. She shrugged into her long johns, sweatshirt, and coat and then sat on the couch. Today was the day when they parted ways. Her throat tightened at the thought of leaving him behind, but then she remembered her nightmare. How would she feel if she saw him gunned down? That idea made her stomach lurch. She needed to be strong and form a plan.

Something nagged at her in the back of her mind, some small detail that she knew would be important if only she could put aside all the distractions. She had to stop her mind from wandering. She was a scientist, which meant she was cerebral. She thought things through and considered the facts. So what where the facts? She had created a solar panel that did remarkably well in tests. Damn it, it did great in tests. It was revolutionary. It could change the world and provide her with the financial independence and professional recognition she craved—and that was why people were trying to kill her.

But what about David, what did he have to do with it? The man who wanted her dead, Marshall Portman, had set David up, and now he was accused of abducting her, and they were being hunted. Twice, David had taken her where she wanted to go, and both times attempts had been made to snatch her, and he had been forced to take action again.

Her mind jumped to the moment at the airport when one of the thug-twins had grabbed her arm. She remembered his sweaty hands and his body odor as he whispered in her ear, *Don't make a sound.* She shook away the memory and forced her mind back to the task at hand. She could fix the kidnapping charge. She could call the police and tell them everything. No, David had heard Portman say he had people in place who would bury the truth. But how far did that influence extend? Granite City and Elkhead County definitely, but what about other jurisdictions? If she went to the police in another county, or state, would they believe her word over that of the Granite City-Elkhead County Police? It was doubtful, especially considering she hadn't heard Portman's claims. David had, which made her accusations hearsay.

Okay, she couldn't go to the police and she trusted David. But he wasn't all-powerful. He was hurt. He had been to hell and back when he'd served in Afghanistan, and now he was in danger again because of her.

She inhaled. What else did she know? Marshall Portman wanted to destroy her prototype because it threatened his way of life. Why she hadn't seen that from the beginning was beyond her. She had been naïve to believe she could develop a new way to harvest electricity and think everyone would welcome it. Where did that leave her?

First, she had to tell the world that David hadn't abducted her. She couldn't go to the police, and the media coverage seemed biased at best. Although there was that one report from Big Sky News that questioned David's guilt...

The fear she'd felt two days ago at the airport rose again unbidden. The reason her subconscious kept replaying that scene escaped her. She needed to conquer this, examine it logically. She repeated the details in her mind. The twins had wanted her to go quietly, but she knew once they had her alone, they would hurt her, so she'd screamed.

That was it. Portman wanted to silence her. What would he do if the whole world knew about her prototype? He would discredit her, and that was fine. He would call into question her qualifications. He would even bring up her past affair with Daniel and her claim on his research. The smear campaign would end her career. Her life as a scientist would be over, but David would be cleared of all charges. If Portman discredited her publicly, there was no point in killing David. She would go on the news and tell the world that he hadn't kidnapped her. She would tell the whole story, and then David could go back to his land and his life as a beekeeper.

The decision about which station to go to was easy—Big Sky News. She even knew their location. She'd seen their ugly neon sign two days ago. They were adjacent to the PDE building. Her stomach rolled at the idea of going back to Granite City. She tensed, straightening her spine. She could do this—for David.

She emptied the purple backpack that held their provisions and loaded it with her possessions from the box. She had meant to sneak away later in the day, but this would be better. Now she had a plan, she wanted to put it into action as soon as possible.

Silently, she picked up the car keys, being careful not to rattle them, and tiptoed to the door. Then she crept out into the snow.

This time she would save herself and the man she loved. It didn't matter what happened to her. She refused to run away from her responsibilities. Her days of being a cowardly mouse were over.

Chapter Thirty-One

"Get up Master Sergeant Quinn."

David shot out of bed. His vision blurred. He needed his weapon and his tack. His hands padded the bed—not there. He felt the wall—

"David, David, it's me Sinclair. Wake up."

He stopped. Sinclair? He wasn't in Afghanistan. He was in a cabin. He'd made love to Marie and then slept. "Sin," he said, using the pet name he knew she hated, "can you give us some privacy?"

"Us? There's just you. I've been trying to wake you for the last five minutes. Your girl cut out."

He spun around and stared at the bed. Empty. In two strides, he was at the railing that separated the loft from the rest of the cabin. He couldn't see the bathroom, but he didn't need to. Emptiness enveloped him, a sucking hole in his chest. Marie was gone.

"Dude, you need to cover up." Sinclair stood at the foot of the bed, her gloved hand covering her eyes.

He grabbed his pants. "Where did she go?"

"How the hell should I know?"

"You're in touch with Michael, and he's doing his computer-geek, surveillance thing."

"Why would I be—?"

"Come on, I'm not blind. You and Michael have always had a—a thing. Tim already told me he's inserted himself into the investigation. If that's the case, then Michael would have called you."

"Well, you're wrong. I called him, and I didn't ask him to get involved. He was already on the inside."

"Okay, so back to my original question. Where is she?"

"Even if I did know, I'm not sure I would tell you. You

were just getting your life back together, and this woman comes along and destroys everything you've worked for."

"It's not her fault. It's Portman. He's behind all this." He tugged his sweatshirt over his head.

"Yeah, I know all about it, but still…"

"I need…I need…" What was it he needed? To keep Marie safe and to make love to her again. Yes, he wanted those things, but they were short term. He needed her in his life. She was intelligent, quirky, totally unique, and at this moment, she was out there without his protection.

"I know about her solar panel. It's not your job to save the world. She left you. Maybe she doesn't want you around."

His gut twisted as if he'd absorbed a blow. She'd probably decided she couldn't be with a man who had blood on his hands. He remembered her at Tim's. The news reporter was doing a number on him. She'd placed her cold hand in his, offering him support. "If that's what she wants, then I'll let her go, but she has to tell me to my face. I've earned that much."

"David—"

"Where is she?" He stood in front of his sister. She was tall, almost his height. Her long, fair hair hidden under a black, thermal knit hat. She wore a Canada Goose parka and snow pants that had to have set her back a small fortune. She was pissed. He could tell by her stance and the way she jutted out her chin and held her back ramrod straight.

He sighed. "Remember when we were in basic, and I requested to see you because I sensed you were hurt."

She frowned. "Yes."

"And you told me I had to back off. We had to distance ourselves from each other if we wanted normal lives. You planned to have a husband and a family, and that wasn't going to happen if I didn't let go."

"Where are you going with this?"

"I want this woman in my life. I want to wake up to her

everyday. I want a home and a family. And I want to get pissed at her because I never know what she's going to do." He shouted the last sentence. "Now, where is she?"

Sinclair's phone dinged. She glanced at the screen and then swallowed. "Michael just texted. She's on the highway heading to Granite City."

Chapter Thirty-Two

"What do you mean the street cams are out?" Marshall Portman stared at the gray fuzz on the screen. He'd walked into the conference room, and there was Marie Wilson, sitting in a light blue beat-up jeep at a traffic light near the Granite City square. Then the screen had gone blank.

"I mean they're all dead." Spider leant back in his chair.

"You're the hacker. Hack us back in."

"I can't. I think it's a short in the wires or something. I can get the feed from the east side of the city—see." He tapped some keys and snow-covered streets came into view. "But the west side is gone." He switched to the gray fuzz.

"Damn it, I saw her. She was in an old rust bucket."

Harper stomped into the room. "You called."

"No, I didn't call, I summoned. This is your mess. You should be in here watching these screens, checking to see if they surfaced, not sulking and whining about your nose."

"It's not my fault."

"Whose fault is it? You were the Syndicate's pick for this job, not mine. I went along with it because you're supposed to be some hotshot, decorated soldier. You said you could take them out. Spider, give Brad the cross streets of her last known location."

"Texting now." The hacker's fingers flew over the keys.

"You've found them?" Brad's eyes widened with renewed interest.

"Not them—her," Marshall spat.

"I don't give a shit about her. I want him."

Harper had allowed his ego to turn this assignment into a personal vendetta.

"She's the job, not him. He's just the distraction."

"Quinn put both of the Paxton's in hospital and is responsible for Mac's death. I owe him." Harper ground his teeth as he talked, trying to seem intimidating, but his broken nose lessened the effect.

"Yeah, I checked the video on that. He was unarmed at the airport, and he threw the weapon he took from your buddy into the garbage," Spider supplied.

Marshall laughed and then said. "He's unarmed? The man who made you look like a bumbling idiot isn't even carrying a weapon."

Harper's face reddened.

Marshall went in for the kill. "David Quinn is a Special Forces soldier who you underestimated, and now I'm paying the price for your incompetence. If you'd killed him at Wilson's place, the way you were supposed to, then we wouldn't be in this predicament."

Harper gasped. "But-but—"

"And if the Paxtons were half as good as I'd been led to believe, then they would've picked Wilson up at the airport. And as for Mac, I'm wondering if you shot him so you could keep the bonus." Harper's gaze darted to the floor, telling him he was on target. "You were supposed to be the best, and one burned-out Green Beret with no weapons has shown you up for the buffoon you are." Maybe mouthing off to Harper in front of Spider wasn't the best idea, but it was damn enjoyable. After all, the idiot had failed at his job and was sleeping with Marshall's wife. He deserved to be humiliated.

"Once I complete the job, can I track Quinn down and kill him?"

"Of course. In fact, I insist on it. If you don't kill him, you won't get paid." This was his chance. With his wife packing to go to Mauritius, Harper was the only link to the Syndicate, the only one left to keep track of his whereabouts.

Harper glanced at his pinging phone. "I've just received Spider's text with her last location. What am I supposed to do with it, drive around until I find her?"

"At least that would be more productive than just sitting around. Spider, there must be more than just street cams. What about security cameras?"

The hacker frowned. "I'll see what I can find. They'd have to be on Wi-Fi for me to access them."

"Get on it. Harper, I want you to do a grid search from her last known location. She was driving a light blue jeep. A vehicle like that will stand out.

Harper strode toward the door. Can I use force?"

"Use whatever firepower you think necessary." Discharging a weapon on the city streets was bound to cause a commotion and would keep Harper tied up for a considerable length of time.

Spider stared at Harper's retreating back. "He's got it bad for this Quinn guy."

Marshall didn't feel the need to reply. He touched the inside pocket of his blazer, feeling for his fake passport. When his phone buzzed, he answered, "Yes."

"This is Notley."

Portman gritted his teeth. He knew who was calling, the idiot's name had flashed on the screen.

The chief continued. "One of my officers just spotted a woman matching Wilson's description going into Big Sky News."

"The station on the square?" His knees threatened to give way. Wilson was here, across the street from the PDE building. *Damn it.* Now there would be people focusing on the square. His car was parked in a premium spot at the front door of the building, visible to everyone. Normally that wasn't a big deal, but with police on the square, watching for Wilson, someone was bound to spot him driving away, unless there was enough chaos at Big Sky News to act as a distraction.

"Do you want me to have my men keep an eye on her?"

"No, that won't be necessary. I'll deal with her." He

hung up and dialed Harper's number. "She was just seen going into the news station on the square. Shut them down. Use whatever force necessary."

"How many of us are going in?" Harper's voice rose, his excitement at the prospect of killing a woman was palpable.

"Just you." The idea of Brad dying at the hands of the police made him smile.

"What?"

"She's alone. Are you saying you need help to kill an unarmed woman?"

"No. I—"

In the meantime, I'll cut the electricity so they can't broadcast."

"You can do that?"

"Of course, I own the power company."

With any luck, Harper would go in guns blazing, and the police would take him out. That was the best-case scenario. Whatever happened, Marshall would escape at the moment law enforcement stormed the building. By the time the dust settled, he would be living under a new name in Brunei.

Chapter Thirty-Three

Marie wondered if screaming might be a good idea. She'd survived a white-knuckled drive on ice-covered roads back to Granite City, only to be thwarted by the receptionist at the front desk. The woman simply refused to allow her in to see Cruz McDonald, or talk to anyone at the station. It didn't seem to matter that Marie's face had been plastered all over the news. The dragon with short, dark hair and buckteeth was not going to budge. "I don't care who you are. Mr. McDonald is busy planning his next news cast."

"But I'm Dr. Wilson. Big Sky News reported that I'd been kidnapped. I've come to straighten it out."

"And I'm the Queen of Sheba," Dragon Woman said, falling back on a clichéd answer.

"Look—"

The phone rang, interrupting their conversation. Dragon answered it.

Marie seized the opportunity to run past her into the darkened studio. "Hello."

"I said I didn't want any interruptions," a voice barked.

Marie blinked her eyes, but the dimness of the interior contrasted too sharply with the bright reception area, making it hard for her vision to adjust. "I'm Marie Wilson. Everyone thinks I've been kidnapped."

Stage lighting above the set flickered on. "Who did you say?"

The hairs on the back of Marie's neck tingled. This was a bad idea. She'd imagined she would be talking to someone face to face, not a bodiless voice. No, she couldn't back out now. She was doing this for David. "My name is Dr. Marie Wilson. Reports say I was kidnapped.

They were wrong. If you don't come out and talk to me, I'm leaving."

Dragon ran into the studio. "I'm sorry Mr. McDonald. She wouldn't listen."

Six people tumbled out of a room at the rear of the sound stage.

A tall, middle-aged man with a round stomach walked toward her. "That's fine, Andrea, I'll deal with this." He held out his hand to Marie. "I'm Cruz McDonald."

There was no need for the introduction. She recognized him from the broadcast she'd seen yesterday.

Cruz called over his shoulder. "Hank, hold the opening spot." The TV studio was a large rectangle with the news set at the back and communication rooms on the left-hand side. The door to reception was in the middle of the right-hand wall and situated behind her was the audience seating. Each row was higher than the next until the last sat eight-feet high. Everything except the set was painted a matte black. Even the seat cushions were dark.

"I'm Marie Wilson," she repeated and then blurted her story. It was strange how good it felt. It was as if she'd punched a hole in a dam and couldn't stop the flow.

"This character, Quinn, has been protecting you?" Cruz ushered her to two chairs on the set.

"Yes."

"Why?"

"Because he's a good man."

"I got some intel on him. He served with distinction and was awarded a purple heart and a medal of honor."

Marie wasn't surprised to discover David was a decorated hero. All his actions and decisions had been selfless. "I want to clear his name and set the record straight."

"You'll have to go on live TV and tell everyone what happened."

She shrugged. "Whatever it takes." It didn't matter what she had to do, or how much misfortune came her way. She was doing this for David.

"I'm not sure you can accuse the president of PDE on air."

"Why not? I heard Portman myself."

"How do you know it was him? Have you heard his voice before? I'm not saying you shouldn't set the record straight about Quinn, but you can't accuse the head of a multimillion-dollar corporation of attempted murder. He'll sue."

Once again her inexperience caused an error of judgment, but she would adjust. "I'll just talk about David, my personal experiences, and show the world my solar panel."

"Sounds good." He smiled and patted her shoulder. "Okay, let's do this. You sit here." He led her to a chair on the set and then he shouted instructions to the production crew.

Marie squinted as the studio lights dimmed. A large professional video camera zoomed in, and a young, scruffy man held a boom microphone over her head.

"Hello, this is Cruz McDonald. Today we have a special guest, Dr. Marie Wilson. As you may know, there have been reports she's been kidnapped. She's here to set the record straight—"

Everything went black. "Hey, get the lights back on," Cruz shouted into the darkness.

"Can't, the power's out," a male voice called back.

"Is it the storm?"

'Not sure, I'll check." The door of the studio opened, allowing daylight to filter in from the lobby.

"All the other businesses in the square are up and running." A man wedged the door open, providing a permanent source of light.

"Hank, is the transmitter down?"

"Yep," Hank answered.

Cruz pulled her out of her seat, propelling her toward the lobby. "I guess we're shut down. Why don't you hang around and see if we can get up and running?"

A tall silhouette appeared in the doorway to the studio. "Marie?"

"David?" He was here. She ran to him, launching herself into his arms. She shouldn't be happy to see him, but she was. She wasn't sure if she kissed him or if he kissed her, but before she knew what was happening, they were locked in an embrace.

He broke the kiss. "We have to leave now."

"How did you get here?" She'd taken the only vehicle, and they'd been miles from the nearest house. In effect, she'd left him stranded, and yet he'd managed to not only get out, but also follow her, which brought to mind another question. "How did you find me?"

"Never mind. We have to go." He ushered her into the lobby where natural light flooded through the windows.

"No, I'm staying and clearing your name. You go." She waved her hand toward the square.

He placed his hands on his hips and shook his head. "Not gonna happen, and don't think about sneaking off again because—"

"I did not sneak off. I decided you'd be safer without me." He was the most irritating man. She wanted to save him, but it was hard when he wouldn't listen.

"Oh, how so?" He gave her a look that suggested she'd gone insane.

"Because everyone thinks you abducted me so you're the target, not me."

"That may be what most people believe, but we both know that isn't true. You're the one with a bull's-eye on your cute little butt."

"Look, I'm going to tell the world everything and get this whole mess out in the open. Then there'll be no point in killing us. And it's easier for people to believe you didn't kidnap me if you're not here," she shouted.

He gave her his death stare.

"Don't give me that look. How do you expect people

to believe you're not intimidating when you make that face?" she ground out.

"I'm angry, and this is my angry face. Deal with it."

"No, you deal with this." She poked his chest. "I'm clearing your name. We can't run forever. Go back to your land and your bees. Live the life you planned."

He bent his head so he was nose to nose with her. "What good is that life if you're not in it?"

Her heart beat hard and she was light headed. Was she hearing things? "Do you really mean it?"

"Yes, I mean it. I want you in my life."

He cared. Whatever was between them was more than a passing affair.

"Say something." He looked down, avoiding her gaze. He was unsure of himself. And that realization made her love him even more.

She cupped his scarred cheek. "I want that, too." Then she stood on tiptoe to kiss him.

A statuesque woman wearing a black knit cap pushed her way between them. "Hi, I'm Sinclair. We'll do the introductions later." She turned to David. "I just got a text from Michael. They know she's here."

"Okay, let's go. Move," he ordered.

"I'm not going," Marie countered.

"What do you mean you're not going? There's no power. They've been shut down. There's no way to broadcast," David shouted.

"Listen to him," Cruz said, entering the reception area from the studio. "Unless you have the mother of all batteries on you, I can't help you."

Marie must've lost her mind. That was the only explanation for her taking so long to think of a solution. "I do…well, not a battery. I have a solar panel. Actually, it's more than that. It works—"

"We don't have time for you to explain. If you're going to do this, you have to do it now." David grabbed her hand.

Marie tugged free. "Listen, you've done your job. You've protected me and kept me safe. It's my turn to look after you."

Sinclair smiled. "I like her."

He nodded to his sister. "Clear the building."

Sinclair punched the fire alarm, which was next to the front door. "I'm on it."

A deafening bell sounded. A few people ran down the stairs, the rest emerging from the darkened studio.

Marie put her hands to her ears in an attempt to diminish the painfully loud ringing. "You need to go, too," she screamed at David.

A couple ran between them through the lobby. Marie was pushed against the reception desk.

David stepped forward, pressing against her, blocking anyone else from coming between them "It's not a question of if they resort to violence, it's when. They've already killed. What's to stop them from coming in here and shooting us?" he shouted in her ear.

He had a point, but what were their options? To keep running. She didn't see that as viable. This needed to end.

"That's all the more reason for you to leave." Marie tried to step to the side, but he put an arm on either side of the counter to cage her. She'd had enough. It was time to set the record straight.

Sinclair stood at the front door. "Everyone's out.

David turned to face his sister. "Already?"

Marie used the distraction to ease away from the desk, but David grabbed her hand.

Sinclair nodded to Cruz. "He said they only have a skeleton staff at this time of day. There's just the three of you. Don't wait too long." she yelled as she stepped through the sliding glass doors.

"We're going around in circles. The sooner you send your message to the world, the better chance we have of surviving this thing." The set of David's jaw told her he wasn't going to give in. She'd known it was a long shot the moment he appeared in the studio doorway.

Cruz McDonald moved to stand in front of her, his tablet in the air.

"What are you doing?" she shouted.

"I'm streaming this live on social media."

"How long have you been doing that?" David asked.

"Since your sister pulled the alarm." Cruz moved to her side, presumably to get a better angle. "This is great."

"You can live stream the news?" She slapped her head. Of course, he could. Sex with David must've made her IQ drop fifty points. She sighed. "Don't answer that. It was a stupid question. So we can transmit from the middle of the square with everyone watching?"

"That's right."

"Great, let's go." Marie headed for the entrance. The glass door fractured as a bullet lodged in the wall behind reception. David leaped, wrapping his arms around her as he flung her across the lobby. They hit the wall. He covered her with his body. She gasped for breath as David's weight forced the air from her lungs. She tried to move but was pinned under him. He grabbed her around the waist and dove for the reception desk. They scrambled under the counter as bullets plowed into the floor. Cement and bits of carpet flew through the air. Cruz was already hunched under the desk. His knuckles were white as he gripped his tablet, filming. Marie couldn't tell that he was recording anything except the noise of the alarm and the sound of gunfire.

We need another way out," David shouted to Cruz.

Cruz shook his head. He was pale, sweating, and his eyes wide with fear.

"Cruz?" She knew how he felt, but they couldn't stay here.

"Don't worry, I see it." David nodded to the stairwell, where EXIT was written above the door in large red letters. He grabbed Cruz's arm and flung him toward the door. He clasped Marie's hand and forced her ahead of him. She hit the door with her shoulder and tumbled down the stairs.

Chapter Thirty-Four

Finn Callaghan had managed to get home to shower and change. He'd also succeeded in getting a few hours' sleep, which had helped clear his head. The corruption in the police department had to start with Chief Notley. That much was obvious. He was the one who had warned Finn off the kidnapping.

"I should get us some coffees." Kennedy perched on the uncomfortable, hard chair.

"That can wait. We need to talk to Notley." He walked to the door.

"You think it's him."

"It's got to be. He warned me off the kidnapping. I don't know why we didn't question him yesterday."

"You're off balance because you have a personal interest in the case." She stood, her hand automatically touching her gun and badge. "You know we still have no evidence of anything. It's Quinn's word against Portman's."

"Yes, but there's also the fact that no one's working the kidnapping. We should at least let them know we're watching. I want to rattle the chief."

They marched through the large central room of the station, heading to Notley's office in the front corner.

Ramirez stood as Finn and Kennedy passed his desk. "I want in on this."

Finn glanced at Kennedy, who gave a faint nod, agreeing to have the detective present for the interview.

Notley straightened in his chair, sucking in his stomach, as the three of them strode into his office. "Haven't you ever heard of knocking?"

Finn got to the point. "Who's working the Wilson

kidnapping?"

Ramirez stood next to Finn as Kennedy strolled to the back of the room. She stopped behind the chief's desk and inspected the photos and awards that hung on the wall.

"I told you this is a police matter." Notley rubbed his bald spot. "The FBI has no jurisdiction."

"I have information that might be helpful, and I'd like to pass it to the detective who's working the case," Finn insisted.

"You can leave it with me. I'll see that it gets to the right place." Notley gave a small squint that revealed a negative response.

"I have information, too." Ramirez said, "but I haven't been able to find a file on it. Who's working the case?"

"Ramirez, you're going to be in deep shit if you keep this up. We're police officers. We hold the line. We do not question each other." Notley pursed his lips, obviously considering his next strategy.

Ramirez pounded his fist on the table. "I'm working the home invasion, and evidence has come to light linking it to the kidnapping. I want to share this evidence. Who's working the case?"

"Are these photos yours?" Kennedy interrupted as she pulled one of the personal pictures off the wall.

"Yes," Notley snapped and then turned his attention back to Ramirez. "I want your badge and weapon."

"I'd hold off on that if I were you." Finn moved so he stood between the two policemen.

Kennedy handed the small photo to Finn. It was the same picture they'd seen in Portman's office. Finn cleared his throat. "You should know we're investigating a charge of public corruption that has been levied against the Granite City-Elkhead County Police."

"I-I-I have never taken a bribe in my life. You can check my financial records." Notley held himself stock-still, as though scared that one false move could give him away.

"Here's what I think." Finn held up the photo. "You're one of the kids pictured here. Portman rescued you from a life on the streets. I don't know if you feel obligated, or if he has something on you. Whatever the reason, you're burying the Wilson kidnapping."

The chief's mouth fell open, and then he averted his gaze. "I'm not burying it. I'm the investigating officer."

"And what role is Public Domain Energy playing?" Finn said through clenched teeth.

Notley hunched his shoulders. "They're helping me with my enquiries." The man telegraphed shame.

"How?" Finn persisted.

"They're looking for this Quinn guy. Portman feels responsible because Quinn went to Marshall House."

"Do you really believe that?"

"Of course." Notley's answer was direct. He didn't flinch or look away.

"We think they're hunting Dr. Wilson."

Notley frowned, but kept silent.

"When they burst into her house, they were trying to destroy her solar panel. She told us that herself," Ramirez added.

"What solar panel?" Notley demanded.

Kennedy tilted her head. "You really don't know?"

"Know what?"

Ramirez thumped the desk again. "How could you let a civilian run a case?" He threw his arms wide. "Every cop in this department is tainted by your actions."

Finn's phone buzzed. He glanced at the caller ID—Sinclair. He hesitated. They were at an important stage in the interview, and he didn't want interruptions. But Sinclair wouldn't call unless it was important. "Callaghan."

"Finn, I need your help."

"Where the hell are you?"

"Big Sky News. They're under attack. The power's out. David and the others were following us out when this guy arrived and started shooting up the place. You have to save them."

"Stay on the—"

She hung up.

Finn stepped into the bullpen. Normally it pulsated with activity; police questioning suspects, conducting interviews, and making phone calls, but all was quiet as everyone seemed mesmerized by the big screen TV.

Dr. Wilson appeared on the screen. The picture didn't have the professional quality of a newscast. It jumped about, going in and out of focus. They appeared to be in a small cement room. Marie sat on the floor with a gold sheet and black box laid out in front of her.

"My name is Marie Wilson. We are hiding in the underground parking area of the Big Sky News building. We need help. There is a gunman shooting at us. I would like to state, for the record, that at no time did David Quinn kidnap me. I chose to go with him because a man employed by Public Domain Energy was chasing us. His name is Harper. He's the same man who's shooting at us now."

Finn flinched as shots echoed in the background.

"Cruz McDonald is streaming this live using his tablet. Power to the building has been cut. This whole thing has been about my solar panel and inverter." She pointed to a gold sheet and a small black box. "I've used it to power this Wi-Fi modem so we can send—"

"Hush," The camera swung to David who was peeking out through a gap in the door. He'd changed his appearance in the last two days. "Stay quiet. I'll lead him away."

"No, stay here. You're unarmed," Marie whispered.

Then everything went dark.

The bullpen was silent. Everyone seemed to be stunned.

Officer Calder ran into the office. "Chief, one of the staff at Big Sky News is here. They've been evacuated. A guy wearing a PDE security vest is in the building taking pot shots."

Finn swore under his breath. "We need to get over there—now."

Members of Granite City-Elkhead County PD all jumped into action at once.

Ramirez grabbed the phone. "I'll get SWAT."

"Kennedy and I are both SWAT certified. We'll follow your guys in."

"No problem." Ramirez nodded.

"I'll get our tactical gear ready." Kennedy strode to the stairs.

Finn pointed to Officer Calder. "Can you cordon off an area around the building?"

"On it." The young policeman ran toward the lobby.

Finn started for his office and then stopped. "Detective Ramirez."

"Yes."

He nodded his head to the chief. "Don't let your suspect get away."

Ramirez smiled. "Don't worry. He's not going anywhere."

Chapter Thirty-Five

Marie flinched at the rat-a-tat-tat of gunfire. David was out there unarmed. She crept to the door and peeked out. The only light came from the ramp, which opened to the street. Handsome knelt on the ground with his back to her, firing at cars parked along the back wall. Bullets tore chunks out of the vehicles. She couldn't see David, but it stood to reason that the vehicles hid him from view.

Silently, she shut the door, but why she was so careful about the sound was beyond her. The noise from the weapon was deafening. Someone could creep... Now, there was an idea. She looked around the room, searching for anything that could be used as a weapon. Shelving stood along the back wall. She pulled a sledgehammer from the bottom shelf, but dismissed it because it was too heavy to swing. A regular hammer would be a great choice, but she couldn't see one. Finally, she discovered an iron bar lying on the ground. She picked it up, judging its weight, and then swung it a couple of time to assess its maneuverability.

Cruz blocked her way. The light on his tablet told her the camera was still on. "Whatever you're planning, it's not a good idea."

"He is out there, and he's unarmed. I cannot let him die." She headed for the door.

She stopped before turning the handle and faced Cruz. "Portman has killed people over that solar panel. I suggest you use this opportunity to escape. Take the prototype with you and hand it over to the authorities."

Marie inched through the door, the bar raised above her head. She crept behind an old station wagon. Then everything went quiet.

She'd heard that silence could be deafening but hadn't realized what that phrase meant until this moment. She had adjusted to the noise of the gunfire and used it to cover her actions. Now that there was silence, she felt exposed. She couldn't help David if the gunman turned on her the minute she moved. Then it occurred to her that she was waiting for Handsome to shoot at David. She forced herself to crawl to the next car.

The gunfire started again. She stood, gripped the iron bar tighter, and edged closer to the shooter.

****

Finn marched into the square, wearing his full tactical gear. He carried his H&K MP-5 submachine gun with his Glock holstered at his side. Kennedy tugged her helmet onto her head.

Detective Ramirez greeted them as they approached the news station. "SWAT will be here any minute."

Finn understood. Being on a SWAT team was essentially a second job. Members of the highly-trained unit were stationed throughout the county, working their regular shifts as police officers until they were required.

"I think it would be best if they split into two teams. One goes in the front and the other should go through the parking garage at the side of the building." Ramirez pointed to the right side of Big Sky News.

Finn agreed. "Kennedy and I will go through the parking garage. How many people are in there?" Splintered glass hung in the door, bullet holes clearly visible. He resisted the urge to dash in and save David. His FBI training told him to stay calm and wait for the rest of the team.

"Four. They only had a skeleton staff when Wilson arrived. The only people in there are the gunman, Quinn, Dr. Wilson, and Cruz McDonald."

"She was the first one there?"

"Yes, Quinn arrived later with a woman."

"Finn." Sinclair waved from behind the barricade.

He walked toward her, and a policeman allowed her to slip under the ribbon. "Give me details." He dispensed with the pleasantries. There was no time and, besides, she wasn't the type to care about idle banter.

She thrust her phone into his hand. "You need to see this."

Emails from Michael with video attachments appeared on the screen. Each one had a title, *Quinn saving woman, David at airport*, and there where documents, lots of them.

"I think we have our evidence," Finn stuffed the phone into the pouch attached to his vest. "I'll keep your phone until we can process it."

A beige armored truck honked its horn as it drove through the square. SWAT had arrived.

Finn nodded and marched back to where Kennedy stood with Ramirez. Finn checked his primary weapon and then waited for Kennedy to do the same. She nodded.

Two officers exited the rear of the truck carrying large, black ballistic shields. The other men fell into formation as they split into two groups and filed toward the building. Finn and Kennedy joined the one headed for the parking garage.

Chapter Thirty-Six.

Marshall walked into the elevator. He was heading for his car parked in front of the building. It was time to escape.

He'd watched from his fifth-floor window as a crowd formed in the city center. Police cordoned off the entrance to Big Sky News. There was still a chance Harper would escape through the parking garage that exited into the alley on the far side of the building, but it didn't look promising.

As an ex-street kid, David's first instinct should've been to keep running, and as Special Forces he would've been trained in discretion. Returning to Granite City and talking to the media must have been Wilson's idea. Her unpredictability was one of the traits that made her so dangerous to the Syndicate.

He tapped his breast pocket, assuring himself, once again, that his fake ID was still there. Calming classical music played as he rode the elevator down to the ground floor. Sinclair Quinn was in the square. Her tall statuesque figure stood out even from his office. With her natural beauty and gift for languages, she could have had a job with any of the top firms in the country, but instead she'd followed her brother into the service.

The door dinged open as he reached the ground floor. Leaving the building, not twenty feet in front of him, was Spider. The hacker was probably absconding before the authorities descended. There was something different about him. He still had the same short, cropped, black hair, the same sweatshirt, but his posture was different. He strode with confidence. There was a military bearing that hadn't been there before. As he marched through the exit, he waved to someone in the Square, and Sinclair waved back. *Fuck.* Spider was working with Sinclair—David's sister.

Marshall ran to his car, which was parked in its reserved spot next to the front door. A red mist clouded his vision. The bastard had been given access to everything: videos, emails, orders, and most importantly, money transfers. Blood pounded through his ears as his pulse quickened. He'd never escape. One lousy hacker would track him down, and it would all be over. He probably wouldn't even make it out of the country before the police apprehended him. He'd have to kill the asshole. He rammed his Mercedes into reverse and then maneuvered on to the street that ran in front of the PDE building. Spider crossed the road twenty feet in front of him. Marshall stepped on the gas and swerved, aiming for Spider as his foot touched the sidewalk. He didn't flinch as the hacker's body hit the front bumper, bounced onto the hood of the car, and then slammed into the pavement.

Marshall didn't check to see if he was dead. He just kept driving.

****

David covered his head with his hands as he crouched in front of a Volvo. Rounds propelled pieces of framework in every direction, and chunks of cement wall peppered him with flying shrapnel. He needed to keep the engine block between him and Pretty Boy because there was a dense concentration of metal in the average engine, enough to stop a bullet. When Harper moved, he had to move, too, always keeping as much material between him and Brad.

It might not have been his best strategy, but it was the only one he had. Hopefully, Finn would come to the rescue. *Fuck.* He should've used Sinclair's phone to call Finn, but he'd been so focused on getting to Marie, he hadn't been thinking straight.

He hadn't caught a glimpse of Pretty Boy's exact weapon, but it was some kind of semi-automatic. He flinched as fragments hit him in the arms and shoulders. What was Harper waiting for? David was unarmed and vulnerable. All Harper had to do was walk over and deliver the kill shot.

It was time to move. David hunkered down near the front tire and peeked under the car, hoping to get a better sense of Pretty Boy's location so he could judge his next step. He was in a kneeling position, his left elbow supported by his left knee. Damn. That was a good position. A shooter could move fast and relocate without taking his eyes from the target. David's heart hammered in his chest as small, black boots worn by a person with pink thermal long johns crept toward Pretty Boy. Marie.

Damn it. What the hell did she think she was doing? He was the distraction. She was supposed to stay safe until Finn arrived. That was the plan, although he might have forgotten to mention it to her. If they lived through this, he'd start working on his communication skills.

Brad fired another round in David's direction, oblivious to the woman creeping up behind him. They were underground, which meant the noise from the semi-automatic echoed off the cement walls, making it impossible for Harper to hear her approach. Unfortunately, it also meant the only light source was from the sloped entrance, which was behind Marie. The angle of her shadow would fall across Harper, alerting him to her presence.

David crouched low, calculating the best time to act. He shrugged out of his coat and then threw it to his left. A spray of bullets followed the jacket as he leapt to the right.

****

Moving fast, Marie stepped to Handsome's side, holding the bar like a baseball bat, and wacked his nose, striking it as if she were trying to hit the ball out of the field. His head rocked back as one hand covered his face, but the other hand continued to pull the trigger. Bullets sprayed wildly. She slammed the iron bar into his nose again. He dropped the gun, both hands stemming the flow of blood from his nostrils. She kicked the weapon away, wanting it out of his reach. It clattered a few feet and then stopped. She stood over him, panting, waiting for him to attack. His back arched and then his gaze slanted to her. His eyes rolled to the ceiling. He crumpled to the grey cement floor without making a sound.

She stepped back, stunned by her own actions. Her hands shook as she held up the bar. She'd beat a man unconscious and she wasn't sorry.

From the corner of her eye, she noticed a flash of movement. David took a step and then collapsed.

"No." A white-hot light blurred her vision. "David?" She threw the bar to the ground and ran to his side.

His whole body shook as he tried to push himself to a sitting position. Sweat gathered on his deathly pale face.

"Stay still." Marie ordered.

There was a small nick above his left eye.

He lay back and closed his eyes.

"Were you shot?" She felt along his arms and torso.

He didn't answer.

"David. Answer me," she shouted, as she reached his legs. Blood pooled beneath him. She ripped open his pant leg. A huge chunk had been carved out of his thigh.

"Yes." His eyes flickered open.

"You are not allowed to die. Do you hear me? I've just found you, and I'm not letting you go. Got that?" She pressed her hands to the wound, desperately trying to stem the flow of blood, but it seeped through her fingers.

"Okay," he whispered, his voice weak and thready.

"Stay awake. That's an order." She tried to put some power behind her words. *Oh, God.* She needed to stop the bleeding.

He closed his eyes.

"No, stay with me." A scream erupted from her throat as she kept pressure on his wound, praying it would be enough to stop him from bleeding to death.

Chapter Thirty-Seven

Finn crept toward the prone body with the battered face. David lay a hundred yards away. Marie yelled David's name as she held her hands to Quinn's leg.

The SWAT team had checked the building. It was secure. They found no other assailants, which didn't make sense, considering Marshall Portman could afford to pay an army of men. Finn added it to the list of questions he would ask the president of PDE once he was arrested.

He suppressed the urge to rush to his friend's side; instead, he followed protocol. The assailant's weapon, a FN SCAR 17 semi-automatic carbine, lay a few feet from his body. Finn flicked on the safety. Kennedy searched the gunman's body, checking for other weapons, and retrieved a Glock and a K-bar knife.

Finn placed his fingers on the attacker's neck, checking for a pulse. It was thin, difficult to detect, but it was there. Big surprise. The man's face was a mess. The remains of a bandage hung from his nose. His eyes were swollen, and one of his cheekbones was dented, probably broken.

He radioed the controller at the police Headquarters. "Situation is contained. I have two, repeat two, injured. Need two ambulances in the parking garage."

Finn strode toward David wondering how he'd managed to beat up the gunman and then walk a hundred yards, bleeding. Then his commonsense kicked in. Women were just as capable of violence as men, given the right motivation. David had been shot, and Marie had attacked the gunman. Yes, that theory fit the crime scene.

He blinked as he neared David. *Oh, God.* That was a lot of blood. *Shit.* If there were even a small nick in the femoral artery, he would bleed to death before help could arrive. Finn discarded his helmet and vest as he ran. He stripped off his T-shirt, elbowed Marie out of the way, and placed the wadded-up clothing over the wound. "There's an ambulance coming. You have to hold on."

David coughed. "Okay." He opened his eyes and stared at Marie. "You're good?"

"No, I'm not good. You're hurt." Her voice cracked.

"He's lucky," Finn said.

"Lucky? You people are mad."

"No, I mean the bullet missed the femoral artery."

"How do you know?"

"He's still alive. There are a lot of blood vessels in the thigh. That's why there's so much blood." He was waffling. He knew he should stop talking, but he couldn't. He needed to calm Marie down. He needed to keep pressure on David's wound to lessen the blood flow. And most of all, he needed to believe that his friend wasn't going to bleed out on the floor of a parking garage.

Chapter Thirty-Eight

Marie dabbed her eyes with a tissue as she stood at the nurse's station. Damn it, a woman could go over twenty years without shedding a tear and then become a crybaby in the space of two days. The gray-haired nurse behind the counter refused to tell Marie anything about David's condition because she wasn't family. The shrew wouldn't even tell her if he was still in surgery.

She'd found herself alone in the Granite City Square, surrounded by emergency personnel and onlookers. David was wheeled away in an ambulance. She'd tried to accompany him. She had screamed and shouted and kicked up a fuss worthy of a toddler, but it hadn't helped.

Agent Kennedy Morris wanted to interview her, but Marie refused. She needed to see David. Nothing else mattered. The no-nonsense agent had driven her to emergency.

The last time she'd been in a hospital was after her mom's attempted suicide. Marie liked to believe that her mother hadn't meant to kill herself with a lethal combination of pills and alcohol, but she didn't really know. Her mom had lingered in the gray space between life and death for days, until there was no hope of recovery. Marie held her nanny's hand, waiting for her mother's life support machine to be turned off. This may as well have been the same hospital, the sterility, the white walls, the antiseptic smell, and worst of all, the same detached, efficient nurses who saw too many patients to care about one brave, strong man who'd been shot trying to save her.

Marie hammered on the desk. "He's wounded because of me. I need to—"

"Look, if you don't quiet down, I'll have you removed from the premises."

Agent Morris marched into the reception area. "That won't be necessary. I'm special Agent Morris." The agent flashed her credentials and badge. "What information do you have on David Quinn?"

The nurse tapped a keyboard. "He's still in surgery. His family is in the waiting room on the second floor."

Agent Morris nodded. "I've just finished talking to hospital security. We have a suspect and several witnesses undergoing treatment at this hospital. I do not want any information released to the media. Do you understand?"

Marie didn't wait for the nurse to answer, but headed for the elevator. Agent Morris dashed after her and grabbed her elbow. "There's something we need to talk about."

"It can wait."

"No, under the circumstances, it can't. First, there was another man named Michael Papin. He went—"

"Michael, yes, he's a friend of David's."

"He was hit by a car leaving the PDE office."

"An accident?"

"No, we believe it was deliberate."

Marie's knees weakened. Michael had put himself in danger because of his loyalty to David, but his sacrifice added to her burden. Two men were dead and two injured because of her invention. How could a solar panel be worth all this? "Is he okay?"

"He has a broken pelvis, a broken shoulder, and a concussion, but he's in stable condition."

"I'll make sure—"

"Do you know there's eighty million dollars sitting in a trust fund under your name?"

"Portman said that, but I don't think… I spent all my money developing that silly solar—"

"First, it's not silly, and second, there were two accounts. The one you use has a balance of eighteen hundred and sixteen dollars, and there's another that's held in trust with eighty million—"

"Are you sure it's mine?"

"Your grandfather on your mother's side set up the trust. Your mother was the beneficiary. You inherited the money after her death. I emailed Rothman's Bank where the trust is held. Apparently, you signed an order authorizing them to send your father yearly checks for the accumulated interest on the account. As far as I can tell, he has kept the money."

"He deposited the interest on eighty million dollars?" She pictured her father, his distance, and his remoteness. He had never had any time for her. Her chest ached. She loved him despite everything, but he would never be the father she wanted him to be.

"That's right, for five years."

"Five years ago, he worked on the patent for my solar panel. He gave me mounds of papers to sign... I must've endorsed the consent form then. I thought he was interested in my work. We were finally connecting."

The agent put a hand on her arm. "Sorry, but you don't get to choose your family."

"How much is the interest on eighty million dollars?"

"It depends on how it's invested, but a conservative estimate would be between two and three million."

It was typical of her father that he'd care more about her money than he did about her, but all the cash in the world wouldn't change the fact that David had been shot. "Look, I'm grateful you told me, but this can wait—"

"I'm telling you this now because it means you can pay their medical bills. You can afford the best care money can buy."

Marie didn't need telling twice. She marched back to the efficient gray-haired nurse. "I'm going to pay for David Quinn and Michael...Michael... She stared at Agent Morris. "What's Michael's last name again?"

"Papin."

I'm going to pay for David Quinn and Michael Papin's care.

****

Finn ignored the tension in his gut as he waited for David to come out of surgery. Marie sat, her face in her hands.

Tim draped a blanket around her shoulders. "It's not your fault."

"No, it's not," Sinclair agreed, coming to sit next to Marie. "Portman convinced David to work for him. He used emotional blackmail to get what he wanted."

"David felt obligated because Portman had taken us in," Tim added.

"We're looking into others who he might have manipulated into doing his dirty work." Finn had talked to his superiors in Salt Lake City. They were arranging a task force of experts to examine the massive amount of data Michael had gathered.

Kennedy had returned to the police station to get started on the paperwork. At least, that was what she'd told him. She was probably taking advantage of his absence to move her desk into his office, which he supposed was now theirs. He didn't object because she had a point. They were partners, and they needed to confer on cases. It made sense they share the space.

"Is there any word on Michael?" Sinclair wrung her hands. It was a sign of stress, which was understandable under the circumstances.

"He's regained consciousness, but he doesn't remember being hit by the car." Finn had been to see his old friend and was appalled at his condition. "He looks like shit, but he's fortunate."

Sinclair's green eyes, a shade darker than her brother's, narrowed on him as if he'd said something outlandish. "Fortunate? Portman aimed at him."

Finn shrugged. "Considering the car didn't slow down, Michael's lucky his back and neck aren't broken. It's early days, but I spoke to him, and he was coherent." That was the second time today he'd qualified his friends' injuries.

"Any news on Marshall?" Tim asked.

"None. His car was abandoned at the Best Western on the edge of town. We have uniforms and highway patrol looking for him, and everyone's on alert at the airports." Finn's attention turned to the television. News networks now ran the full video of Marie and David escaping the PDE building under fire. It was good to see the whole scene and know that the truth was out in the open. The Department of Defense had released the details of Quinn's actions under fire. He was being hailed as a hero.

"What about that guy?" Marie pointed to the TV. "The blond with the broken nose. Did I kill him?"

"No, he's unconscious, but he's expected to recover. He'll be charged once he wakes up."

"Pity, I wanted him dead." She clutched the blanket tighter around her shoulders.

Despite the grave situation, Finn smiled. Marie Wilson was just what David needed, a woman with enough guts to keep him in line.

****

Marie could finally breathe. David was out of surgery and doing well. He'd lost a lot of blood, suffered a compound fracture of the femur, and muscle damage. The surgeon had pinned his bone fragments together and warned them his recovery would take at least six months and would include extensive physical therapy.

David lay in the recovery room. His face was deathly pale. She wanted to see his eyes light up and be graced with a smile. The rhythmic beep from the myriad of machines that monitored his condition comforted her. Even when she closed her eyes, she could hear his heartbeat and know he was alive.

The others had gone to get some food and check on Michael, but she wouldn't leave. She couldn't. The last couple of days had been a whirlwind of fear, trauma, and love. She could live without the guns and peril, but she couldn't be sorry it had happened. Without the danger, she would have never met David. She wouldn't know what it was like to love, or that love meant you had to be prepared to give up everything. And she had.

She had left her precious prototype at Big Sky News. She had no idea what had happened to it and, at this moment, she didn't care.

She squeezed David's fingers, taking comfort from the warmth of his skin.

"Marie, there you are." Her father's commanding voice made her spine tingle with anger.

Standing, she patted David's hand and then faced the man who was supposed to love her, but didn't. "Why are you here?"

"Why am I— There's the kidnapping and the home invasion for a start. You've really made a mess of things, Mouse. Don't worry, I'll make sure you get the best defense—"

"Do. Not. Call. Me. Mouse." She spat the words, her hands balling into fists.

He shut his eyes and then opened them, then took a step closer. "I won't have you—"

"Shut your mouth. Did you or did you not withhold my inheritance from me?" She straightened, ready to fight.

"I never—"

"The FBI explained everything. You've been living off the interest and—"

"I see the little mouse has come out of her hole. Why shouldn't I get paid? I've put up with you. Raised you. I deserve some recompense." His upper lip lifted in a sneer.

For the first time, she saw the real man, the grasping, self-absorbed cheat who hid beneath a handsome face, a veneer of civility, and expensive suits. He wasn't concerned about anyone except himself, and he most definitely didn't care about her.

"There are people all over the world who raise their

children and don't feel the need for a financial reward."

"After your mother—"

"You mean after you drove her to commit suicide." In a flash of insight, she questioned whether his lack of affection and empathy had broken her mother's heart and caused her to go into a downward spiral of drugs and alcohol. Perhaps he wasn't capable of love. It didn't matter. She wasn't a little girl, and she didn't need him in her life, but she did want him to know the consequences of his actions. "Everything that has happened to me in the last two days is your fault."

"What? You being in Montana and getting—"

"Do you know why I came here?" She didn't wait for an answer, but carried on with her tirade. "To get funding so I could complete my work. I asked you to help, and you turned me down. You refused to give me what was rightfully mine. Marshall Portman heard about my solar panel because I sent emails to anyone who might be interested in keeping my project alive. I could've used the trust, or maybe the interest you stole."

He flashed a cold smile. "It was all there. You just didn't read the documents I asked you to sign. You should always read before you sign."

And there it was, his admission of guilt. He had deceived his own daughter for personal gain. "You're my father. I trusted you."

"You can't trust anyone when it comes to business. Now, get your stuff, we're leaving."

For as long as she could remember, she had wanted him to accept and love her, but he never had. Everyday of her sad, lonely life, she had worked hard and excelled, hoping that one day he would acknowledge her achievements. She realized now that it would never happen, not because she wasn't worthy, but because he wasn't capable of caring about anyone but himself.

"Do you see that man lying in bed?" She pointed to David. "He's worth ten of you. You're fired as my lawyer, and any personal relationship we had is over. I'll be getting legal and financial representation and will control my trust fund myself from now on."

"Good luck with that," he scoffed. "I'll have that money tied up in legal loopholes faster than you can blink. You have a history of unstable behavior. You accused your former professor, who was also your lover, of stealing your work."

Every muscle in her body tensed. She wanted to hurt him, to crumple his perfectly pressed suit, and pound his face into the dirt. "Try it. I just beat a man unconscious with an iron pipe. I'd be happy to do the same to you."

His mouth fell open. "Is that a threat?"

She gave him her sweetest, fake smile. "Of course not, I've been through so much in the last few days. I've had a gun held to my head, I've been shot at, and the man I love was injured. It's a lot to deal with. I'm sure any judge will understand I'm overwhelmed, and sometimes a woman simply needs to hit a bully."

Special Agent Callaghan stepped between them. He pressed a piece of paper into her hand. "Here's the name of a good lawyer. I heard the whole thing and would be happy to testify on your behalf." Then he glared at her father and pulled his credentials from his pocket. "I'm Special Agent Callaghan with the FBI. I suggest you leave—now. You can expect a visit from our agents in Seattle."

Patrick Wilson paled. "You-you can't—"

"I'm unable to comment on an ongoing investigation." The agent placed a hand on her father's shoulder, turning him toward the door. "Although, if you want, I can take you in for questioning now."

Patrick Wilson walked away without saying goodbye. Marie watched his retreating back. She would miss him from her life. He was, after all, her only relative. Her world would be even more isolated than it had been before...

No, it wouldn't. If David didn't want her around—

"Did I hear you say you love me?" David croaked, reaching for the button to raise his bed.

"David?" She rushed to his side. "You're awake."

"Of course, I'm awake. Who can sleep with all this noise?"

She gave a shaky laugh. "You heard—"

"He deserved it." He placed his hand over hers.

"Yes, he did." She kissed his scar.

"Don't cry." He brushed a droplet from her cheek.

"Those damn tears. I never cry, honest." She wasn't sure if they were tears of joy because David was awake or if she was crying because her only living relative had admitted he didn't love her.

Sinclair patted her shoulder and passed her a box of tissues. Marie hadn't noticed the others return, even though Agent Callaghan had intervened in the argument. Her fight with Patrick had consumed her. She couldn't call him her father, not anymore. He didn't fill that roll, never had. Agent Morris was right. You couldn't pick your family...but you could pick your friends.

"Back to my original question, you love me?" David's voice was groggy and thick.

She glanced around the room. Agent Callaghan and Tim stood by the door, smiling, and Sinclair sat on the other side of David's bed. A little privacy would have been nice, but none of them looked like they had any intention of moving. In fact, they were all listening intently. It didn't matter. She loved David and didn't want to hide it. "Yes, I do. I love you very much."

"You'll stay?" He gripped her hand, surprising her with his strength.

"Yes." She would stay as long as he wanted her.

"Good, because it's a pain in the ass when the woman you love isn't around."

Her eyes leaked again. She bit her lip. She had to get her act together and get her emotions under control.

"What's wrong? I thought you'd be happy?" He sat up

straighter, his face blanching with the effort.

"I am. I'm crying because you love me, and I'm more than happy. I'm overjoyed, ecstatic, and thrilled." She laughed, suddenly not caring about the tears that rolled down her cheeks.

"Oh, damn." He lay back, folding his arms across his chest.

"What," she sniffled.

"I never know what you're going to do next."

Chapter Thirty-Nine

Marshall breathed a sigh of relief as his chartered jet took off from a private airfield in Elkhead County. His first stop would be the Cayman Islands where he would transfer his remaining funds into an account under his new identity. From there, he would make his way to Brunei.

A blond flight attendant stood with her back to him, fussing with the coffee pot. She wore a miniskirt so short it revealed her stocking tops. As she talked to the pilots, she swayed her curvaceous bottom. He didn't bother looking at her face. He wanted to enjoy the view. Besides, once he glimpsed the indifferent gaze women normally gave him, the fantasy would be over.

The plane leveled as it reached cruising altitude. She turned and walked toward him, swaying her hips. He took in her long legs, the white, creamy flesh of her upper thigh that was visible with every step. His gaze traveled up. The top buttons of her blouse were undone, revealing her bust, which was full and generous.

His penis twitched. He'd never been unfaithful to his wife. Not because he'd never been tempted, but because she was a scary bitch, and he knew he would never get away with it.

The woman stood in front of him, legs slightly apart. She held her hands behind her back, which pushed her bust forward. He leant back, appreciating the view of her deep cleavage, unable to tear his eyes away from her magnificent breasts. Her luscious nipples poked through her shirt, begging for attention.

She lunged, shoving him back, and straddled him. "Hello, darling."

He froze. It couldn't be. He stared into Lucy's cold,

calculating eyes.

"Did you forget something?" Her breath warmed his ear, sending shivers of fear down his spine.

"N-no, I would've met up with you eventually. I just didn't want you involved. I was trying to protect you."

"I think you made a mess of things. There were those on the Syndicate who said you weren't up for the job, and they were right.

"The Syndicate? You told them?"

"Of course, did you know Daddy was a founding member, and when he died his responsibilities were passed to me?"

"But your father's been dead for ten years. Ouch." He glanced down in time to see her empty a syringe into his arm. He pushed her off and then stood as he yanked out the needle. His knees buckled, and he landed in a heap in the aisle.

"That's a little poison. It's succinylcholine, or SUX for short. The good news is that it doesn't take too long to kill you. Your muscles become paralyzed so you can't move. Once it reaches your respiratory system, you'll suffocate and die. The bad news is that you'll be conscious until the end."

He tried to move his arms, but they refused to work. He yelled, but no sound came from his throat. He thought she might have kissed his cheek, but he couldn't feel her touch.

"It's a good poison. I used it on Daddy because it's virtually undetectable. Everyone thought he'd died of a heart attack. They'll probably assume the same about you."

She undid her blouse, letting it fall to the floor near his head. "You know you could've avoided all this if only you planned to take me with you. I would've protected you from the Syndicate. After all, being stupid is forgivable, being disloyal is not."

He willed his arms and legs to move, but they wouldn't cooperate.

"I'm going to fuck each of these pilots while you watch. Of course, you'll be done before I am." Her skirt slipped to the floor, and then her underwear.

He tried to breathe, but his lungs wouldn't expand. Lucy dragged one of the pilots from the cockpit and guided him to the center of the cabin. She unzipped his pants and let them drop to the floor. Marshall tried not to look but he couldn't close his eyes. Lucy straddled the pilot after he lay on the floor. Marshall didn't want to watch, didn't want to hear her screams of pleasure as she rode the man in uniform. He tried to cover his ears with his hands, but his arms wouldn't move. Nothing worked. All he could hear was his own shrieking in his head as the world dimmed and blinked out.

Chapter Forty

David hobbled on crutches down the hospital corridor. It'd been a week since his surgery. His leg ached like a bastard, and the crutches chafed his armpits, making every movement a lesson in pain. He'd refused the pain meds because they made his mind fuzzy. It was one thing to be immobile, quite another to be a babbling idiot. He hated the inactivity of being injured. He'd walk, or rather hobble, to Michael's room every day, but after an hour's excursion, he would collapse exhausted into bed and sleep for hours.

"I'm going to hit them on the nose with an iron pipe when I get my hands on them." Marie sauntered beside him, not the least put out by their slow pace.

Despite his own discomfort, he laughed. She had taken the news that her home had burned down pretty well.

"It's not the research. I have that compiled on a memory stick in my bag." The backpack she'd taken to Big Sky News had been returned to her, including the solar panel. She hadn't looked at it. In fact, the only time she seemed sad was when someone mentioned her prototype. "It's not even the furniture or any of the other stuff."

"What's got you in a snit?" He leant against the door jam, taking a breather.

"I had photos of my mother." There was a distant, empty look in her eyes.

He understood. If he had a picture of his parents, he would cherish it, too. "Sorry." As gestures went, it was inadequate, but what could he say? He'd never been good with words.

She straightened, forcing herself to brighten. "You're here." She waved her hand toward the hospital room. "I'll see you in an hour."

He watched her walk away. Despite his condition, her heart-shaped behind still did a number on him. She wore a pair of jeans, a soft cotton shirt that clung to her breasts, and a bra. He tried to persuade her she didn't need the undergarment, but she'd just laughed.

"You got it bad." Michael sat in a chair next to his bed. His face was paler than usual and a fine mist of perspiration covered his forehead. They were small signs, but ones David instantly recognized as pain.

"They got you out of bed today. I'll bet that hurt."

"Yeah, like a bitch, but I can't lie on my back forever."

"Have they given you a timeline for your recovery?" David hobbled to the bed and sat, shifting the weight off his injured leg.

"My bones should knit within three months. After that I'll have to do some major physio. Complete recovery should take six to nine months."

"Tim told me that your bosses at the CID questioned you yesterday, and you've been fired."

Michael shrugged. "I was ready to move on. There's only so much undercover work a man can do before he craves the light." Despite his words, there was a tension in him that hadn't been there the day before. David suspected it had nothing to do with the pain of sitting on a broken pelvis.

"I understand the two of you have plans," Michael said, changing the subject.

"She wants to build a house on my land with running water and a bathroom. I'm good with that." David allowed himself to be sidetracked.

"What about the future?

"There's a lot of stuff to be sorted. Her dad's trying to gain control of her trust—"

"And the solar panel?"

"I want to develop it, but she's hesitant. There's been a lot of interest after what happened at Big Sky News."

"Is she scared another Portman will come out of the

woodwork?"

David nodded.

"She's not wrong to be scared. Portman wasn't the brains behind the operation."

"He wasn't?"

"No, there were hints in some of the documents I uncovered."

"Hints to what?"

"A group called The Syndicate. Who they are and what they do, I couldn't find out, but I know they were the ones pulling Portman's strings. He even mentioned them. By the way, did you hear about Marshall?"

"Yeah, heart attack." David wasn't sure how he felt about the death of his mentor. Marshall had been instrumental in making him the man he was today. There were moments when he was grateful they had met. Then, at other times, he wished he'd been left on the streets.

"You going to marry her?" Michael said, lightening the mood.

"I would marry her in a heartbeat, but…"

"But what?"

"She's worth eighty million dollars."

"Oh, boohoo. The woman I love is too rich." Michael said, in a mocking imitation of a crying child.

David laughed and then said. "You're right. I need to get a grip."

"Do you love her?"

David pictured Marie, refusing to leave him in the barn, and then the next day in the parking garage creeping up on Pretty Boy. He'd never been so scared in his life. He didn't know how he would cope if he lost her. "Yeah, I love her."

"Then go for it. You can always sign a prenup." Michael had cut through the irrelevant details to the heart of the matter.

David smiled and changed the subject. "I owe you a debt. I would never have asked you to put yourself in the line of fire the way you did. You took a big risk working for Portman at PDE. I'll never be able to repay you."

Michael shrugged, dismissing David's gratitude.

"Why'd you do it?" The question had been burning a hole in David's mind. His friend had risked his career, and his life. He'd been injured and was now in constant pain. The way David saw it, Michael had paid a high price so that they could live.

He swallowed. "I had to. I'm responsible."

"How can you—"

He gazed at the floor. "I'm the one who put the three of you in Marshall House."

"You weren't even there. You'd already returned home."

"I went home so I could find a way out for you." Michael's brow furrowed. He still didn't make eye contact.

"I don't understand." David had always believed that joining Marshall House had been pure, dumb luck.

"Once I had access to a computer, I did some research on the best way to get you off the street. I decided Marshall House was a good fit and contacted Portman. I told him about you, how you and Sin were good at languages, and how Tim helped little old ladies. I told him you avoided the homeless shelters and persuaded him to find you."

"Why?" This was shocking, but at the same time it made sense. The things Portman had known about them, David had assumed Marshall's charisma was instinct and he was good with kids.

"Sinclair couldn't survive on the streets much longer. She was done. She'd lost hope—"

"And she would never have left without us." David remembered his sister at sixteen. She was gaunt, despondent, and had given up on life. For a while he was scared he'd lose her.

"No, she wouldn't." Michael shifted, trying to get comfortable. He had got them off the streets to save his sister, and whether he admitted it or not, he had probably gone undercover at PDE for the same reason. As a teenager, Michael had been infatuated with Sinclair, and those feelings had grown into something deeper over the years.

"You should tell her," David said baldly.

"Tell her what?

"That you love her."

"I don't know what—"

"Don't deny it. You've loved Sinclair since you were fifteen years old. It's time you faced up to that."

"Easier said than done."

"Yeah, but you deserve to know if she feels the same way about you." David had never concerned himself with his sister's love life. It was none of his business, but Sinclair had never had a serious boyfriend, and now he had to wonder if it had something to do with Michael. Whatever happened between Michael and Sinclair, Michael was his friend, and he deserved to be happy.

"And if she doesn't?" He could see the fear in his friend's eyes.

"Then you can move on. No matter what, I'll be there for you." Using his crutches, David levered himself off the bed. He'd go and find Marie. It was time to start planning their life together.

Epilogue

Marie lay on her stomach with her head resting on David's shoulder. She was exhausted. After two months together, their lovemaking was still a wild, desperate thirst that couldn't be quenched.

This bout of sex had been provoked by a particularly heated quarrel about their prenuptial agreement. She didn't want one. He on the other hand refused to marry her until he had signed away any claim to her money.

She tried to reason with him, but he wouldn't budge.

"You know," she said, using her last logical argument. "There's no point in keeping our finances separate. I paid for the house, but you own the land. They can't be divided. Like us."

Their log home was simple rather than ostentatious. It was a three-bedroom house with two outbuildings: a garage and a workshop. Everything was powered by her solar panel which, strictly speaking, wasn't legal. The prototype was still going through the national fire code certification to ensure it was safe. Ironically, the publicity caused by Marshall Portman's actions had ensured an interest in her work. She had received job offers from around the globe, and orders for her solar panel were pouring in. David dealt with the business side of things. With his education, he understood the complexities of a business enterprise, whereas she was content to go to her workshop and concentrate on her next project.

David's hand trailed down her spine and then patted her buttocks. "Nice try, but you know my terms."

She leant on her elbow so she could see his face. "I thought you might say that. Okay you win. We'll get a prenup." She'd make an appointment with her lawyer to draw up a will, naming David as the beneficiary. He wouldn't like it so she wouldn't tell him. It was a little lie of omission, but it would give her some piece of mind, knowing that he would be financially secure if anything happened to her.

"It's about time. I thought I was going to have to drag you to the lawyers and force you to sign the damn thing. Let's get married tomorrow."

"No, that's too soon."

"The next day then."

"No, we'll get married when I have a dress."

"Do you want a church wedding? Cause I'm not sure I want to wait that long."

"No, but I'd like to wear a wedding dress. Besides, Sinclair, Tim, Michael, and Finn are your family, and I want them there on our special day to celebrate with us."

His intense green gaze caught hers. "Okay, we'll get the license and then make the arrangements. I can't wait to call you Mrs. Quinn."

Her breath hitched. She wanted him again. It was always the same. The scar didn't matter. She was drawn to the power of his personality and his strength, coupled with his good heart.

He smiled. "Stop looking at me like that. I need to recover before we make love again. Besides I don't think we have time. I have a guy coming by this afternoon." He rolled out of bed, grabbed his pants from the floor, and strolled to the bathroom. A slight limp was the only sign he had been shot two months ago.

She clipped her bra into place and then sat on the side of the bed to pull on her jeans. "What guy?"

"He's bringing a pair of personal protection dogs for us to look at. We don't have to buy them, but this is big acreage, and I can't be with you twenty-four hours a day. I figured a friendly, well-trained dog can spend time with you in your workshop."

"We'll see." Since the incident with PDE, she had been

nervous about being in her workshop alone, but she'd never had a dog and didn't want to make the commitment without meeting one first.

She tugged on her T-shirt and headed for the door. Soon she would marry the man she loved, and she had friends who were like family. She belonged.

Turn the page for an exciting preview of book two in
The Gathering Storm Series,
Fire Storm.
Due to be released winter 2018

Fire Storm
Chapter One

Ben North clutched a hand to his heart in an effort to control his racing pulse. The woman sat at his kitchen table, displaying her magnificent naked breasts. He hadn't seen a bosom that superb since he'd served in Vietnam.

Her knee-length skirt had ridden up to her thighs, exposing her shapely legs. He should send her on her way, but the chance to spend time with a beautiful woman would be gone soon enough. He was two weeks away from his seventieth birthday and had more days behind him than ahead of him.

Besides, it would be rude to tell her to leave. To get to his cabin on Molly's Mountain, she'd had to drive past protesters and negotiate a steep, narrow trail that, at times, teetered on the side of a cliff.

"Don't you want me?" the woman at the table purred.

He wasn't sure if he could pleasure her. It had been years since his last sexual adventure. He licked his lips. "Of course I do, but are you sure? What about your husband?"

She stuck her bottom lip out in a pout. "He's having an affair."

"And I'm your revenge?" He had no time for her weasel of a husband, and there was poetry in the idea of him being used as an instrument for retribution.

Her gaze slanted to the floor as she swallowed and then licked her dry lips. "You're not the only one, but yes, you're payback."

There was something in her manner that was off. She could be lying, or maybe she felt guilty over her adultery. Yes, that was it. She wouldn't lie about having other boyfriends, but still, it was a surprise. "You have other lovers?"

She nodded and met his gaze, seeming direct and honest.

He'd always thought of her as uptight and unyielding. Maybe she showed the world the strict and conservative side of her nature, but in the privacy of the bedroom she was a wild woman. He liked that idea.

She smiled, straightened her back, thrusting her chest forward, and then curled her index finger, beckoning him closer. "I want you to lick my breasts and suck on my nipples."

His cock sprang to life, which was comforting. Maybe he would be able to satisfy her. He stepped closer and knelt on the floor in front of her, ignoring the pain in his arthritic knees.

As he leaned in, she held up a hand to stop him. "Before you start, I need to get something out of my purse." She plucked her bag off the floor and placed it in her lap. She was probably looking for a rubber. That was the way of it these days. You couldn't have sex without protection, even if there was no chance of pregnancy.

She pulled out her compact mirror, and lipstick and then placed her bag back on the ground.

He smiled. She wanted to make sure she looked good. Maybe she would primp her hair or touch up her makeup. He leant closer. He loved watching a woman put on lipstick. It was a feminine and intimate gesture. One he didn't know he'd missed until this moment.

She pursed her lips as she opened the compact, held it level with his face, and blew.

He coughed when a fine, white powder flew into his nose and eyes. He tried to wipe it away, but it just smeared.

She blew again.

A chemical taste coated his tongue. He spat as he pulled away, trying to rid his mouth of the dry, bitter substance. Then the world tilted and swayed. The floor seemed to buckle under him. He cried out and grabbed the table, trying not to fall over.

A pretty she-devil with the largest breasts he had ever seen moved toward him. Horns grew out of her fair hair. "Where's the gold?"

He held his arms wide in an effort to prevent the walls from crushing him. "Why are the walls moving?"

"They're not moving. You're hallucinating. It's a side effect of the drug I blew into your face. I know you found a can of gold coins because I heard you telling Jack. Where is it?"

Jack? Jack Morgan was his oldest friend. Jack would chase the devil away the same way he'd chased away Ben's other demons. He tried to move to the door. He needed to get out of the house, to feel solid ground beneath his feet. But the floor slanted into an abyss. He gripped the table, scared he'd slip into the dark, inky blackness. "Help me," he screamed at the devil-woman.

She smiled. Her evil eyes shone with blue fire. "I'll help you if you tell me about the gold."

He'd been tricked. The devil knew Ben's weakness and had disguised himself as a beautiful woman.

"You'd better get out of here before she kills you," the chair said.

The world righted itself, and he started for the door, ignoring the fact that chairs couldn't talk. The furniture levitated, floating slowly around the room. His mouth was dry, so dry he thought his tongue would crack. Blood pounded in his ears. He took another step, but didn't have the energy to continue. He tried to inhale, but his lungs wouldn't expand. And the damned furniture was spinning faster.

"Just tell me where the gold is!" the she-devil shouted.

"It's on Morgan land," he yelled. He didn't want to tell, but was compelled to reveal everything. The devil controlled his mind.

"Where?" she insisted.

He opened his mouth to speak, but a crushing pain in his chest made him double over. He fell to his knees.

Tim—he was supposed to meet him tomorrow and tell him about the gold. Now it was too late. He was a thief. He'd stolen from the Morgans, and the devil had come to claim him.

"Where is it?" The she-devil was on the ground next to him. "I need to know," she screamed, grabbing him by the collar.

Her words stabbed at him, coalescing into a dark, sharp knife that pierced his heart. The pain extended through his chest and down his left arm. His world exploded into a white light of pain, and then nothing.

Chapter Two

Officer Dana Hayden gripped the steering wheel of her patrol car as she negotiated the treacherous, narrow road to Ben North's cabin that was perched on the side of Molly's Mountain.

The homes on this part of the Hopefalls Highway were geographically isolated. The only way to reach them was to drive through the town. There were no other roads to this part of the county. Ben's only neighbors were the Kootenai National Forest and the Morgans, who owned the adjacent ranch.

She'd been to Molly's Mountain a number of times to deal with trespassers. Ben was embroiled in a particularly nasty lawsuit, one that had captured the attention of the press. Third Estate Mining Corporation claimed to own the mineral rights to Molly's Mountain and were using Montana's Eminent Domain Laws to force Ben from his land. Activists supporting both sides were camped out at his gate on the Hopefalls Highway, which was a twenty-five-minute drive to the cabin.

Strictly speaking, the properties west of Hopefalls came

under the jurisdiction of the Elkhead County-Granite City Police Department, and she had no power to arrest anyone, but she could talk to people as a private citizen. She'd been motivated to act as an intermediary for Ben since the town of Hopefalls had suffered of spate of vandalism. The graffiti painted on the side of the police station, town hall, and post office suggested a link to Ben's supporters. What had started off as defacement had escalated into arson when someone set fire to the mayor's shed.

Most of the protesters were respectful of Ben's privacy. She'd had very few problems when she spoke to them face to face so she'd been unable to pinpoint a culprit.

Ben hadn't been grateful for her efforts. He was crotchety and gruff, but there was a spark in his eye that told her he was intelligent and alert, and she had instantly taken a liking to him.

She parked on the grassy ledge in front of the rundown cabin. Her boss, Police Chief Levi Booley, had parked his new Jeep Renegade close to the front door. Positioned beside it was the mayor's newer model Ford Explorer, which meant she had to park next to a sharp precipice. She inhaled as she took in the view. It was stunning, but it was also a long way down, and heights had never been her thing. She wasn't exactly scared; she just had a healthy respect for Newton's law of gravity.

She climbed out of the patrol car, flinching as the skin at her waist caught between her Kevlar vest and gun belt. As a newly appointed officer for the town of Hopefalls, she'd been back in uniform for only two months. She couldn't get used to the starched white shirt, the polyester pants, and wearing two belts—her gun belt and a belt to hold up her pants. The gun belt was bulky and awkward, but necessary since it carried most of the tools needed for the job: two sets of handcuffs packed neatly into two handcuff cases, an expandable baton, a flashlight, Taser gun, her portable radio, and two spare, fully loaded magazines, which ensured she carried at least forty-six rounds of ammunition.

As she ascended the three steps to the front door, her hand automatically went to her SIG Sauer, a reflex from her twelve years as a law enforcement officer. Booley had been cryptic when he'd phoned the station. He had refused to tell her the nature of the call, but claimed the area was secure.

She stood at the entrance and blinked, allowing her eyes to adjust to the dark interior. Ben lay near the door, flat on his back, with his arms by his side. A revolver lay on the ground next to him. His face was white, bloodless, and his eyes cloudy and opaque. She could tell at a glance he was dead. Whenever she encountered a body, her first instinct was to look away, but she resisted. Before moving back to Hopefalls, she'd worked in Spokane as a homicide detective for six years and knew the drill.

"There you are." Police Chief Booley stood in the center of the room, a tall rangy man with sharp eyes and a ragged face that revealed a lifetime smoking habit. "It took you long enough to get here." He wore muddy work boots, jeans, and a white cowboy hat. A lit cigarette dangled between his fingers.

Paul Harris, the mayor of Hopefalls, paced near the fireplace. He wore his usual uniform, a suit and tie. As always, his hair was perfectly combed, not so fussy as to be feminine, but not rugged either. His wife, Zoe Harris, sat on the old, duct tape-patched couch. She dabbed at her eyes with a crumpled tissue. Her short fair hair and gel nails were perfect, as always. Her eye makeup and mascara were also flawless despite the fact she'd been crying.

Dana bit her lip and counted to ten. Damn it, Booley had over thirty years experience. He should know better than to contaminate the scene. He should've asked Mr. and Mrs. Harris to wait in the car instead of letting them trample all over the cabin. They needed to clear the room.

"Have you already called the Granite City-Elkhead

County police? Or do you want me to do it?" It was her way of reminding her boss there were procedures to follow.

Booley gritted his teeth. "Yes."

She gave a curt nod as she snapped on a pair of latex gloves, hoping he would take the hint and extinguish his ash-trailing cigarette, which was contaminating the scene. "Then I'll have to ask you all to wait outside while I preserve the evidence."

Booley's face flushed. "I'm your boss. I can do whatever I want."

Dana ignored his outburst. Her job was to protect the citizens of Hopefalls within the confines of the law, and she didn't care whose toes she had to step on to do that. "We need to secure the area and allow the Granite City-Elkhead County police to investigate. I need the three of you to wait outside. Who found the body?"

Zoe raised her hand.

Dana softened her tone. "Why were you here?"

Zoe sniffled. "I deliver food to the elderly."

"Did you touch Ben?"

The mayor's wife shook her head.

"You'll have to wait until the GCEC PD arrive. They'll want to question you."

The mayor, who had been silent to this point, stomped past her and out the door. "I'm taking my wife home. They can find us there. There's no need for all this fuss. We know who did it."

"We do?" Dana ground her teeth together. She wanted to blast Booley and the mayor. She didn't like having a civilian tell her who'd committed the crime, even if he was, technically, her boss. The three of them had stomped all over the crime scene, leaving footprints, fingerprints, DNA and cigarette ash. She doubted Booley would want to explain to the Granite City-Elkhead County police the evidence was tainted.

Booley pointed to the gun on the floor next to the

body. "That's a limited edition Colt six-shooter. It was made in 1984 and jointly purchased by Jack Morgan and Ben North. The two had a falling out, and Jack Morgan kept the weapon."

Zoe rose and walked toward Dana, not looking at Ben. "I'll wait outside."

Dana nodded as the mayor's wife inched past her. Of the three of them, only Zoe Harris' behavior was understandable. She was distressed and probably in shock. She had found the body so her presence in the cabin was justifiable. They other two should've known better.

Dana pushed the thought aside, grabbed her notebook from her back pocket, and started documenting the crime scene. It didn't matter what Chief Booley or Mayor Harris said. She would work the case and hand her notes to the detective in charge of the investigation.

Ben North lay on the floor a few feet from the door. Dead. His lips were a faded shade of blue. In her twelve-year career as a policewoman, she had viewed more dead bodies than she cared to remember, but she never got used to seeing a soulless corpse. Everything Ben had been was gone. All that was left was an empty husk. She forced herself to focus. Four bullet holes punctured his chest. In her experience, a body never fell neatly. After being shot, people normally landed in a crumpled heap on the floor. They did not lie there as if they were waiting to be placed on a stretcher. Ben's body had been moved.

Booley peered over her shoulder at her notes, puffing on his cigarette.

Dana snapped the book closed, her patience at an end. "Sir, please extinguish that outside."

Booley grunted, knocking her shoulder as he passed through the door.

She ignored his juvenile antics and flipped open her notebook, concentrating on the task at hand.

A trace of a white powdery substance covered Ben's face. A chair near the small kitchenette lay on its side. The kitchen cupboards and drawers were all open. Someone had been searching for something. From her position at the door, she couldn't see if the loft had been ransacked, but the living area seemed to be untouched. Maybe the assailant had found whatever they were looking for in the kitchen and hadn't gone through the rest of the house.

Booley's heavy footsteps thudded through the door. He didn't bump into her as he entered, which was a relief. Booley was a jerk. Dealing with his attitude was a challenge at the best of times. She didn't need the distraction while working a case.

"So you think Jack Morgan killed him?" Dana hadn't met Jack and hadn't wanted to. It was better for her peace of mind if she stayed away from the Morgans. It helped that their ranch was on the other side of Molly's Mountain, away from Hopefalls and in Elkhead County.

Booley hunched down next to Ben. "It's doubtful. Jack's suffering from Alzheimer's. He's in a care home in Granite City, but he has a son, Timothy."

"Tim Morgan? The same Tim Morgan who killed Aunt Alice?" She backed through the door, but stopped before she stumbled down the steps.

Booley straightened and then nodded.

An invisible vice tightened around Dana's chest. Tim Morgan had devastated her family when he'd caused the car accident that had taken Aunt Alice's life. Unable to deal with his sister's death, her father had moved the family to Spokane, a place where she, at thirteen, had been an outsider. It was the beginning of a dark time in her life, one that had lasted until she'd joined the Spokane police force in her twentieth year.

Dana straightened her shoulders. "I need you to leave the scene now."

"Sounds like you mean business."

"Yes, sir." She took one last look at the body. Although four wounds punctured the chest, there was very little blood. *Damn.* No blood meant Ben was already dead when he was shot. No, she couldn't draw any conclusions. All she could do was wait for the medical examiner's report and go from there.

She marched to her car, opened the trunk, and took out some crime scene tape and paper bags. The bags were to preserve any evidence on Ben's hands. She was doing this by the book. This was their chance to get Timothy Morgan. Nineteen years ago, he'd gotten away with killing Aunt Alice.

He wouldn't get away this time.

Sun Storm